MW01633414

Kalb Hollow

A Nashville Story

R.W. NAPPER

LifeRich
PUBLISHING

LifeRich Publishing is a registered trademark of
The Reader's Digest Association, Inc.

LifeRich Publishing books may be ordered through booksellers or by contacting:

LifeRich Publishing
1663 Liberty Drive
Bloomington, IN 47403
www.liferichpublishing.com
844-686-9607

Because of the dynamic nature of the Internet, any web addresses or links contained in this book may have changed since publication and may no longer be valid. The views expressed in this work are solely those of the author and do not necessarily reflect the views of the publisher, and the publisher hereby disclaims any responsibility for them.

Any people depicted in stock imagery provided by Getty Images are models, and such images are being used for illustrative purposes only. Certain stock imagery © Getty Images.

ISBN: 978-1-4897-4880-5 (sc)
ISBN: 978-1-4897-4881-2 (hc)
ISBN: 978-1-4897-4879-9 (e)

Library of Congress Control Number: 2023914983

Print information available on the last page.

LifeRich Publishing rev. date: 08/22/2023

Contents

Author's Note

The early 1960's was a tremendously interesting and consequential period of history. Locally, nationally, and internationally, the sixties were a period of change and challenge. This held true for a working-class neighborhood in Nashville, Tennessee known as Kalb Hollow. Through the interaction and personal struggles of its characters, *Kalb Hollow: A Nashville Story* depicts the attitudes and prejudices of that time and place—the good, the bad, and the ugly. The novel also relays several major historical events of the time and local reactions and attitudes toward those events. Specific historical information for the novel was obtained from copies of the *Nashville Tennessean* newspaper that are archived at the Metropolitan Nashville Public Library.

The reader should keep in mind that the views, values, and attitudes expressed by the characters are in keeping with the time and place of the novel and are not necessarily those of the author or publisher.

R.W. Napper

Chapter 1

Spring/Summer, 1961

Frontier Justice

The usual feelings of boredom and anticipation burned deeply as I sat in the pew staring at the wooden clock high on the wall. It was Brother Cullom's Sunday to preach. His speaking in our small country-like church always slowed the clock. Brother Cullom was an old-fashioned hell-fire preacher whose stern appearance and fiery speech made each third Sunday of the month particularly lively. Our church had a different preacher every Sunday of the month, and the third Sunday belonged to Brother Cullom. Although he could certainly hold my attention, I watched the clock. I was thirteen years old; it was Sunday. I had bigger fish to fry.

I was always intimidated by Brother Cullom and gingerly shook his hand as I descended the meeting-house steps. I looked across the gravel parking lot. My dad was usually waiting to pick me up after church, but he had not arrived yet. What car would he be driving today? The '55 Chevy? The '57 Ford? The '38 Oldsmobile? As I walked across the gravel parking lot toward the street, the green '50 DeSoto pulled up. He rarely drove that one. My dad owned and operated a grocery store, but he also had bought and sold cars for as long as I could remember. He would buy a car and immediately use white liquid shoe polish to write a price on the windshield. At times he would have four or five cars sitting on the street or parked on the side parking lot beside the grocery store. On Sunday, it was kind of exciting not knowing which car dad would choose to drive. One thing was always for sure: he always picked me up.

I was an only child, and I loved being the focus of my parents' attention. There had never been any question regarding their commitment to me. When I was two or three years old, my mother hired an older lady to keep me during the day. She lived across the street where she also kept her grandson. My days at Mrs. Kirby's house were miserable. I was not allowed to play with the grandson's toys, and I was constantly being hit, kicked, and punched. When Mrs. Kirby, the grandson, and I took our daily afternoon nap, I was made to lie in the opposite direction, my head at the foot of the bed. I was absolutely miserable and always bolted into my mother's arms each evening when she arrived to pick me up. It was not long before I started crying each morning when mother took me to Mrs. Kirby's house. When it became apparent to my mom and dad that I was not happy, Mom quit her job. She remained a stay-at-home mom until I started school at age six. At that time, I did not understand the financial sacrifice my parents had made because of their commitment to me. At that time, my dad had a very low-paying job sanding cars in a paint shop at a local Chevrolet dealership. Money obviously became tight with only his income. Understanding the love my parents had for me may have been the reason I always tried hard to please them. I was always obedient and compliant. When I started school, my grades were always tops, and I was always polite and helpful. My teachers bragged on me to my parents. So did the Sunday school teachers; so did the neighbors; so did our relatives. I loved it! My dad was born in 1908 and almost finished the second grade. Mom was born in 1911 and completed the eighth grade. My parents were not educated, but they were extremely hard-working—and they knew how to love a kid.

My dad had lost his job in 1959 and soon after jumped at an opportunity to enter the grocery business. Stone's Shop and Save Market was in a rectangular two-story red brick building with a flat roof. The store was on the first level and the apartment that I called home was on the second. The store was located at 500 Clay Street where Fifth Avenue North came to a dead end at Clay. If a car did not turn at the intersection, it would roll right into our front parking area. As Dad and I pulled into the parking area in front, the upstairs windows looked like big square eyes surveying the neighborhood. The green awning was down over the concrete porch to block the afternoon sun. As we entered, it was almost closing time. Business hours were 8:00 a.m. to 1:00 p.m. on Sundays. The other six days of the week were long ones – 6:30 a.m. to 8:00 p.m. It was my Sunday chore to help Dad sweep up and get necessary stock on the shelves for Monday. At one o'clock sharp, Myrtle yelled "good-bye" and walked down Fifth Avenue to her home. Myrtle was a light-skinned Black lady who worked as a part-time cashier. She was a retired schoolteacher and was around sixty-five years old. After we had finished cleaning and stocking, Dad locked the front door from the inside and he and I went up the back stairs to the Sunday dinner that Mom had waiting. Skillet-fried steak, mashed potatoes, brown gravy, green peas, and cornbread – my mom could really cook. Because of the work schedule that a small grocery store demanded, Sunday was the only day that we could sit down at the kitchen table and enjoy a meal together.

I not only enjoyed the food, but I also enjoyed the conversation. For people lacking in formal education, my parents were very knowledgeable about current events and had strong opinions regarding the issues of the day. I listened intently to the wide range of topics from the difficulty of running a small business to opinions about the job performance of President Kennedy, the first Roman Catholic president. When Kennedy defeated Richard Nixon in the election of 1960, one would have thought the world had come to an end. My parents were sure that the President of the United States would soon be taking orders directly from the Pope. My mom was sure that, with a Democrat in office, another war would be just around the corner.

Sunday afternoons were neat. The store was closed and I was free to play with my buddies. Behind the alley that ran behind the store was a large field enclosed by a wire fence. Since ponies used to graze on this area, it was called the "pony field." The pony field was a couple of hundred yards long before it became a wooded area that ended abruptly at the "cliffs," an abandoned rock quarry that descended to a huge, wooded area that everyone called the "bottoms." The bottoms ended at the Cumberland River which wound through Nashville. If you saw that area today, you would see a Cadillac dealership, the Maxwell House Hotel, several restaurants, and a large office complex. In the early sixties, however, it was a sprawling area of low- lying tree studded bottom land.

Harold lived in the house next to the store. He was a fifth grader, three years my junior. He was a skinny little kid with a million freckles. His brown rimmed glasses and extremely short haircut gave him a rather ridiculous look, but he was fun to play with when nobody else was available.

Bucky lived in the next house, and he was my best friend. He and I were the same age, and we were always together when possible. Bucky was tall and thin with blonde hair and green eyes. His legs were extremely long and out of proportion to his upper body. His gangly appearance made him resemble a big grasshopper. On Sundays Bucky was always waiting around outside the store for me. We usually got Harold and went down to the cliffs to play and mess around. The cliffs were neat. We had found a cave in the quarry wall large enough for three or four people to sit comfortably and made a club house out of it.

As I came down the outside steps of the apartment over the store, Bucky was sitting at the bottom of the steps with Harold. As they looked toward me, I could see tears streaming down Harold's face.

"Hey, what's wrong?" I asked.

"The son-of-a-bitch killed my cat," Harold yelled. He was fond of colorful language.

As he tried to console Harold, Bucky explained that the new boy who had moved in across the street had killed Harold's big yellow cat. The murder weapon had been a brick. Bucky tried hard to keep Harold settled down, but Harold's violent temper was out of hand. I was afraid that my parents might hear Harold's cursing and screaming, so Bucky and I led him down the street beside the store to the pony field. We talked to Harold for a long time. Just when we thought we had him settled down, the red-headed cat-killer came out of his house and started playing in his front yard. Harold went berserk, yelling obscenities that a fifth grader isn't supposed to know. Bucky grabbed him and pulled him to the ground.

"Shut up, Harold!" Bucky ordered. It was clear that Bucky had grown frustrated with Harold's tantrums. "Shut up, or I'm going to give you something to cry about!"

Harold rose to his knees. His face was flushed, and tears filled his eyes. His chest rose and fell angrily with each breath as his clinched teeth locked his jaw in place. Harold broke his cold, angry stare by breaking away from Bucky. He jumped to his feet, bolted out of the pony field, and dashed down the street. We watched as Harold ran across his back yard, leaped to his porch, and disappeared inside his white clapboard house. The screen door slammed behind him.

"Harold is a real little jerk," Bucky declared.

"Yeah, but that little red head had no business killing his cat," I said.

Bucky sighed. "He'll get over it. Let's go down to the cliffs."

We were walking across the pony field toward the cliffs but sat down under a large sycamore tree with low-hanging branches. This was a favorite sitting place. As an April breeze swept across the pony field, we could smell the wild onions that seemed to sprout up everywhere.

"Maybe we ought to go and tell Little Red's mamma about the cat," I declared.

"Do you really want to do that?" Bucky replied. "Let's just hold off and maybe it will blow over."

"Hey," yelled a voice from over the fence. Bones stepped over the short wire fence and started walking toward us. Bones' real name was Randall Martin, but due to his slight build, everyone called him "Bones." The same age as me, he was short, wiry, and sandy haired. When not wearing a shirt, every rib could be counted. As usual, his face and hands were covered with dirt and his clothes were wrinkled and tattered. Bones lived in the next block on Fourth Avenue in one of the poorest areas of Nashville. Right at the pony field, an alley connected Fourth and Sixth Avenues. Bones lived in a house on the corner of Fourth Avenue and the alley. Past his house were two other houses just like his. These were the last three houses before the street led into the "bottoms" and became a dirt road. Bones' house was what people called a "shot gun" house. It was a long, narrow, three-room clap-board house with one room right after the other. You could look in the front door and see out the back. In this small house lived Bones, his mom and dad, his older brother, an older sister, and two younger sisters. The house was unbelievably dirty. Old dingy wallpaper was pulling off the walls and ceilings. Cobwebs hung from the corners, and there was a dirt floor. That's right! A dirt floor! The kitchen had trash everywhere and the free-standing sink was always filled with dirty pots and pans. The toilet facilities were located about fifty feet from the back door in an "out-house." The smell of urine always filled the house. The other two houses at the end of Fourth Avenue were just like it. It is hard to believe that such conditions existed in Nashville, Tennessee in 1961—but I promise they did.

"Where's weird Harold?" asked Bones.

Bucky and I told him the whole story as we sat under the big sycamore tree. As we sat there, we saw Harold walking back up the street carrying an empty bushel basket that he must have taken from the stack behind the store.

"I'm gonna kill that little bastard," declared Harold as he walked up to us and dropped the basket at our feet. Inside the basket was a grass rope. Harold picked up the rope and headed back down the street.

"Don't leave," he said coldly. "I'll be right back."

"What are you up to, Harold?" yelled Bucky. "Are you crazy?"

Bucky turned to me. "You know what he's going to try to do, don't you?"

"Well," I hesitated. "Not really."

Bucky shook his head and gave me an intense stare. "Horsehead! Don't you ever watch television?"

I just looked at him. I had no idea what he was talking about.

Bucky pointed at the basket and turned it upside down under a tree branch. "Harold is planning a lynching!"

"What?"

"A hanging…… Get it? Rope. Basket. Tree."

Bones really thought this was funny. He sat down on the ground and started laughing wildly.

"This ain't funny," said Bucky nervously. "Harold really is crazy."

When Harold did not return, we grew a bit more at ease and fell into our familiar habit of sitting under the sycamore tree, chewing blades of grass, and telling jokes and tall tales. It had appeared to me that Bucky had been in a foul mood all day. As our conversation under the tree progressed, it became apparent that Bucky was upset about issues that had nothing to do with Harold.

"I've got to watch Linda and Lynn again tonight," complained Bucky. "Every time mamma and daddy go off, I get stuck."

It appeared to me that Bucky had a legitimate gripe. Ever since his momma had had the twins, Bucky often stayed in the house to help in some way. When the twins first arrived, he had to help clean the house and prepare meals. Now that they were toddlers, it seemed he was baby-sitting all the time. Not only was he left with the twins, but he also had a seven-year-old sister and a six-year-old brother that required almost as much attention. He watched his siblings every day immediately after school for several hours and a lot on weekends. I didn't think about it at the time, but he did not get paid for the baby-sitting. Bucky did not even receive an allowance or spending money. I worked in my dad's store quite a bit, but my parents paid me ten dollars every week. For a kid in the early sixties, that was a lot of money. It was embarrassing to Bucky when I paid his way into the movies or bought him an RC Cola. Even I had become self-conscious about it. Of course, Bucky's parents probably did not have much money with which to pay him. His dad worked at a cotton mill as a laborer and his mom stayed home with the kids. That may be why Bucky only complained about having to spend so much time babysitting, never about not having any spending money.

We sat under the tree for most of the afternoon and were about to go our separate ways for the day when we heard a commotion. Coming toward us was Harold dragging the red-headed cat killer whom he had bound with the grass rope. The scene I witnessed that day was both unbelievable and unforgettable. Holding a carefully constructed noose in one hand, Harold tried to stand Little Red up on the peach basket that he had left under the tree branch. As Little Red struggled, Bones jumped in to help Harold. Bucky and I gave each other an astonished look. All the while, Harold was crying and cursing as he and Bones struggled to get the condemned cat-killed on the basket. Suddenly, Bucky sprang to his feet and pushed Bones away. He grabbed Harold and flung him to the ground. As he pinned Harold to the ground, I grabbed Little Red and started trying to free him from his bindings. Bones, lying on the ground, just continued to laugh as Bucky sat on Harold's chest and pressed his hands to the ground until his violent display of temper slowly became a whimper.

"Hey, what's going on?" shouted a distant voice.

Tommy must have heard the commotion as he walked up the alley near the pony field. Tommy was Bones' eighteen-year-old brother. He had dropped out of school and was working for a construction company. He still lived at home but was nothing like the rest of the family. He was always clean, and his clothes were always neat with a nice crease in his starched Levi's. He was tall and lean with a short flat-top haircut.

"What's going on, men?" He really did not have to ask, especially when he saw Harold lying on the ground with Bucky sitting on his chest. Tommy knew that Harold was crazy and really disliked him.

When Harold saw Tommy, he stopped crying and relaxed.

"You can let me up now," he said matter-of-factly to Bucky.

Bucky thought for a few seconds. As he got off Harold, he watched Tommy help me untie Little Red. As we struggled with the knots, Tommy and I could feel the trauma that permeated Little Red. Harold slowly raised himself from the ground as Bucky backed up to give him some room. Suddenly, Harold bolted! He dashed to where Red lay on the ground and kicked him in the chest……….and quickly kicked him again. Tommy lunged at Harold and knocked him to the ground before he could kick Red a third time. As Bucky took out his pocketknife to cut the ropes and free Red, Harold escaped from Tommy and ran down the street toward his house.

After we freed Red from the rope, we attempted to console

him, but to no avail. There were rope marks all over his arms and neck. Tommy took the terrified little redhead home and talked to his parents while Bucky and I remained under the sycamore tree feeling bewildered at the ludicrous events of that afternoon.

All hell broke loose between Red's dad and Harold's family. Red's dad ran across the street to Harold's house and pounded on the door while his mom called the Nashville police. Red's dad screamed and yelled, but Harold's dad, of course, protected his son by keeping the angry father out of his house. The day ended with the police ordering Harold to stay completely away from Little Red and telling his dad that he was responsible for whatever crazy thing Harold might do. When the police left, Harold got the belt-whipping of his life as Little Red's dad looked on approvingly. As for Bucky and me, our parents told us not to play with Harold anymore. My dad told me—in no uncertain terms—to avoid Harold completely. Within a month, Little Red's family moved. I don't know if their move had anything to do with what happened that Sunday afternoon, but everyone else assumed that it did.

Later that spring, Harold and his family also moved. Harold's dad had worked for a local auto body shop painting cars but had been put out of work when the company's business slowed. I heard that he had gotten a job in Detroit. One thing was for sure—the neighborhood felt safer with Harold in Michigan.

*****

The Apprentice

With great happiness and anticipation, Bucky and I stormed out the front door of North Nashville High School. The brightness of the mid-morning sun caused us to squint a bit as we skipped toward home. It was the first Friday of June—the last day of school. Summer vacation was before us. As we walked briskly up Clay Street, we clutched our report cards in our hands. Both of us had been promoted to the ninth grade. I was in a hurry to show off my grades to my mom and dad: History-A, Health-A, Music-A, P.E.-A, Math-A, English-B. Five A's and a B. Not bad. Bucky didn't volunteer his grades, and I didn't ask. The important thing was that we were free from the 3 R's until after Labor Day. I looked forward to playing baseball at the Little League field, messing around at the cliffs, and wandering through the bottoms.

"Hey, slow down," ordered Bucky. "I've got to babysit when I get home, and I am in no hurry."

I completely understood and immediately brought my exuberance under control. Although Bucky would get some free time during the summer, he would be hampered by his babysitting duties. As we continued to walk toward home, my mind turned toward the wonders of summer vacation.

Although I looked forward to the next three months, summer vacation was somewhat bitter-sweet. I would not see Judy again until after Labor Day. Judy was my squeeze—the love of my life. She had been my girlfriend since the seventh grade. Of course, I was the only one who knew it. I was so shy around girls that I had never said more than a few words to her. When I saw her in the hall or in class, I could only muster a smile. Even though she always returned the smile, I could never get up enough nerve to speak.

The first time I saw Judy was in the library on the first full day of school at North High School in the fall of 1959. My first period class was physical education which met every-other day. On the off-day, I was assigned to the library for a study hall. So was Judy. As I sat alone at one of the many golden oak tables that were neatly arranged in rows of three, I watched her as she placed books in their proper places on the shelves. Judy spent her library period working for Mrs. Brown, the school librarian and stern taskmaster. Where-ever Judy went in the library that day, my eyes followed. She wore a red, green, and blue plaid dress. Her silky brown hair flipped up at the back of her neck, and her eyes were the bluest I had ever seen. She was beautiful. As she walked by my table pushing her cart of returned books, she smiled at me. That was it—I was immediately and incurably smitten.

"Hey, Horsehead," Bucky interrupted. "What are you thinking about?"

"Nothing." I sighed. I could not let my secret out, not even to Bucky. I changed the subject. "If you can get out today, come on over to the store."

"Maybe." Bucky said doubtfully.

As we reached our destination, Bucky and I peeled off, each going our separate ways. Bucky went into his house to face his baby-sitting duties, and I reported to Stone's Shop and Save

Market. As I opened the screened door and entered, my mom was sitting behind the check-out counter and Dad was standing behind the meat-counter in the rear of the store. I handed my report card to Mom. She looked at it and smiled.

"You did good, Jimmy," she said.

"How good?" my father inquired as he approached the check-out counter at the front of the store.

Mom handed him the report card. As he scanned the card, he nodded his head and broke into a smile.

"I'm proud of you, boy," he said.

He handed the card back to Mom, gave me a pat on the shoulder, and headed back to the meat-counter. At that moment, a customer came into the store and ordered a pack of Winston's. I removed myself to the soft drink box at the rear of the store. I slid open one of the many doors to a very large drink box and pulled out a 12-ounce bottle of Double Cola. I liked the harsher taste that it offered. Pepsi tasted like it had been run through a rusty pipe; RC was too sweet and syrupy; Coca Cola came in only a six-ounce bottle. Double Cola's slogan was "Double your measure, double your pleasure." That is exactly what I was doing. I opened the bottle with the opener attached to the drink box and walked up to the check-out counter where I placed a dime on the counter in front of my mother. With a wry smile, she rang up the ten-cent sale on the cash register.

I walked back out onto the porch of the store and sat down on the concrete steps. The front porch of the store was large, spanning the entire width of the building. Both steps from the front parking area spanned the width of the porch. As I sat on the top step gazing down Fifth Avenue, I saw Mr. Gates mowing his yard. He lived across Clay Street from the store on the corner of Fifth Avenue. He was a tall, gray-haired Black gentleman who often visited our store and engaged in long conversations with Dad. Mr. Gates was a Dodger fan; Dad was a Yankee fan. Mr. Gates was a Democrat; Dad was a Republican. Despite those deep philosophical differences, they had become good friends.

As Mr. Gates pushed his power mower through his front yard, I heard the screen door open behind me. As I looked around, my dad walked out and sat down beside me and gave Mr. Gates a wave. I could hear Dad take a deep breath as he reached into his shirt pocket and pulled out a pack of Lucky Strike cigarettes. As he lit a cigarette, his physical closeness took my mind back to my early childhood. On Sundays, my dad always took me into his lap and read the Sunday funnies to me. My favorites were Blondie and Dennis the Menace. As he read, I could feel the strength in his arms, the muscles acquired through years of tough physical labor. I remembered how the warmth and strength of his body gave me a wonderful feeling of safety and security. Although he was still over six feet tall, he had acquired a little stoop in the shoulders over the years. As he sat next to me on the store step, it was obvious that he was not the same man who had held me in his lap. His coal-black hair had turned gray. His steel-gray eyes had lost their sparkle and had become deeply set into a gaunt face. My dad, once strong and powerful, had become terribly thin. His weight had dropped to 135 pounds. His face had become filled with deep intersecting lines. The fingers of his right hand were stained yellow from nicotine. He was only 52 years old, but the ravages of cigarettes, hard physical work, and long hours at the store had given him the appearance of a man in his 70's.

As smoke exhaled from his nostrils, he turned his head toward me, "Hey, Jim. You are going to turn fourteen in just a few days. I want to give you more responsibility here at the store this summer. Are you interested?"

"Sure." I said. "Just tell me what you want me to do."

"You have been doing a good job sacking groceries and helping people get them to their cars. Everybody likes you. I think it's time you started working the front counter. I want you to learn how to use the adding machine and cash register. The extra time and responsibility comes with extra pay. What do you say?"

"Yeah."

My dad continued. "I want you to work the front counter from 6:30 to 11:30 on Monday through Friday. You will be completely off the rest of the day. Myrtle will work from 11:30 to 3:30. Your mom will work from then until close. You will need to be available on Saturday to sack and help people with their groceries, just like you have been doing. I'm raising your pay to twenty dollars. What do you think?"

"Sure, Dad," I already felt rich. "But what about when school starts again?" I did not want to lose my new-found wealth.

"We'll adjust your hours. Let's cross that bridge when we come to it."

"When will this start?" I asked.

"Monday. I want you to work on Monday morning with your mother. Business will be slow enough for her to teach you how to work the counter. When she thinks you're ready, you will be on your own," he smiled as he gave me a big pat on the head. "Can you handle it?"

I just nodded as he tossed his cigarette butt down and snuffed it out with his foot. Dad got up and went back into the store. As I continued to gaze down Fifth Avenue, I felt confident. I had worked at the front counter sacking groceries and had watched Mom as she added up items on the adding machine and rung up the sales in the cash register. I knew working the counter would be no problem. I was actually anxious for Monday to roll around.

That weekend passed slowly. Not much happened. Bucky was watching the kids the entire weekend. I worked as sack-boy on Saturday morning and spent the afternoon in the upstairs apartment watching the Yankees on the CBS Baseball Game of the Week with Dizzy Dean and Pee Wee Reese. Thinking about Monday morning made it difficult to concentrate on the game. I did perk up when Roger Maris and Mickey Mantle hit back-to-back home runs in the fifth inning. After the adrenalin rush that came from that, I again lost my concentration on the game. I felt confident in my new position, but the butterflies would not go away. It was a long weekend.

***

Mornings came early at Stone's Shop and Save Market. By 6:15 a.m. on Monday morning, Dad was already behind the meat counter slicing bacon. Mom had already shown me how to put the money into the cash register and had made sure I knew how to use the adding machine and ring up sales in the register.

"Jimmy, it's very important to handle a customer's money in the right way. When a customer gives you the money," she went on, "do not put it directly into the cash register. Put the money on the ledge over the cash drawer and leave it there while you give the customer his change. When the customer seems to be satisfied with the change, then—and only then—do you put the money into the cashdrawer."

Actually, I had observed both Mom and Miss Myrtle handle transactions in that manner and I knew the reason, but I continued to listen.

"Jim, there are people out there that will give you a five-dollar bill and claim that they gave you a ten or a twenty. If you leave the money that they give you on the ledge, you can show them what they gave you." Mom continued, "Always do it that way. Never put the money into the cash drawer until they have their change."

"Yeah, Mom. I get it." I did understand. There were all sorts of dishonest people out there, and we had to protect ourselves.

At 6:30 a.m. on the dot, Mom sent me to open the front door. There were a handful of customers on the porch waiting for us to open. Most of them were men who had stopped to buy cigarettes on their way to work. Others purchased other sundries: milk, bread, coffee, or twinkies. The first customer was a tall man with a thick black stubble on his face wearing a pair of Duckhead overalls. He ordered two packs of Pall Mall cigarettes.

"That'll be sixty cents," said Mom.

The man gave her a dollar bill. As Mom rang up the sale on the register, the cashdrawer opened, and Mom put the dollar bill on the ledge of the drawer. She took from the cash drawer a dime, a nickel, and a quarter. She gave the customer his change in a particular way. "Sixty cents." She gave the man the dime. "Ten cents make seventy." Then she gave him the nickel; "Seventy-five and a quarter makes one dollar. Thanks, and come back and see us."

The man dropped the change into his pocket and opened a pack of Pall Malls on his way to the door. Mom turned back to the register and put the dollar into the cash drawer and closed it. She handled each transaction the same way. By 7:00 a.m. the store was empty of customers.

"Well, Jim," she said, "do you think you can handle it?"

I just nodded. I was confident.

"Get over here, then," she ordered. "I'll just watch you for a while."

Just as I had switched places with Mom, the screened door opened, and two little blond-haired girls entered. They were five or six years old and were wearing only white cotton panties. Their hands, arms, face, and legs were covered with dirt. They were Bones' little sisters. One of them put a dime on the counter and handed me a note which read: "Dimes worth of boloney and please slice it thin."

Bones' family was among the poorest of the poor. The

dad, Mr. Martin, worked every day, but he spent most of his income—which was probably very meager—on alcohol. When not working, he was drinking. Unskilled and uneducated, the mom was trapped in a horrible situation. I rarely saw Mrs. Martin, but her appearance is burned into my memory. She was extremely thin, and her tattered clothing just hung over her slight frame. Her long brown hair was heavily streaked with gray, and she was missing several teeth. She almost never came into the store herself, opting to send the girls with a note.

A dime's worth of bologna at thirty-nine cents per pound would be about three slices—four if thinly sliced. Dad brought up a small package wrapped in white butcher paper with "10 cents" marked on it. When he handed it to me, I could tell from the thickness of the package that it contained much more than four slices. I put the package into a small brown bag and gave it to the girls who waved "good-bye" as they left the store.

By mid-morning, I had handled enough business that Mom was confident enough to go upstairs and do her housework. As she headed toward the apartment stairs in the back of the store, the phone rang. The business phone was a coin-operated phone secured to a post a few feet from the front counter.

"Stone's Shop and Save," I said as I answered.

It was Steve. He was my cousin who lived on Ninth Avenue across from the Little League baseball field at White City Park. Steve was two years my junior, but he loved baseball almost as much as I did. During prior summers, a bunch of us had played baseball almost every day; however, with my new role at the store, I knew my play would be limited.

"Hey, Jimmy Stone," he barked. "Are you up for some baseball today?"

"Absolutely. I'm working until 11:30, but I'm good after that."

"Doug, Jew-Baby, Melvin, and bunch more are showing up at one o'clock," said Steve.

"What about Roger?" I inquired. Roger was Steve's older brother—and a real prick. He and I were the same age, and there was not a lot of love lost between us. Whatever anyone could do—especially me—Roger could do better; if you didn't believe that, just ask him; he would tell you.

"Who knows?" Steve retorted. "He might show up. Say, do you think you could get Bucky or Bones or anybody over around the store to come too?"

"Don't know, but I'll check. Hey, customer's coming in; gotta go."

As I hung up the phone, the screened door opened and in walked Bucky.

"Hey, Horsehead," he chided as he eased the door shut and proceeded to the meat counter.

"Hey, Mr. Stone," he said as he approached the meat counter. "I need a pound of boloney and ten slices of American cheese."

He proceeded over to the drink box and gathered a carton of six RC colas and brought them to the check-out counter and set them down. As he grabbed a loaf of Colonial Bread off the bread rack, I asked, "Can you play some ball this afternoon?"

"Yep. I'm pretty sure I can." As he walked back to pick up his bologna and cheese, he said," Can I borrow your glove again?"

"Yeah," I said as I added his purchases on the adding machine. "OK, Grasshopper. That'll be a dollar and forty-three cents."

Bucky gave me two one-dollar bills. I gave him his change and sacked his groceries. "Come over about noon and we'll walk over to the ballpark."

***

As we approached the baseball field, Bucky and I saw six guys throwing baseballs around. Steve and Roger were there along with four other regulars. Bucky and I would make eight players, which was a borderline number needed to play a real game. After throwing for several more minutes, Roger made a suggestion—actually, coming from Roger, it was a demand, "Let's play 'fly and a bounce.' I'm first up. I wanna try out my new bat." Roger had a new 38-ounce bat. It was brown and the size of a small telephone pole. Not really, but it was a huge baseball bat.

"Fly and a bounce" was a game that included a pitcher and a batter. Everyone else played in the field. If a fielder caught a ball on a fly or one bounce, he became the batter.

"Hey, Stone; you pitch," Roger demanded. I did not like Roger telling me what to do, but I was the best pitcher—no brag, just fact. Pitching a game of "fly and a bounce" was not difficult. The pitcher just lobbed the ball over the plate so that the batter would have no trouble hitting it. I disliked Roger, but I had to admit that he could hit a baseball a long way with that telephone pole he called a bat.

We hoped that more guys would show up during our game, but none did. After an hour or so we divided into two 4-man teams. We made teams of four work by eliminating first base. When a batter hit the ball, he would run directly to second base—then to third—then to home. Any ball hit to the right side of second base was an automatic out. The team in the field had a pitcher, a shortstop, and two outfielders. Of course, the games were usually high scoring, but it did not matter who won. We played baseball for the sake of playing baseball.

After several innings, shadows started stretching over the ball diamond signaling that it was time to go home. All of us were hot, thirsty, and very dirty. It was great!

"Same time tomorrow, guys," shouted Steve. "And find somebody. We need more players."

As Bucky and I left the field and started walking back home, I asked, "Hey, Buck. Do you think you can play tomorrow?"

"Don't know, but I'll try. Probably won't know until tomorrow."

Bucky may have tried, but he did not succeed. He was again called upon to watch his little sisters and do some chores around the house. When I got to the ball field on Wednesday afternoon, it was the same guys minus Bucky. Being only seven, we played "fly and a bounce" for a couple of hours and left. We promised ourselves that we would find more players for the next day, Thursday.

***

Thursdays were busy at Stone's Shop and Save Market. About 9:00 a.m. a big box truck pulled up in front of the store. A sign on the side of the truck read, "C.B. Ragland Wholesale Groceries." Ragland supplied the store with canned foods, paper goods, sugar, salt, flour, and other basics. As I sat on the stool behind the counter, I watched through the window as James Patterson opened the back door of the truck and put boxes onto a two-wheel hand-truck. Mr. Patterson handled our deliveries from Ragland. He was a tall, muscular Black man who was tremendously strong. He had no trouble pulling the fully loaded two-wheeler up the front steps and into the store, all the while chewing on an unlit cigar. He wheeled the boxes into the store until the middle of the far grocery aisle contained twenty to twenty-five boxes.

"Hey, Stoney," he shouted in a deep, gravelly voice. "I'm ready to check this stuff off."

Dad walked from the meat counter as Mr. Patterson handed him a yellow sheet of paper that listed the items of the delivery. As Dad took the paper, Mr. Patterson retrieved a black marker from his pocket.

"Northern Tissue, white," Dad said as he put on his eyeglasses.

"Check it," Mr. Patterson loudly exclaimed as he put a big black check mark on the box of tissue.

"Northern Paper Towels," Dad continued down the list of items.

"Check it."

"24 cans of Green Giant cream style corn."

"Check it."

"48 cans of Bushes cut green beans."

"Check it."

"24 boxes Kellogg's Frosted Flakes."

"Check it."

So it continued until delivery of all items were confirmed.

Actually, James Patterson was more than a delivery driver; he was a neighbor. He and his family lived on Sixth Avenue just a few houses down from Clay Street. He and his wife had two sons, Paul and Silas. The older son, Paul, had graduated from Pearl High School, a legendary all-Black school. Like the rest of the South, Nashville was a Jim Crow city in which racial segregation was the order of the day. Blacks and Whites attended separate schools, drank from segregated water fountains, and used separate restrooms. When I was small, Mom took me with her to the downtown shopping district which centered on Church Street and Fifth Avenue. We rode the city bus, and a small sign attached to the top step of the bus read: "Colored people please move to the rear of the bus." I marveled at the restroom arrangements in the department stores. There were four separate restrooms: "White Men," "White Women," "Colored Men," "Colored Women."

Paul was currently in his junior year at Tennessee State A&I College, an all-Black college in Nashville. Paul had become a celebrity in the Black community near the store. His fame rested on the fact that he had been arrested and jailed. That's right—arrested. What was his crime?" Paul and other Black college students had had the nerve and audacity to sit down at lunch counters in downtown Nashville on Fifth Avenue. Of course, Blacks were not allowed to eat at the "White only" lunch counters in Nashville. Hundreds of Black students, including Paul, had participated in well-organized, non-violent demonstrations to protest the injustice of Jim Crow laws regarding restaurants and lunch counters in downtown Nashville. Known as the Nashville Sit-ins, these protests occurred from February through May of 1960. On February 13, 1960, one hundred and twenty-four students, including Paul, entered the Woolworth, Kress, and McClellan stores on Fifth Avenue just north of Church Street. The students seated themselves at lunch counters as if waiting to be served. They were refused service but remained in the stores for a couple of hours before leaving without incident. A few days later, February 18, two hundred students, including Paul, entered Woolworth's, Kress, McClellan's, and Grant's. After they took seats, the lunch counters were immediately closed. A sign was displayed reading: "Fountain Closed in the Interest of Public Safety." After thirty minutes or so, the students left— again without incident. On February 20, approximately three hundred and fifty students entered the same stores in addition to the Walgreen's drug store. Several White youths gathered in the stores along with a strong police presence. The protesters were denied service and left the store after a couple of hours. Again, there were no incidents.

Tensions rose as the daily news reported sit-in demonstrations in other southern cities. In Chattanooga, a sit-in exploded into violence. Several Whites were arrested for their part in what had become the Chattanooga Race Riot of

1960. Viewers of the nightly news witnessed police armed with batons beating un-resisting demonstrators. Things had become ugly in cities throughout the South.

On February 27, Nashville experienced its fourth major sit-in. Hundreds of demonstrators took seats at all the major lunch counters on Fifth Avenue. Paul was among the group that entered the Woolworth store. The students at McClellan's and Woolworth's were immediately heckled and harassed by a growing group of White youths. Unfortunately, there was no police presence, and the sit-in became violent. Some of the demonstrators had soft drinks poured over their heads as they sat at the counters. Others were dragged from their stools and pulled out the door onto the sidewalk. At the Krystal on Fifth Avenue, Krystal employees attempted to disrupt the sit-in with water hoses and insect spray. At Woolworth's, Paul was pulled from his lunch counter seat and dragged along the floor. Although strong and muscular like his father, Paul did not resist. Like the other protesters, he just covered his head with his arms to avoid injury. Just as Paul was being dragged onto the sidewalk, the police arrived. The White attackers fled, and none were arrested. The police ordered the demonstrators to leave the stores. When they refused, they were arrested. As they were loaded into police vehicles, a large group of White on-lookers broke into applause. Eighty-one students, including Paul, were charged with loitering and disorderly conduct. Of course, Mr. Patterson placed bond for his son's release. The next week, Paul appeared in court where the loitering charge was dismissed, but he was found guilty of disorderly conduct. Like the other students, he paid a fine of fifty dollars.

There were several other sit-ins in Nashville throughout the spring of 1960. They were covered in graphic detail by the local news and television networks. Many more arrests took place. In fact, Paul was arrested two more times, forcing Mr. Patterson to pay a lot of money in bail and fines. Serious violence took place in Nashville in mid-April when the home of a key organizer suffered a stick of dynamite being thrown through a window. Although the residence was completely destroyed by the blast, no one was injured. This incident may have been the catalyst for a series of meetings between the leaders of the protests and local merchants. The meetings were arranged by Nashville mayor, Ben West. My dad believed that Mayor West deserved a lot of credit for ending the protests with the merchants of Nashville agreeing to desegregate their lunch counters and restaurants. On May 10, 1960, stores in Nashville opened their lunch counters to Black customers for the first time.

Although much still had to be done to totally desegregate Nashville's public accommodations, Paul had emerged as a hero to the Black segment of our North Nashville neighborhood. James Patterson was extremely proud of the role his son had played in a major civil rights milestone. He was proud—and afraid.

Mr. Patterson feared that Paul would become involved in a protest demonstration that had just begun the previous month, May 1961. He feared this new protest would prove to be more dangerous than the sit-ins. Known as the Freedom

Rides, demonstrators were riding Greyhound and Trailways buses into bus terminals of cities in the deep South in order to protest the non-enforcement of a Supreme Court decision the previous year. The court had found segregation of buses and bus terminals to be unconstitutional and that travelers had a right to disregard local segregation ordinances. In May, a group of Black and White students from several colleges in Nashville boarded a Greyhound bus headed to Birmingham, Alabama. The protest involved pairs of students, one Black and one White, sitting together on the bus while at least one Black protester would take a seat in the front of the bus.

After he had completed his paperwork on the delivery, Mr. Patterson walked to the back of the store where Dad had resumed preparing the meat counter.

"Stoney, I'm really worried about my oldest boy."

"Is Paul taking part in that bus thing that started?" asked Dad.

"Not yet, but he's thinking about it. We got into a little scrap the other night. I told him that it's just too dangerous to take something like that into the heart of Alabama. Things got a little out of hand here in Nashville. Something bad is bound to happen down South."

Dad really did not know what to say, but it was clear that Mr. Patterson genuinely feared for his son's life.

"Pat, I hope your boy doesn't go either. If he does, he's a big boy who can take pretty good care of himself. All the same, I hope that you can talk him out of it."

"Just pray for him, Stoney." He turned toward the door, "Have a good one. See you next week if not before."

As Mr. Patterson walked toward the front door, he stopped at the check-out counter and purchased a five-cent Have-A-Tampa cigar.

"Hey, Little Stoney. You know my boy, Silas, don't you?"

Silas was my age, and he came into the store from time to time.

"I know him when I see him," I said. "He comes in sometimes."

"Well, he's a lot like you. He's really into baseball. You guys ought to get to know each other and throw the ball around a little bit," he said as he walked out the door.

As I watched Mr. Patterson walk out to his delivery truck, I could not help but think about the idea of throwing baseball with Silas. I only knew him by sight, and he was Black. Other than working in the store, I had almost no contact with Black kids. The neighborhood around Stone's Shop and Save was about 60% Black. Although the neighborhood was certainly integrated, the races had little to do with each other. Dad's friendship with Mr. Patterson and Mr. Gates was limited to conversations at the store. Otherwise, there was no social contact. In addition to Silas, there were several Black kids of my age in the neighborhood, but my time was spent with Bucky, Bones, and other White kids. I had never even thought of playing baseball—or anything else—with a Black guy. I had never been in the same classroom with a Black student. In 1961, Nashville schools were only partially integrated. After the

Supreme Court ordered schools to be desegregated in 1954, the court approved a grade-per-year plan for Nashville that began in 1957. That year, Black students were allowed to enroll as first graders in previously all-White schools in their neighborhoods. By 1961, Nashville schools had only been integrated through the fifth grade; therefore, North High School was still an all-white school with grades seven through twelve.

As Mr. Patterson drove away, I thought of Miss Myrtle. I had known her for most of my life. I had never really thought of her as a Black lady—just Miss Myrtle. The same was true of Mr. Patterson, Mr. Gates, and the many Black customers who patronized our store. Obviously, I knew that they were Black people, but I just thought of them as *people.* For the first time in my life, I was wondering why segregation of the races was such a big deal. I was also questioning myself: why did I only hang out with White guys?

***

Her eyes were like sparkling pools of blue. I put my arms around Judy's waist and pulled her closer to me. She responded by embracing me around the neck and shoulders. She ran her hand through my hair as I drank in our closeness. I moved my head toward her and gently kissed her lips. Judy closed her eyes, and we held each other tightly. This was the moment of which I had dreamed.

"I love you," I said.

"I love you too, Son, but we've got to get to the market. It's Friday, and it's already 4:30," Dad said as he pulled back my bed covers. I awoke with Dad sitting on the side of my bed gently shaking my shoulder. "Come on, buddy," he said. "It's time to get up."

"Okay, Dad. I'm moving." With an ocean of disappointment, I let go of the pillow that only seconds ago had been Judy. I had been shaken into reality.

Dad and I got into his 1957 Ford Country Squire station wagon and headed to the market. The Farmers Market in Nashville was located between Seventh and Eighth Avenues just south of Jefferson Street. It was about a ten-minute drive from the store. When we pulled into the Farmers Market, there must have been twenty-five to thirty pickup trucks parked next to each other. Men in bib overalls stood beside open tail gates of trucks stocked with all types of farm produce: corn, green beans, squash, new potatoes, turnip greens, and more. Dad bought three bushels of turnip greens, six dozen ears of yellow corn, one bushel of green beans, six heads of lettuce, and a half bushel of squash. We loaded our purchases tightly into the station wagon.

"Look, Jim," Dad said as he pointed across the market. "Strawberries are coming in." I looked and saw a pick-up truck loaded with strawberries in quart containers. Dad bought twelve quarts that we somehow squeezed into the station wagon. When we arrived at the store, it was already six o'clock, so we scrambled to unload the wagon and put the baskets of produce near the produce bins. We would have to stock the bins later because we had to open the doors for business at 6:30 a.m. I opened the front door and greeted the group of regulars that stopped at the store almost every morning for cigarettes, milk, bread, or lunch meat. The Martin girls came in with a note for a dime's worth of bologna. When the early morning rush was over, I went to work at the produce bins. I put about thirty pounds of potatoes into the dry bin. I put a half bushel of turnip greens into the cold bin along with a half bushel of green beans, a dozen ears of corn, and the half bushel of squash. I made a special display for the strawberries. The produce that was not put into a bin was taken to the walk-in cooler behind the meat counter. As I worked on the produce display, Dad was busy butchering a side of beef into roasts and steaks. He would spend most of the day slicing sides of bacon, cutting pork chops, preparing trays of ground beef, and arranging the showcase at the meat counter. Friday nights and all day on Saturdays were times of heavy grocery shopping, and most of our profits came from the sale of meat and produce. Those areas had to be made ready.

As I worked to prepare the produce bins, I stopped several times to wait on customers, but by ten o'clock or so I had finished the bins and had taken my station behind the check-out counter. When there were no customers, I sat on a wooden stool behind the counter and read a Superman comic book. I loved DC Comics including Batman, Green Lantern, and Aquaman; however, Superman had always been my favorite. When I was younger, I had coveted superpowers. I had wondered what it would be like to have x-ray vision and see through walls or be able to fly around the world to exotic places like New York or Miami. Traveling is something that I really wanted to do.

In reality, I had never been outside the state of Tennessee; in fact, I had rarely been outside the city limits of Nashville. My family just did not take vacations. When I was little, my family simply could not afford to take trips. Since opening the store, there wasn't time. My family had overcome poverty, but we had become chained to Stone's Shop and Save Market.

My reading about the exploits of the "man of steel" was interrupted when the Gibson girls entered the store. Margie was my age and Allie was a couple of years younger. They lived with their parents a few houses down Clay Street. They rarely came into the store and were seldom seen out in the neighborhood. Both sisters were wearing print dresses that came down to their ankles and up to their necks. Margie and Allie were very pretty, but I do not ever remember seeing them smile. They always carried a blank expression on their faces—never happy, yet not sad either. Their expression seemed almost trance-like.

At the end of the check-out counter, we had a glass case filled with penny candy. Margie laid a nickel on the counter and pointed at the box of Tootsie Rolls.

"Five Tootsie Rolls?" I asked.

Margie nodded. I retrieved five Tootsie Rolls from the candy case and handed them to Margie.

"Thanks," I said as I picked up the nickel, "and come back."

In response, Margie lowered her head and turned toward the door with Allie close behind. As Allie was about to exit the doorway, she turned and looked me in the eye. Her face was expressionless and there was no sparkle in her eyes.

"You're welcome," she said softly. She then turned and walked out of the store.

I believe that was the first time I had heard either of the sisters speak. As I watched them walk across the parking lot and turn up Clay Street, I could not help but wonder why these girls acted so strangely. Margie had been in a few of my classes at school, but I had never given her much thought. For some reason, this encounter had caused my heart to go out to these girls. As I watched them slowly walk up Clay Street, a puzzled sadness enveloped me. Why were these girls so detached? I made up my mind that I would engage in a real conversation with them the next time they came into the store.

As I watched the Gibson girls walk down Clay Street, Tommy entered the store. He was wearing a light blue polo shirt and a pair of Levi's that were starched and neatly creased. He wore penny loafers and white socks which were the popular footwear of the time. It was hard to believe that he had just spent the night in the horrible living conditions of the Martin house.

"Hey, Jimmy," he said as he walked by the counter and headed to the back of the store. I knew that he was going to the soft drink cooler. On his days off work, he always stopped in at mid-morning for a Dr. Pepper. He liked Dr. Pepper as much as I liked Double Cola.

"Have you seen my little brother?" he asked as he placed a dime on the counter.

"I haven't seen Bones since yesterday," I said, "but your little sisters were in here this morning."

"If you see him," Tommy continued, "tell him Buzz is looking for him."

"Okay, but if you see him before I do, tell him that I'm looking for him. I'm looking for people who want to play baseball this afternoon."

"I'll do that," he said as he took a sip of his Dr. Pepper.

"Hey, Tommy. The Gibson girls were just in here. Do you know them very well?" I knew that the Gibson's backyard backed up to the alley across from the Martin house.

"I don't think anybody knows them very well. They almost never come out of their house. I've seen them in their backyard a few times, but they just mope around. They don't talk much; in fact," he said with a little laugh. "I don't think that I've ever seen them talk to each other."

"Well, I was just wondering. They always seem so.......... bland."

"I know what you mean." With that, Tommy put his empty bottle into the collection cart at the rear of the store. As he exited the store, he said, "Don't forget to tell Randall that Buzz is looking for him."

"Okay."

As the door closed behind Tommy, I realized how much I had come to like him. Although he was four or five years older, he never treated me like a kid. We talked a lot during his visits to the store, and he always conversed with me as an equal. I think we had come to regard each other as friends. Even so, there was one thing that puzzled me. Why would Tommy continue to live with his parents in absolute squalor?

My thoughts were interrupted when I saw Miss Myrtle walking up Fifth Avenue toward the store. Her long, wiry, silver-gray hair was parted in the middle and long, braided pigtails hung down the front of her cream-colored blouse. She was wearing knee-length pants called "pedal-pushers," a popular style of the time. Miss Myrtle was one of the most well- spoken, sophisticated people I had ever known. She was a very kind woman and was always cheerful. In her mid-to-late sixties now, she had taught English at Pearl High School for over thirty years. As a retired schoolteacher, she worked on a part time basis at the store. I was always glad to see her for two reasons: I really enjoyed talking to her and –of course—she was my relief. When she took over the check-out counter at 11:30 a.m., I was free for the rest of the day.

"Hello there, Mr. Jim," she said as she entered the store. "You surely look chipper today!"

There was one thing that I really did not understand. Miss Myrtle always referred to me as "Mr. Jim." Since I was more than fifty years younger, her calling me "Mr." made me feel a little strange.

"Have you been busy today?" she inquired.

"Oh, not really."

As I was answering and Miss Myrtle was moving behind the counter, the door opened, and a young Black guy came in.

"Hey, man. Where's your pimento?" It was Silas Patterson.

"Hey, man. They are right over there," I said as I pointed to the shelving near the check-out counter.

He went over to the shelf and returned with a small can of pimento. "My dad said you're a pretty good baseball player."

"I'm okay at baseball," I said. "Good or not, I love to play. Your dad told me that we should get together and throw it around a little bit."

"Maybe so."

Just as Silas was saying that, the door opened, and Bones and Buzz entered. Both had their baseball gloves.

"Tommy said we're playing ball today," Buzz said.

I looked at Silas wondering whether I should ask him to come along. He would be the only Black kid at the Little League Park. As I gave him his change, Silas bailed me out of this decision.

"Well, I gotta go. I'll see ya later," he said as he hastily exited the store with his can of pimento.

***

After retrieving my glove from the apartment, Bones, Buzz, and I stopped by Bucky's house to see if he could play. Unfortunately, Bucky had chores and baby-sitting duties and could not go with us. As we left his house, I could feel Bucky's disappointment with being stuck with kids and chores. I was upset for him; this was the third day in a row that Bucky had been unable to leave his house. I felt Bucky's frustration.

When Bones, Buzz, and I arrived at the Little League Park, a game was already in progress. There were two teams of four players each.

"Hey, we got Stone!" Steve shouted as he saw us arrive.

"No! "We got Stone," Roger shouted. "Steve, you know that you had last pick. It's our turn, and we're picking Stone."

"But you guys got first at bat. We should get this pick," argued Steve. As he looked at me, Steve shouted, "What do you think, Jimmy Stone?"

"I think I'm on your team," I said to Steve as I ran out to play shortstop. I did not want to be on Roger's team.

"All right," Roger surrendered with some frustration. "We've got Buzz."

"What about me?" inquired Bones.

"You'll have to wait until another player shows up," said Roger. "We've got to have even teams."

"But I could pitch for both teams," Bones retorted.

"Nope. Just wait for somebody else to show up," said Roger forcefully.

Actually, Bones was an extremely poor baseball player and a terrible pitcher. With him pitching, a batter would have to wait a long time for a pitch to hit.

With a great deal of frustration, Bones accepted that he would have to wait. He sat down on one of the park benches under some trees behind the backstop and began to pout. A couple of hours passed as Bones watched the game hoping in vain for another player to show up. Between innings, I sat on the park bench with him, and I could sense his growing anger. Several half-gallon glass milk bottles filled with water had been placed on a picnic table behind the backstop. It was such a hot day that it did not take long for those bottles to empty.

"Hey, Bones," said Roger. "Why don't you go down to

my house and fill these bottles? There is a water hose in the backyard."

I looked at Bones. He was fuming.

"Screw you, Roger. Fill up your own bottles," shouted Bones angrily.

Roger walked threateningly toward Bones. With Roger's advantage in size and strength, Bones would be no match for him in a fight.

"Come on, Bones," I said. "Buzz and I will help you."

Bones got up from his perch on the park bench and walked over to the picnic table and picked up a couple of bottles. I picked up two bottles, and Buzz picked up one that had Roger's name written on a piece of tape that was stuck to the bottle. Evidently, Roger didn't want other guys drinking from his bottle.

As we walked across the outfield to Ninth Avenue to Roger's house, Bones was furious. By the time we arrived in Roger's backyard, Bones could scarcely contain himself.

"That smart-ass bastard always has to have his way," fumed Bones.

As I started putting water into the bottle that had Roger's name on it, Bones grabbed it out of my hand.

"Come on, Bones," I protested. "It's only half full."

"You guys fill up the other bottles. I've got something special for this son-of-a-bitch," Bones said with a sly smile.

Bones poured the water out of Roger's bottle. With a big grin, he unzipped his pants and started peeing into Roger's bottle. After he had put about a quarter inch of urine into the bottle, he gleefully took the hose and completed filling the bottle with water.

"This is gonna be great!" Bones said with a broad cheerful smile.

After we filled all the bottles, Bones continued to smile as he handed me Roger's bottle.

"I'm giving you the honor," he said.

I accepted it with great pleasure, and we returned to the ball field.

"It's about time," shouted Roger as we put the bottles on the picnic table where they were immediately seized by dry baseball players. Roger turned up his bottle and drank thirstily. Both Bones and Buzz turned their backs to hide ecstatic smiles.

After he had taken three or four large gulps, Roger took the bottle from his mouth and licked his lips. He held the bottle up toward the sun and looked at it intently. The subtle smile on my face faded as Roger studied the bottle in the sunlight. He continued to lick his lips as he looked in my direction. I sensed that he suspected foul play; however, my fears melted away when he turned the bottle up and began drinking as thirstily as ever.

As Bones, Buzz, and I walked back from the Little League field that day, we did so with a joyous pep in our step. We had just witnessed the biggest jerk in North Nashville drink Bones' pee.

***

When we got back to the store, we found Silas sitting on the front steps with a baseball and glove.

"We'll see ya, Jimmy," said Bones as he and Buzz continued walking down Clay Street. "This has been a great day!"

I could only smile in agreement as I looked at Silas.

"Hey, man," he said. "You wanna throw some ball?"

I was hot, tired, and dirty; however, I could not turn Silas down. We went to the pony field and threw baseball until the sun went down.

***

Saturday mornings were busy at the store. As usual, I opened the store with Dad at 6:30 a.m. Mom took over at 7:30 and I assumed the duties of a sack-boy. I took a break at noon and was not expected to be back until 3:00 p.m. We did not play baseball at the Little League field on Saturdays or Sundays because Little League games were scheduled. Since the Yankees were not playing on the CBS Game of the Week, I decided to walk down to the cliffs. As I exited the store, I met Bucky walking across the parking lot.

"Hey, Horsehead," he said. "Are you off?"

"Yeah. Gotta be back at 3 o'clock. Are you free today?"

"Yep."

"Let's go down to the cliffs and mess around for a while," I said.

We didn't make it all the way to the cliffs. We stopped in the pony field and sat down under the big sycamore tree.

"Who was that nigger you were throwing with yesterday?" Bucky inquired.

"His name is Silas Patterson. He lives up on Sixth Avenue. His dad delivers groceries to the store for C.B. Ragland," I explained.

"Is he any good?"

"He can throw and catch. Yesterday was the first time I pitched with him. He may come back tomorrow after church. Come out and throw with us if you can."

"I don't know," said Bucky. "I thought niggers like to play basketball. I didn't think they cared about baseball."

"Silas told me that a bunch of older colored guys play two or three afternoons a week down at Morgan Park. Silas goes down there to watch. He says that they are real good. I may go down there with him one day this week. You wanna go?"

"I'll see if I can. I've never seen niggers play baseball except on TV," he snickered.

"Let's go down the cliffs, Buck."

The End of a Career

On Sunday morning, Brother Cullom was in rare form. His hellfire and brimstone sermon was taken from the books of Corinthians and Revelation where he enumerated the sins that were deserving of everlasting punishment. From First Corinthians, he read: "Do you not know that the wicked will not inherit the kingdom of God? Do not be deceived. Neither the sexually immoral nor idolaters nor adulterers nor male prostitutes nor homosexual offenders nor thieves nor the greedy nor drunkards nor slanderers nor swindlers will inherit the kingdom of God." After expanding on that he quoted from Revelation: "Blessed are those who wash their robes, that they may have the right to the tree of life and may go through the gates into the city. Outside are the dogs, those who practice magic arts, the sexually immoral, the murders, the idolaters and everyone who loves and practices falsehood."

Brother Cullom ended his sermon with an invitation to those who needed prayer to come down to the front. Several individuals responded as the congregation sang *Just as I Am.* Although I could not remember committing any of those sins, it was all I could do to resist going down front. As I stood singing, I clutched the back of the seat in front of me. I was greatly relieved when Brother Cullom ended our service with a closing prayer.

I wasted no time getting down the steps and across the gravel parking lot to where Dad was waiting for me. I quickly got into Dad's '55 Chevy. Of all his cars, this one was my favorite.

"Hey, Jimmy Boy! How was Sunday School?"

"Sunday School was fine, Dad, but the preacher gave a humdinger of a sermon today."

"Really? What did he preach on?"

"Sin."

"Sin?"

"Yeah." I said. "Sin."

"Well, what did he say about it?" Dad inquired.

"Dad...," I hesitated, "I'm pretty sure that he's against it."

Dad just chuckled. "That sounds reasonable."

As we drove down Clay Street toward the store, I asked, "Hey, Dad. Where did the word, 'nigger,' come from?

Dad did not answer right away. Although taken by surprise by the question, he displayed an intensely thoughtful look.

"I'm not really sure, Son. The proper word for a colored person is 'Negro.' I'm pretty sure that it's just a play on that word. It probably grew out of slavery." Dad continued to look intensely thoughtful. "It's probably a good idea not to use that word. It was used a lot in the old days, but its offensive to colored people. Today," Dad went on, "it's a word that is used to put people down—or even hurt their feelings."

"A lot of people call colored people 'niggers.' They don't seem to mean anything by it." I said.

"Yeah, I know. I've used that word and so has your mother. We used it out of ignorance when we were younger. We grew up calling colored people 'niggers' because everybody else did. We didn't consider it a hateful term; we just didn't know any better. Does that make sense?"

"Yeah, I guess."

"Do you use that word?" Dad asked.

"Sometimes. I've heard colored boys around the store call each other that."

"Yeah, I know, but they would take it differently if a White person said it." Dad glanced at me with an inquiring look. "What brought this on anyway?"

"Well, I was telling Bucky that Silas Patterson might come up to throw baseball after church today. Bucky said that he didn't think that niggers liked baseball." I paused and said, "He didn't use the word to be mean, though."

"Bucky is just like a lot of White people," Dad said. "It's just a term he has heard all his life, and he doesn't think about it as a word that hurts people. But….," Dad hesitated, "I bet you have never heard him use it around a colored person because he knows that they wouldn't like it. I bet the same is true for you."

"Yeah," I confessed. "Even though White people don't mean anything by it, why do they use it knowing that it hurts people?"

"What do you think?" Dad asked.

I hesitated and took a deep breath. "Because White people believe that they are better than Black people?"

"I think you've got it," Dad said.

After a few moments of silence, Dad looked at me and said, "Another thing, Jim. A lot of colored men play baseball. Look at Willie Mays and Hank Aaron. A Black man is the catcher for the Yankees."

"Yeah. Elston Howard is a great catcher; but there's not that many of them."

"Well, at any rate, it's a good idea not to use the 'n' word. Most of our customers are colored………….and they are good people who do not deserve that kind of disrespect."

"Yeah. That's right."

"Son, if you are so interested in the meaning and history of the word, why don't you look it up in the dictionary?"

After we arrived at the store, I helped Mom and Dad close up and clean up. After our Sunday afternoon dinner, I went right to Webster's Dictionary. It defined "nigger" as: "used as an insulting and contemptuous term for a person of color. It is derived from the Spanish Portuguese for a black person, "negro."

Dad was right. The word was a put-down that Mr. Gates, Miss Myrtle, Mr. Patterson, or any of the people in our neighborhood did not deserve. I decided that I would never use it again.

***

The sun was setting as Silas, Bucky, and I were walking up the alley that ran from the Morgan Park baseball field to Clay Street. On Monday, Bucky and I skipped the afternoon game at the Little League field to go to Morgan Park with Silas. The three of us had spent all of Sunday afternoon throwing ball and climbing on the cliffs. Silas had convinced Bucky and I to accompany him to Morgan Park on Monday afternoon. We were glad we did. Bucky and I were amazed at what we witnessed. Fourteen or fifteen young Black men had put on an astonishing exhibition of baseball skills. The game began around 5 p.m. and did not end until almost dark. Most of the players were high school or college age, but a few were older guys in their late twenties.

"I told Ya'll," chided Silas as we briskly walked up the alley.

"What do you think about that, Buck?" I chimed.

"Those guys can play!" exclaimed Bucky excitedly. "I don't understand why that tall lanky pitcher isn't playing for the Vols. Did you see that curve ball?"

Nashville had a minor league team called the Nashville

Vols. I had to agree with Bucky; that pitcher could be a pro. Of course, the Nashville Vols was an all-White team in 1961.

Walking up the alley, we had almost reached Clay Street when a small Black boy climbed onto the top of a wooden fence that bordered the alley. He may have been seven or eight years old. Just before we reached his perch, he shouted, "You white crackers!" He immediately jumped from the fence and ran up the alley toward Clay Street.

"You better get out of here," shouted Silas. "You little dumb-ass alley-running nigga!"

"Wow!" said Bucky. "I don't believe you said that!"

Silas just shook his head and laughed. "You gotta talk to 'em in the language that they understand, Buck."

I was dumbfounded. "Hey, Silas. Just what is a 'cracker' anyway?"

"Horsehead!" Bucky interrupted. "You gotta get out of that grocery store more often if you don't know what a cracker is!"

"Cracker?" I puzzled. "Like 'cheese and cracker' or 'peanut butter and cracker'?"

Silas just cracked up laughing and looked at me. "Hell, man. You don't know that you are a cracker?"

"Damn, Horsehead," Bucky exclaimed. "Cracker is what colored people call White people."

I gave Bucky a puzzled stare for a moment and then said, "That makes no sense. How is a White guy like a cracker?"

Silas kept laughing. "No, man. We're not talking about saltines. The White man was the slave driver. He cracked the whip on the back of the Black slaves. He's the cracker."

"Oh," said Bucky. I could tell that he did not know the meaning either. Both of us learned something that day.

***

The next day, I was really looking forward to baseball at the Little League field. I already knew that Bucky would not be going, but I felt certain that Bones and Buzz would show up at the store by noon. As usual, I opened the store with Dad at 6:30 a.m. For a Tuesday morning, we had become quite busy. From the time we opened until a little after 8:00 a.m., there was a constant line of customers. Following the morning rush, the Gibson girls came into the store. Margie and Allie went to the dairy case and picked up a half-gallon of Jersey Farms milk and proceeded to take a loaf of Colonial Bread from the bread rack. They sat the items down on the counter.

"Will that be all?" I asked.

Margie nodded.

"That'll be sixty-five cents."

Margie handed me a dollar bill. While I made change, I decided to engage them in conversation. As usual, both girls wore dresses that spanned from the neck to the ankles. They also wore that familiar blank expression.

"Hey, Margie," I said. "Are you girls doing anything special this summer?"

Margie continued to look down and glumly shook her head. Allie uttered a very soft "No."

I really did not know what else to say, but I wanted to find out more about these two.

"What are you doing with your time this summer?" I continued.

Margie just shook her head again and turned toward the door with Allie close behind. As Allie exited the store, she looked toward me and said, "Nothing......Bye."

***

Bucky could not play baseball that afternoon, and Bones did not show up either. When Buzz and I arrived at the Little League field, we joined Steve, Roger, and a few others. There were only nine players, so we divided into two 4-man teams. To keep the teams even, I did the pitching for both teams. Although there were few of us, we played until the afternoon shadows were long.

As we were leaving the park, Steve said, "We need more guys!"

"Does anybody know somebody?" shouted Roger.

"Well," I said. "Bucky can come sometimes and sometimes he can't."

"What about that little scrawny-ass Bones Martin?" Roger demanded.

"I know I can get him to come," I said.

"With Bucky and Bones, we'll have eleven players," said Steve. "One more player and we can have six on a team."

The nine of us just stood looking at each other. I thought of Silas.

"There's one more guy that I might can get to come," I said.

"Get anybody you can," insisted Steve. "Everybody be here same time tomorrow."

***

Silas was not very comfortable about playing baseball with a bunch of White guys that he didn't know. Buzz and I had put the question to him as we stopped by his house on the way back from the Little League field. Although somewhat hesitant, Silas agreed to play. We decided to meet at the front of the store the following day.

After we left Silas and were walking toward the store, Buzz voiced concern about Bones.

"I don't know about Bones," said Buzz. "He's not a very good player and he hates Roger. He may not want to play."

"Yes, he will," I insisted. "You'll see him later today. When you do, tell him to be at the store at noon tomorrow. If he refuses, let him know that I will tell Roger about him peeing in the water bottle."

"That's blackmail, Jimmy," Buzz snickered. "He'll be there." Buzz stopped laughing and looked at me. "What about Bucky?"

"I'll see him later today, but he probably won't know if he can play 'til tomorrow. That's usually how it works with him."

***

Just before noon on the following day, Bucky was the last to arrive at the store. He had managed to escape babysitting for the day. He was in great spirits. He joined Bones, Buzz, Silas, and me as we sat on the front steps of the store. Silas was also in great spirits. His love of baseball had stretched his comfort level regarding playing ball with a bunch of crackers.

We walked up Clay Street and turned onto Ninth Avenue toward the Little League field at White City Park. The houses on this section of Ninth Avenue were shotgun houses and were set very close together. Out of one of those houses came Gooch Davis. His real name was George, but everyone called him Gooch. He was slightly taller than I and, like Bucky, extremely slim with bushy brown hair and a pre-mature mustache. Gooch was an excellent baseball player.

"Hey, Stone," he said as he stepped through the gate of his fenced front yard. As he acknowledged me, he noticed Silas. He squinted his eyes and gave me a strange look –like I had just arrived from another planet.

"We've got another player, Gooch. This is Silas, a friend of mine from over around the store."

"Hey, man," said Gooch as he gave a nod toward Silas.

As we approached the Little League field, I noticed a few more new faces. One of them was throwing with Roger. When Roger saw us walk onto the playing field, he stopped throwing and gave me the "stink eye."

"Hey, Roger," I said. "This is Silas. He's a friend of mine from over at the store, and he is a good baseball player."

"If you say so," retorted Roger with a cold stare.

I could tell that Roger was not the only one that had a problem playing ball with a colored boy. Jew Baby, Melvin, and several others gave the same "stink eye" look, but Steve walked over to Silas and gave him a friendly tap on the back of his shoulder.

"Hey, Silas. I'm Steve," he said with a smile. Steve just loved to play baseball. When it came to baseball, he was color blind. Not Roger.

As Buzz and Silas started warming up by playing catch, Roger walked over to where I was throwing with Bones. "Didn't know you were a nigger-lover, Stone," he said.

"Come on, Roger," I pleaded. "We need players and Silas is a good one. He's a good guy."

It was decided that Roger and Gooch would be captains to choose teams. Of course, Roger had the first choice, and he picked Melvin. The very last player to be chosen was Silas. He was on Gooch's team. Unfortunately, Bucky and I were picked by Roger.

As our team took the field, Bucky ran next to me and quietly said, "I've got a bad feeling about this."

"We'll see," I said with some trepidation.

When the game started, the stink eyes and cold stares melted away. Enough guys had shown up to enable each team to have eight players. Each team had a player for every position except catcher. Since the pitcher just looped the ball slowly over the plate, a catcher was not needed. We played for hours. Silas proved to be an excellent baseball player, and several of the guys followed Steve's example and warmed up to him.

When the shadows grew extremely long, we decided to call it a day. We were tired, dirty, and sweaty, but we had enjoyed our very best day of the summer. We all sat down on the grass behind the backstop to cool off and rest. Everyone was smiling, talking, and laughing. After a period of recuperation, I stood up to leave along with Bucky, Buzz, Bones, and Silas.

"Great game, guys," I said. "Hey, who won anyway?"

Everyone just laughed as we looked at each other. At some point, we had just stopped keeping score. We played baseball for the sake of playing baseball.

"We gotta go, guys," I said. "Same time tomorrow?"

"Absolutely," Steve shouted gleefully.

"Hey, Stone," said Roger as he sat in the grass. "Same time tomorrow," he said coldly, "…. but leave your nigger at home."

The laughing and smiling immediately stopped as everyone looked at Roger and then at Silas. The silence was overwhelming. The sudden tension in the air could have been cut with a knife. The only sound was the wind rustling through the trees. I could not believe what I had just heard. I looked at Silas. He was staring menacingly at Roger with both fists clinched and taking short angry breaths.

"Why don't you shut-up, asshole," Steve shouted angrily at Roger.

"No. You shut up, Steve," barked Roger as he scrambled to his feet. Jew Baby, Melvin, Gooch, and a few others slowly walked over and stood beside Roger.

I walked over to the seething Silas and took his arm. "There's too many of them," I whispered.

Silas jerked his arm away from me, picked up his ball glove, turned and walked toward Ninth Avenue. I followed with

Bucky, Bones and Buzz close behind. As we reached the edge of the Little League field, Bones stopped and looked back.

"Hey, Roger," he shouted. "You are a sorry-ass son-of-a-bitch. Guess what!!!" he shouted even louder. "I pissed in your water bottle the other day……and you drank it!"

We were too far away for Roger to give chase, but we quickened our pace as we walked up Ninth Avenue. When we turned onto Clay Street, we slowed and just looked at each other. Silas' eyes were red and tearful. I could feel his anger and hurt.

"I knew this wouldn't work," he sobbed as he gave me an angry look. "I can't believe you asked me to do this!"

"I'm really sorry," I said as tears came to my eyes. "There's no way I thought this would happen."

The five of us walked in silence down Clay Street. When we reached Sixth Avenue, Silas turned toward his house. I wanted to say something, but I could think of nothing to say. As I sadly watched Silas walk down Sixth Avenue, I made a decision: I would never go back to the Little League field. I never did. Never.

***

Independence Day

A week or so after the fiasco at the baseball field, Mr. Patterson's C.B. Ragland truck pulled up at the store for his usual Thursday delivery. As he loaded the boxes onto his hand-truck, I could not help but wonder if Silas had confided to his dad what had transpired. As he pulled the loaded hand-truck up the steps of the store, I hurried around the front counter to hold the door open for him.

"Thanks, Little Stoney," he said as he entered the store chewing on the usual unlit cigar.

"Hey, Pat," Dad's voice rang out from the meat counter at the rear of the store. "Do you need some help?"

"Nah. Just one more load."

After Dad and Mr. Patterson finished checking the boxes and signing the delivery receipts, Mr. Patterson said, "The Fourth of July is right around the corner. Are you gonna be ready for me?"

"Pat," Dad said, "I've got a whole herd of goats coming in here from Jacobs Packing Company. I'll be more than ready for you."

Mr. Patterson had already put in an order for two complete sides of goat for Dad to butcher. Barbeque goat was a Fourth of July staple in the Black community of Kalb Hollow. It had been a tradition for several families on Sixth Avenue to gather in Mr. Patterson's backyard to feast upon barbequed goat and chase it with Pabst Blue Ribbon beer.

"Little Stoney," he said as he approached the door to return to his truck, "I know your daddy is too old and too worn out to walk a block and a half to my house, but you come on over on the Fourth. Have you ever eaten goat?"

"No, Sir….I don't think so."

"Well, we'll fix that. Come on over."

"Well," I hesitated thoughtfully, "maybe.......... or… maybe not."

At that, Mr. Patterson let loose a big belly-laugh as he exited the door and walked to his truck—all the while chewing on that unlit cigar.

As Mr. Patterson was laughing his way to his delivery truck, the phone rang.

"Stone's Shop and Save," I said into the receiver.

It was Steve.

"Hey, Jimmy. We need ballplayers. Are you up?"

"I just can't do it, Steve," I said. "You saw how shabby my friend, Silas, was treated. I'm out for baseball."

"Come on, man. That was all Roger. The other guys wish they had backed you up. What do you say?"

"Can't do it. I know that you did not stand with Roger, but almost everyone else did. I'm sorry, but I won't be back to the Little League field. I appreciate your call, but…."

"Okay," Steve interrupted. "I hope you change your mind, but I really don't blame you. My brother is a jerk."

"Yes, he is," I agreed. "I'll see you sometime."

With that, I hung up the phone.

***

On July 4th, I did not go to the Patterson house to eat barbequed goat. I had always been a finicky eater, and the thought of eating a goat just did not agree with me. After the store closed at 1;00 p.m., Mom, Dad, and I grilled hamburgers in the backyard behind the store. We spent most of the afternoon just relaxing under the shade tree in the backyard. After Mom and Dad went up into the apartment to rest and watch the CBS Evening News, I got my glove and a baseball-sized rubber ball and played catch with myself by throwing the rubber ball against the side of the garage and catching it on the rebound. I imagined that I was playing shortstop for the New York Yankees as I fielded hard ground balls and threw strikes to the first baseman getting the runner out by a step.

"Who's winning?" asked a voice from beyond the gate in the fence.

"Hey, Silas!" I exclaimed. "What's up?"

"I was hoping to watch you eat some goat today," he said jokingly, "but I forgot that crackers don't like goat."

"Well, this cracker don't," I retorted smartly.

Silas was wearing his baseball glove on his left hand and was tossing a baseball up and down in his right.

"Put that rubber ball up, and let's pitch some real ball," he ordered.

And that's exactly what we did. We threw baseball—talked a little—threw baseball—and talked a little more. As we engaged in throwing and talking, the ugly event at the Little League field was never mentioned—nor was it ever mentioned again.

✳✳✳

The Red Menace

Although I really missed playing baseball at the Little League field, the summer of 1961 was a fun time. Bucky, Bones, Buzz, and I spent a lot of time throwing baseball, climbing the cliffs, walking through the wooded "bottoms," and telling tall tales while sitting under the big sycamore tree at the pony field. We were often joined by Silas. The summer was certainly not lost due to the lack of baseball. Bucky and I had walked downtown to the movies a couple of times that summer. Of course, Bucky never had any money, and both of us found it a little embarrassing that I had to pay his admission. Embarrassing or not, I was glad to make the movies my treat. Although the city bus stopped right in front of the store, we saved the seventeen-cent fare by walking down to Church Street where a whole line of movie theaters was located. We had seen *The Absent-Minded Professor* starring Fred MacMurray as well as *The Parent Trap* starring Haley Mills, Brian Keith, and Maureen O'Hara. Both were Disney movies that had been shown at the beautiful movie palace on Church Street known as The Tennessee Theater. Even in early childhood, I had loved going to the movies in downtown Nashville. Mom always took me shopping, and we always went to a movie. My mom and I had seen *Tea House of the August Moon* with Glenn Ford, *Badmen of Oklahoma* with Randolph Scott, *Moby Dick* with Gregory Peck, and *Foxfire* with Jeff Chandler. In fact, I think Mom and I had seen almost every Jeff Chandler movie ever made. He was Mom's favorite actor, and she had been saddened by his death that summer of 1961. Mom liked to go to the movies for a couple of reasons. With admission only 70-cents, movies were an inexpensive escape from the daily chores and concerns of a relatively poor family in the 1950's. Just as important, if not more so, was the fact that the movie palaces were air conditioned. Very few, if any, homes in Kalb Hollow had air conditioning. Summers in Nashville were very hot and humid, and an afternoon in one of the cool and comfortable movie palaces was a welcome relief.

My dad was a news junkie. He had the morning newspaper, *The Nashville Tennessean,* delivered to the store every morning. During the course of a day, Dad read the entire paper. My dad was very lacking in formal education, but he was not ignorant. Whenever he could, he slipped upstairs into the apartment to watch *The CBS Evening News with Walter Cronkite.* Dad loved the way that Cronkite delivered the news, and he always wondered whether Cronkite was a Democrat or a Republican. Some days, Dad was convinced that Cronkite had to be a Democrat; other days, Dad was certain that he was a Republican. In truth, no one could really discern the political beliefs of Walter Cronkite; he really was fair and balanced in his newscasts.

On a Saturday morning in mid-August, Dad and I opened the store at 6:30 a.m. as usual. While I unlocked the front door, Dad busied himself in the back dressing up the meat counter and preparing for a busy day. Since there were no customers waiting at the door, I filled the produce bins. As I was spraying down the turnip green bin, I looked out of the front window and saw the paper boy cruise by on his bike throwing rolled-up newspapers right and left. He threw a paper onto the store porch, and I immediately went out to retrieve it. I walked the front-page section of the paper to Dad, and I kept the sports page. The *Nashville Tennessean* had a great sports page in those days, and I devoured it daily. I was keeping close tabs on the

American League pennant race in which the New York Yankees enjoyed a slim lead over the Detroit Tigers. A lot of interest was added to major league baseball that summer of 1961 due to a historic assault on Babe Ruth's record of 60 homeruns in a single season. The record was set by Ruth in 1927 and had held for decades; however, two Yankee outfielders were making a serious run at Ruth's mark. As I read the paper dated August 19, 1961, I found that both Mickey Mantle and Roger Maris had clobbered forty-four homeruns each. Both players were hitting homers at a faster clip than Ruth's 1927 pace. Like me, most fans were rooting for Mantle, the Yankee super-star of the time. To me, it was only fitting that he was the one to break Babe Ruth's record.

As I was reading the sports page and admiring the picture of Maris and Mantle holding a jersey with "44" on it, Mr. Gates entered the store carrying the newspaper that he had just picked up in his front yard.

"What's up, Jim?" he said as he entered the store. Before I could respond, he looked toward the back of the store. "Hey, Stone!" he shouted. "Have you seen the morning paper?"

"I'm looking at it right now," retorted Dad. "This don't look good."

Dad was referring to the headline on the front page: "JFK Sends 1500 Troops to West Berlin."

"Stone, we are about to go to war over Berlin," Gates said.

Since no one else was in the store, I listened intently to the conversation. Growing up during the Cold War was a frightening time. The Soviet Premier, Nikita Khrushchev, had made a well-publicized and chilling speech in which he vowed, "We will bury you!" Statements like that one—in the nuclear age—got the attention of even a fourteen-year-old.

"This won't be like any other war," Gates continued. "When the damn Russians start firing those atomic missiles at us—and we throw ours at them—it's Armageddon."

Although I was only a kid, I knew about the war of words and threats that had been passing between the United States and Soviet Union since the end of World War II. I was aware that a Cold War crisis had been building all summer centering on the divided German city of Berlin. East Berlin was a part of Soviet-controlled East Germany; West Berlin was a part of pro-U.S. West Germany. The entire city of Berlin was located in East Germany; however, West Berlin was a part of West Germany. West Berlin was an island of freedom amid a communist police state. This situation had become a major sticking point of the Cold War. By the late 1950's, relations had become more tense regarding Berlin. The Marshall Plan—the brainchild of American Secretary of State, George Marshall—had provided billions of American dollars to the rebuilding of war-torn Europe since the late 1940's. The countries of Soviet-controlled Eastern Europe, including East Germany, had declined American aid. With American economic aid going to the West, the contrast between Western Europe and Eastern Europe had become stark. By the late 1950's and early 1960's, Eastern Europe was largely still in ruins with lagging economies and general poverty. In Western Europe, including West Germany, the Marshall Plan had transformed war-ruined cities into gleaming metropolises with robust economies and widespread prosperity. This proved to be a problem for the Soviet Union because large numbers of people were leaving Eastern Europe for the West using West Berlin as a conduit. Many of the refugees were professors, scientists, and mathematicians. From the Soviet perspective, this "brain drain" had to be stopped. Before dawn on Sunday, August 13, 1961, the twenty-five mile border between East Berlin and West Berlin was sealed by heavily guarded barbed-wire fencing. This was the beginning of the Berlin Wall which would imprison millions of people to a life under Soviet communism. Soviet-controlled East Germany threatened to go further and close the autobahn which connected West Germany to West Berlin. This action would leave West Berlin isolated from West Germany.

"It says here," said Dad as he scanned the newspaper story, "that Kennedy sent troops to patrol the autobahn connecter to West Berlin. It was in the paper yesterday that Kennedy had warned Khrushchev about trying to blockade West Berlin."

"That's what I'm talking about, Stone," said Mr. Gates with a worried look. "If the damn Russians try to blockade West Berlin, the shooting is going to start—maybe an atomic war.

Mr. Gates had good reason to be especially worried. His son, Frederick, was a U.S. soldier stationed at one of the military bases in Germany. He was definitely in harm's way.

"When did you last hear from Freddy?" asked Dad.

"We got a letter from him last week. He was fine, but that was before this Berlin shit hit the fan."

With that, Mr. Gates left the store visibly upset. I watched through the front window as he crossed Clay Street to return home. I had taken in the entire conversation, and I was worried too. I was worried about Freddy—and about surviving a nuclear war.

***

Over the next few days, the Berlin Crisis seemed to subside. American troops were continuing to patrol the connecter highway into West Berlin, but things had settled down. The Berlin story was no longer on the front pages of the newspapers, and it was no longer the lead story on the television newscasts. Mr. Gates had received a letter from Freddy who was serving at a military base near Frankfurt. Knowing that his son was not in West Berlin gave Mr. Gates a measure of relief. As the August days were waning, my mind turned toward the upcoming Labor Day holiday, Maris and Mantle, and the beginning of a new school year.........and seeing Judy again.

Chapter 2

Fall, 1961

School Daze

Labor Day was always bitter-sweet. It was the best of times and the worst of times. It was the best of times because the store closed at noon giving my mom and dad a badly needed afternoon of relaxation at my Uncle Henry's house. It was the worst of times because school started the very next day.

My Uncle Henry and Aunt Elise lived on a beautiful eighty-acre estate in Whites Creek, a rural suburb of Nashville. The house was a huge 2-story red brick colonial home with six round white columns spanning the front of the house. It was a mansion right out of *Gone with the Wind*. It was my visits to Uncle Henry and Aunt Elise that taught me how the "other half" lived.

Aunt Elise was my mom's younger sister and –just like Mom—grew up dirt poor in Kalb Hollow. Most people referred to the North Nashville community as Kalb Hollow because a large group of people of German descent had migrated there from Dekalb County, Tennessee in the early 1900's. Uncle

Henry earned his wealth from a couple of very profitable taverns that he owned in a seedy part of East Nashville. In his younger days, he had greatly profited from bootleg whiskey. That being said, Uncle Henry and Aunt Elise were awesome people. Hardworking and prosperous, they were also kind and generous. Family was very important to them. On holidays and special occasions, they loved to fill their impressive home with family. A Labor Day cook-out had become a traditional event. Uncle Henry had two brothers; each attended with their wives and children. Including Mom, Aunt Elise had three brothers and three sisters who attended with their families. Including Henry Jr. and I, there were well over twenty kids of various ages running around and having the time of their lives. At ten years old, Henry Jr. was four years my junior, and he was a cool little kid. Neither of us had brothers or sisters, but Fran also lived with my aunt and uncle. Fran was my cousin, the daughter of my mom's youngest sister, Naomi. Naomi had tragically lost her first husband in World War II. According to Mom, that sent her over the edge mentally. She suffered a line of failed marriages, one of which produced Fran. Since Aunt Naomi was unable or unwilling to care for Fran, Uncle Henry and Aunt Elise took her into their home and raised her as their own. Fran was a year older than me. She had a great personality and was very pretty. Slender with dark brown hair and brown eyes, her appearance was striking. Since we were toddlers, I loved Fran – not like I loved Judy – but loved her just the same. Of course, I loved visiting Henry Jr. and Fran because I experienced such a different world from the one in which I lived. Not only did visiting allow me to sleep in a beautiful mansion, but Henry Jr., Fran, and I could roam the fields and the woods playing games that were only limited by our imaginations. Uncle Henry had two horses. "Jim" was a solid reddish-brown horse while "Lady" was stunningly beautiful—reddish brown with a blond mane and tail and four white-stocking feet. Jim was gentle and easy to ride—Lady, not so much.

Even though I lived in the poor neighborhood of Kalb Hollow, Henry Jr. seemed to enjoy visits there as well. In our visits, each of us experienced a different world.

"See ya, Squeaky," said Henry Jr. as Mom, Dad, and I were about to leave for home. Henry Jr. was referring to the change that was taking place with my voice giving evidence that I was becoming a teenager. I was also developing an Adam's apple and beginning to grow hair where there used to be none.

***

I sat in the back seat of Dad's '50 DeSoto as we traveled home that Labor Day evening. Dad peered at me through the rear-view mirror and said, "Hey, Jim. Now that school is starting tomorrow, we need to talk about your new hours at the store."

"Sure, Dad," I said. "I will work anytime you need me." I did not want to lose my twenty dollars weekly pay to which I had become quite accustomed.

Mom turned her head and looked at me. "You will open the store with your dad and work the register until Myrtle comes in a 7:30. That's Monday through Friday. Are you okay with that?"

"Sure, Mom. When Miss Myrtle shows up, I'll head off to school."

"Good," said Dad. "On Monday through Thursday, you will work after school from 3:30 'til 5:00. On Friday, 3:30 'til 8:00." He hesitated. "If you want to go to a football game or something on Friday nights, just let me know and we will work around it."

"Okay. What about Saturdays?" I asked.

How does 9:00 'til noon sound?" retorted Dad.

"Yeah. That's okay."

"But, Jim," Dad added, "we might need you if things get really busy on Saturday nights, so be where we can find you."

"Sure, Dad." I hesitated a moment. "Say, Dad. These are fewer hours than I worked this summer. I was just wondering…"

"Don't worry," interjected Mom. "Your pay stays at twenty dollars a week. Just be available when we need you."

"No problem," I said happily. My wealth was preserved.

***

On Tuesday morning, Miss Myrtle arrived at 7:30 on the dot. Bucky had already arrived at the store sporting a new pair of Levi's and a "ducktail" haircut held neatly in place by a liberal application of Brylcream.

"Good morning, Miss Myrtle," I said as I picked up my spiral notebook and two pencils. There usually wasn't any written work on the first day of school, but I wanted to be prepared.

As we walked up Clay Street toward North High School, we saw a big yellow and black school bus parked on the corner of

Sixth Avenue at Clay Street. A long line of black students was filing onto the bus which would take them to Wharton Junior High School, the all-Black school for grades seven through nine in our Kalb Hollow neighborhood. We saw Silas as he moved toward the door of the bus, and I gave him a friendly wave. He acknowledged me and boarded the bus. It had been just the past Sunday afternoon that he and I had met after church and had climbed down the cliffs to the "bottoms." It was a great time winding our way through the woods all the way to the bank of the Cumberland River. As the bus pulled away, Silas put a hand out of the window and gave a little wave. It's interesting that in 1961 two kids could be friends and play together, but they were not allowed to attend the same school.

***

Mr. Potter was a short bald man of about forty years old. As my homeroom teacher, he checked for daily attendance, gave us our class schedules, and made sure that the emergency contact information was filled out on the back of the schedule cards. As Bucky and I copied our class schedules into our notebooks, I was disappointed to find that we had only two classes together: fifth period P.E. and sixth period Civics. We wished that we had more classes together, but we started each day in homeroom and ended together in Civics.

Homeroom period was from 8:05 to 8:30 a.m. A student could come into class as late as 8:20 and not be considered tardy, but everyone was usually in the room promptly at 8:05.

Every school day at exactly 8:20, a voice came over the public address system.

"May I have your attention for a moment please?" It was the authoritative voice of Mr. J.W. Arrington, the principal. As he spoke these words, Mr. Potter's eyes scanned the room to ensure that the students were giving proper attention.

"Welcome back, everyone," Mr. Arrington continued. "I know we are all looking forward to a great school year. We will begin today with our daily invocation which will be delivered today by our student body president, Danny Hall…………. Danny."

We could hear the rustle of pages as Danny accepted the microphone from Mr. Arrington.

"Today's reading is Psalm 23," said Danny. "'The Lord is my Shepherd, I shall not want. He maketh me to lie down in green pastures; he leadeth me beside still waters. He restoreth my soul….'"

After reading the psalm, Danny continued, "Please bow your heads and repeat the Lord's Prayer with me." 'Our Father who art in heaven, hallowed by Thy name. Thy kingdom come; Thy will be done on earth as it is in heaven. Give us the day our daily bread and forgive us our trespasses as we forgive those who have trespassed against us. Lead us not into temptation but deliver us from evil. For Thine is the kingdom, the power, and the glory forever.'" Along with Danny, everyone concluded with a healthy "amen."

"Please stand for the pledge," said Danny. With that Danny led the student body in pledging allegiance to the flag.

This was my third year at North Nashville High School, and every school day had begun in the same manner. The Bible reading changed, but the Lord's Prayer and the Pledge of Allegiance were recited daily.

With the conclusion of the invocation, Mr. Arrington ordered, "Let's move to our first period class." At that moment, a bell rang, and the students grabbed their notebooks, exited the room, and spilled into the hallway.

As I entered my third period class, I did so with great trepidation. I had always been very good at math, but I feared algebra. I had been told horrific stories regarding its difficulty; however, my fears faded as I entered the classroom. My heart pounded as I saw Judy sitting at a desk on the front row. Wearing a blue print dress that accentuated her sparkling blue eyes, her silky brown hair was flipped up at her shoulders. As our eyes met, she smiled. A warm sensation welled up inside me. The desk behind her was vacant; I immediately claimed it.

"Hi, Judy." These were the first words that I had ever spoken to her. Although I had loved her passionately since that day in the school library two years earlier, I finally mustered enough courage to speak.

"Hi, yourself," said Judy as she turned to face me.

"How was your summer?" I asked nervously, searching for small talk.

"Very nice, but way too short," she replied with a smile that made my heart melt.

Talking to Judy caused my heart to pound so hard that I

feared she would hear it beating. Trying to think of something to say, I thought, "Mouth—don't fail me now!"

"Summer was short, but I'm glad that school is starting back," I said.

"Yeah. Me too. I miss a lot of my friends during the summer," she said with a smile.

"I know what you mean." I really did know what she meant. A summer day had not gone by without Judy entering my thoughts. "Are you helping Miss Brown in the library again this year?" I asked.

"Yep," she nodded. "The fifth period on Monday, Wednesday, and Friday."

"Great," I said—barely catching myself from showing too much excitement. I was also scheduled for the library at those times.

"All right, class," interrupted Mr. Robertson. "Please answer the roll when your name is called."

As Judy and I averted our attention from each other to Mr. Robertson, I vowed to myself that I would hurry to algebra class every day and claim the seat behind Judy.

When class was dismissed, Judy rose from her desk and proceeded toward the door carrying her newly issued algebra textbook. In a warm daze, I could only sit and watch her—my cup running over.

I was walking on air when I left algebra class and briskly walked down the hall to the cafeteria for lunch. As I entered, I saw Bucky sitting alone at one of the tables opening his brown paper lunch bag. I walked over to his table and set my algebra book and notebook at a place across the table from him.

"Save me a seat, Grasshopper," I said as I turned to take my place in the cafeteria line.

"Corn, peas, and potatoes," I said to the server. She put ample servings on the plate and handed it to me. I placed the plate on a tray and continued down the cafeteria line where I grabbed two half-pint cartons of milk and a piece of fudge cake. The North High cafeteria provided the world's greatest fudge cake. After giving the cashier thirty-five cents, I joined Bucky who had almost finished his lunch.

"Hey, Horsehead," he said as I sat down. "If you will look to the third table directly behind me, you'll see your best buddy."

I looked past Bucky and several tables down sat Roger. He was eating his lunch with Melvin, Jew-Baby, and a few others.

"Yeah," I chuckled sarcastically. "My buddy."

I quickly became quiet as I looked at a couple of tables beyond Roger. There sat Judy with two of her friends, Claudia and Rella. She did not see me, so I took this opportunity to just gaze at her. I loved everything about her: her beauty, her smile, her laugh, her mannerisms….

"Wake up, Horsehead," said Bucky as he turned in his chair to see where my attention had strayed. "You're not looking at girls, are you?"

"Just one," I said with a smile.

"Which one?"

"I'll never tell."

***

After I left the cafeteria, I proceeded upstairs to room 223 for English class. As I entered the room, only a few students had arrived, but Margie Gibson was sitting at a desk at the back of the second row. I gave her a big smile as we made eye contact. With her usual blank expression, Margie just buried her head in her arms folded upon the desk. I interpreted her body language as "leave me alone," and "don't talk to me." I took a seat on the front of the first row by the door, but I could not help looking back at her and wondering why she was so sadly isolated. As other students entered the room and took seats, Margie continued to keep her head buried in her arms.

After the tardy bell rang, Mrs. Acuff arose from her desk at the front of the room and closed the door. Mrs. Acuff was an older lady in her late fifties or early sixties. Her hair was jet black with wide steaks of white. It was probably quite long, but she wore it up in a bun. She was wearing a black skirt that came down below her knees. Hanging down the front of her cream-colored blouse was a pair of reading glasses suspended by a stylish little chain from around her neck. Her appearance and her body language conveyed that she was all business. That proved to be true.

"Good afternoon," she said strongly. "If you are sitting on the front of your row, I need for you to count the people in your row including yourself." Pointing to stacks of books in the front corner of the room, she said, "Then come up and get a grammar book for each person in your row."

There were six students in my row, and I distributed a book to each of them. After each student in class received a book,

Mrs. Acuff continued with instructions. "Open your books to page five," she said. "Read pages five and six about proper and improper nouns. When you think that you know the difference in the two types of nouns, turn to page seven and do exercises one and two. While you are working," she went on, "I will call each of you up to my desk one at a time. Bring your book, and I will write your name in it and issue you a literature book as well. Are there any questions?"

I looked around the room. Either no one had a question, or everyone was afraid to ask.

"All right, then. Helen Blackwell, come on up," she commanded.

One by one, each student went up to Mrs. Acuff's desk. By the time she had finished issuing books, everyone had completed the assignment and was sitting quietly. It was absolutely amazing how Mrs. Acuff had almost instantly created a classroom climate that was orderly and respectful. She did not give the students a list of rules and punishments that ninth graders usually needed to hear. Her mere presence and aura created an extremely excellent educational atmosphere. As the school year rolled by, Mrs. Acuff's class was awesome.

"I'm going to call the roll again," she said. "When I call your name, let me know if you completed the assignment……….. Helen Blackwell."

"Yes, ma'am," replied Helen.

"Charles Bilbrey."

"Yes, ma'am."

"Rex Cothern."

"Yes, ma'am."

And so it went.

"James Stone."

"Yes, ma'am."

When she had completed the roll call, she said, "All right. Make sure your name is on your paper and pass your paper up to the front of the row where I will collect them."

As we passed our papers up, I could not help but wonder if everyone had been truthful about completing the assignment. I started feeling sorry for anyone who had not.

***

Boy's physical education met in the gymnasium. Bucky and I, as well as the other students, gathered in a section of the bleachers where Coach Pinkston called the roll and explained the expectations of the class. Coach was a large man who wore his red hair in a short flat-top style that was popular at that time. He had graduated from North High back in the early '50's, and he was a school legend as a football player. Coach Pinkston had no trouble commanding the respect of the boys at North High School. Being ninth and tenth graders, the students knew the requirements of the class, but Coach told us anyway. We were required to wear blue shorts, a white tee shirt, and tennis shoes. Showering after the day's activity was optional, but your grade suffered if you did not shower. On my P.E. days, Tuesdays and Thursdays, I stuffed my blue shorts in one tennis shoe, the white tee shirt in the other, and I tied the strings of one shoe to the strings of the other. Until it was time for P.E. class, I left the shoes draped over the open door of my school locker. One could look down any hallway of North High and see open lockers filled with books and other supplies with coats and gym shoes hanging on open locker doors. Nothing was ever taken. With less than 350 students spread over six grades, North High School was a special place.

As Coach Pinkston was taking roll, I looked up at the bleachers behind me. There sat Roger. Crap! He would not only be in my P.E. class two days per week, but he would also be in the library on Monday, Wednesday, and Friday. Double crap!! As I was looking toward him, our eyes met, and he gave me the middle finger salute. I turned away quickly pretending not to see him. "Crap," I whispered as I gave Bucky an elbow to get his attention. "Look up there."

"Oh, hell," he said with a sarcastic look. "It looks like fifth period is going to be real special."

***

As Bucky and I were walking from the gym to our 6th period class, I noticed that Bucky was giving me a strange look.

"What are you looking at, Grasshopper?" I asked.

He answered slowly and methodically, "I am looking at a young man in love."

"What are you talking about?"

"I'm talking about the girl you were looking at in the cafeteria. That's what," he said with a chuckle.

"What girl?" I asked with a grin.

"You know what girl," retorted Bucky.

I responded slowly and methodically, "Yes……. I do……………but you don't."

At that moment, we arrived at Mrs. Jolly's room. We entered the classroom, and I took the first seat on the row beside the door. Bucky took the seat immediately behind me.

Mrs. Jolly sat behind her desk at the front of the room greeting the students as they entered the room. She was a very nice looking lady in her mid to late forties with shoulder-length reddish brown hair and bright blue eyes. She was a little heavy; some might say pleasingly plump. She wore a broad smile which tended to make me like her immediately.

After she had dispensed with roll call, distributing textbooks, and conveying her expectations concerning behavior and deportment, she gave us a brief explanation of what she hoped we would be learning in her civics class. Civics was a ninth-grade requirement in Nashville at that time. The purpose of the course was to learn about the government and foster good citizenship.

"When the school year is over," she said, "I want each of you to leave this class with a working knowledge of federalism and what it means to be a constitutional republic. The United States is a constitutional republic based upon federalism. Shortly, you will know what that means."

All of that sounded a little boring to me, but Mrs. Jolly was not finished.

"Also," she continued, "we are living in very interesting times. History is being made every day, so I want you to have some knowledge of current events—the things that are going on in our country and around the world. Each Monday, you are to bring to class an article clipped from the newspaper dealing with a national or international event. In addition to the clipping, I want a one-page summary of the news event described in the article. As I said, this will be due each Monday. Now, don't bring me some report about some local store being robbed or somebody's barn burning down. The news event needs to be about a significant national or international event." She looked slowly around the room, then asked, "Are there any questions?"

Two or three hands went up, and Mrs. Jolly called on a student who asked, "What if we don't take the newspaper?"

Mrs. Jolly just stared at him for a moment sarcastically shaking her head. "That's your problem," she said. "If your family does not subscribe to the *Nashville Banner* or *Nashville Tennessean,* find a neighbor or someone who does. The first current event article isn't due until Monday, so you have almost a week to work that out. There are no excuses for not having this assignment each Monday."

It was obvious to me and everyone else that Mrs. Jolly –like Mrs. Acuff and all my teachers—were serious and meant business. There wasn't a soft touch in the bunch.

On the walk home with Bucky, I was actually looking forward to the next school day. I liked all of my classes—despite having to deal with Roger. I was especially looking forward to seeing Judy in algebra class the third period and in the library the fifth period. I could feel a great year beginning.

***

The first day of school had been awesome. When the school day was over, I practically skipped down Clay Street toward my afternoon shift at the store.

"What are you so happy about, Horsehead?" inquired Bucky as he tried to keep pace with me.

"I love school. Don't you, Grasshopper?" I said with a grin.

"Not really."

When we got to the store, we went our separate ways. Bucky walked to his house for his afternoon chores, and I entered Stone's Shop and Save Market with air under my feet; however, when I entered the store, I immediately noticed something odd. Miss Myrtle was still working the front counter. She normally leaves the store at noon. Mom was behind the meat counter at the rear of the store. Dad was nowhere to be seen.

"Come on back here, Jimmy," ordered Mom.

Where's Dad?" I asked as I approached the meat counter.

"He started feeling bad this morning. He was a little dizzy and sick to his stomach. He went upstairs to lie down. Go up and check on him, then come back down so we can let Myrtle go home."

"Okay, Mom." I went up the back stairs into the small, enclosed entry that opened into the kitchen of our apartment. I walked through the kitchen and living room into my parents' bedroom. Dad was lying on the bed asleep. I moved a chair to Dad's bedside. I sat for several minutes making sure that he was okay. I felt his forehead and found no sign of fever. His breathing seemed even and normal. As I sat watching him, I noticed the deep lines on his forehead and face. He looked pale and ashen. His hair was thin and completely gray, almost white. He had a receding hairline and a bald spot on the back of his head. I was looking at a man who was almost completely worn. Long hours at the store were taking a toll on my dad.

I returned to Mom at the rear of the store. She had a worried look on her face. She turned to me and said, "Jimmy, your dad needs rest. He works way too many hours. He has got to cut back." She hesitated before continuing, "I've been trying to get him to hire another meat cutter who can take some of the load off him, but he won't listen to me." After another hesitation, she said, "You stay back here and work the meat counter. I'll relieve Myrtle."

***

"How's your daddy today, Mr. Jim?" asked Miss Myrtle as she moved behind the counter.

"He seems a lot better today, Miss Myrtle." It still bothered me that she called me "Mr. Jim."

Dad was feeling much better that Wednesday morning. He and I had opened the store as usual, and I had worked the front counter until Miss Myrtle arrived. As I moved from behind the counter, Bucky came in the store.

"Are you ready, Horsehead?" he asked.

"You don't know how ready," I responded. "Good-bye," I yelled to Dad as he was working behind the meat counter. He looked up and waived. "Bye, Miss Myrtle," I said as Bucky and I left the store.

As Bucky and I were walking up Clay Street toward school,

the big yellow bus was pulling away from the corner of Sixth Avenue taking Silas and the other Black kids to Wharton Junior High. Further up Clay Street, we walked in front of St. Cecelia Convent at Eighth Avenue. In those days, Eighth Avenue North made a huge left turn in front of the convent and merged with Clay Street. Along the sidewalk in front of the convent was a huge white stone wall protecting the grounds from trespassers. Since the nuns were often customers at the store, I knew a few of them. The older nuns came into the store dressed in full habits with crucifixes around their necks. The habits of the younger nuns were a cream color with no head-covering. Many of the younger nuns were very pretty and always very nice. Bucky and I had sledded down the big hill next to the convent the previous winter with some of them. We had been amazed at their dare-deviltry.

Since I was really looking forward to seeing Judy in third period Algebra, Wednesday morning was a slow crawl. When second period Science class was over, I went straight to Mr. Robertson's room for Algebra class. Since I had my textbook with me, I did not stop at my locker. I wanted to get to class quickly in order to claim the seat behind Judy.

When I entered the classroom, Judy had not yet arrived, so I claimed the same seat as I had the previous day. I could not help smiling as I looked at the empty seat in front of me. In just a few moments, Judy would be sitting in it. Suddenly, my smile vanished as I experienced a very disturbing thought: what if she sat somewhere else? If she did, would that mean she didn't really like me? Would she rather sit near someone else? As I scanned the room, I noticed an empty seat behind her friend, Claudia. Would she sit there? My fears were alleviated when Judy entered the classroom. She smiled as our eyes met, and she took the seat in front of me.

"Hi," she said as she turned in her desk to face me. "Did you save this seat for me?"

"Yes, I did."

"That's sweet of you. I love to sit on the front row."

"I know you do." I tried to quickly say something suave, debonair, or just flirty—but to no avail.

She smiled with a little giggle as we looked into each other's eyes. I drank in the moment which was interrupted by Mr. Robertson closing the classroom door. As Judy turned to face the front, she gently touched my cheek with her fingertips. A warm sensation billowed up inside my chest, and my hands began to quiver. Yes, I was hopeless.

***

The end of the fourth period found me leaving English class and wondering about Margie Gibson. The entire time that Mrs. Acuff had been teaching, Margie sat motionless in the back row staring toward the front of the classroom. When the lesson was over and our homework had been assigned, she buried her head in her arms which were folded on her desk. I still wanted to converse with her, but I only saw her once per day, and she isolated herself at the rear of the classroom. I promised myself that I would try to talk to her when—or if—she came into the store again.

The library was located just down the hall from Mrs. Acuff's room, so I was the first to arrive. The library spanned from a hallway on one side of the school to another hallway on the opposite side of the school. It was huge. Down the long expanse were two rows of 12 tables with four chairs each. As I entered from the hallway, Mrs. Brown was sitting at her desk just to the left of the table rows. As she sat facing the tables, she was inserting library cards into a stack of books. Across from Mrs. Brown on the other side of the tables was a large alcove. This was the reference section of the library which accommodated two more rows of three tables each. Each wall of the library featured bookshelves from floor to ceiling. The North High School library was awesome featuring all the classics, modern novels, numerous biographies, and books on almost every subject.

After entering the library, I took a seat at a table directly in front of Mrs. Brown.

"Hi, Mrs. Brown," I said.

"Hello, Jimmy. Good to see you."

The cool thing about attending a very small school like North was that the students knew most of the teachers and most of the teachers knew the students. As I watched the other students enter, Bucky arrived and took the seat directly across the table from me.

"What do ya say, Grasshopper?" I quipped.

"I'm just wondering what you're going to say in about ten seconds," he chuckled in a mysterious manner.

As I gave Bucky a dumb-founded look, a hand was placed

on my left shoulder. I turned to see to whom the hand belonged. Damn!! It was Roger!

"Hey, nigger-lover," he whispered.

As he started to take the seat beside me, I grabbed the chair and shoved it under the table.

"Don't even try to sit here," I said in such a threatening tone that I surprised Roger, Bucky, and myself.

"Roger," Mrs. Brown said strongly, "only two to a table. You will have to sit elsewhere."

"Yes, ma'am," said Roger. He looked at me in a menacing way. "See ya 'round, nigger-lover," he whispered as he moved to a seat several tables away.

"Were you really going to fight that son-of-a-bitch?" Bucky inquired softly.

Before I could answer, my attention was diverted to Judy who had taken her seat beside Mrs. Brown. She immediately assumed and completed the task of inserting the cards into the stack of books on Mrs. Brown's desk. While Judy placed the books onto a wheeled cart, Mrs. Brown checked the roll and read us the riot act: no talking whatsoever; you may get up to browse the shelves quietly; you may check out a book for one week; there is a late-return fee of one penny per day; the seat that you are now occupying is your assigned seat; you must stay in your seat until roll is checked. "Any questions?" she quipped. Mrs. Brown knew that there would be no questions. All the students had prior experience in the library. We knew the rules, and we knew that they would be strictly enforced. Unlike Bucky and several other students, I did not leave my seat to look for a book. I worked to complete my English homework while intermittently gazing at Judy as she pushed her cart around the library placing books on the proper shelves. As I watched her, I was taken back to the first time that I had seen her: a very pretty, yet skinny, little girl wearing a red, blue, and green plaid dress. This innocent memory was jolted from my mind as I watched Judy stand on tip- toe to place a book on one of the higher shelves. As she stretched to reach the shelf, I noticed something for the very first time. Judy was no longer a skinny little girl. She had developed curves.........and in all the right places. The warm gushy feeling in the center of my chest became bigger, hotter, and more intense. My breathing picked up as my mind raced to places that it had not been before. Brother Cullom would label these ruminations as "impure thoughts." He would be right. I was having a bushel of them.

***

Chasing Ruth; Chasing Judy

I was almost saddened by the arrival of Saturday. The first week at school had been great, and I was already looking forward to Monday. By 6:30 a.m., I had filled the cash register, dusted the shelving, and opened the front door of the store. Being Saturday, no one was waiting to enter, so I sprayed the cold bins and made sure that the soft drink box was loaded with RC's and Double Cola's. As I was putting a few Pepsis into the drink box, Tommy entered the store followed by his two young sisters.

"Hey, Mr. Stone," he said as he walked to the drink box. "We need a half-a-pound of baloney."

"Hey, Jim," Tommy said as he retrieved his daily Dr. Pepper from the box. He was wearing his work boots and construction hat.

"You working today?" I asked.

"Afraid so, Jim," Tommy said.

"Here you go, Tommy," said Dad as he placed the white butcher-paper package on top of the meat counter.

After Tommy retrieved his package of bologna, we walked up to the front counter. As we walked by the bread rack, Tommy grabbed a loaf of Colonial Bread.

"That'll be fifty-one cents," I said.

Tommy placed a half-dollar and a penny on the counter.

"Hey, Jim. Could you put this stuff in separate sacks?" asked Tommy.

"Sure."

Tommy gave a bag to each sister, and they hugged his leg and left the store.

"Where are you working today?" I asked.

"I'm working at the new municipal auditorium down on 4th Avenue. It's supposed to be opening sometime next year. We're working six days a week to get back on schedule."

"Hi, Tommy," said Mom as she took my place behind the counter relegating me to sack-boy.

"Hey, Miss Bess," said Tommy. "Uh-oh," he continued. "There's the bus. Gotta go."

Tommy put his half empty Dr. Pepper bottle on the counter

and hurried across Clay Street. The bus stopped at the corner of Fifth and Clay in front of Mr. Gates' house. Mom and I watched as Tommy boarded the bus for his ride downtown.

"Hey, Mom, how does a guy like Tommy keep living in that filthy house?" I asked.

"Lord only knows, Jimmy."

***

Saturday mornings were extremely busy, so time passed quickly. Mom was checking groceries, and I was sacking them and helping customers get their purchases to their cars. Just before 10:00 a.m., Mrs. Anderson and her daughter entered the store. Mrs. Anderson was a plump older Black lady in her late mid-to-late sixties whose sole income was a monthly Social Security check. Her daughter, Mattie Anderson, was in her late thirties or early forties. Mattie had four children ranging in age from six to twelve years. Mattie was employed as a laundry worker at the Andrew Jackson Hotel in downtown Nashville. Mrs. Anderson, Mattie, and the four children lived on Fourth Avenue, a few houses down from Clay Street. They came into the store every Saturday morning to stock up on groceries for the week. Stone's Shop and Save Market usually operated on a cash-and-carry basis, but Dad had sympathy for the struggling Andersons and extended credit to them during the week. Mrs. Anderson, Mattie, or one of the older children often came into the store during the week to pick up grocery items, usually perishables like milk or bread. In lieu of payment, Dad would hold the paper receipt. Mattie always settled the bill every

Saturday when the week's groceries were purchased. The bill rarely exceeded ten dollars, and the groceries purchased on Saturday usually totaled around twenty dollars.

In 1961, twenty dollars in groceries would fill five or six large grocery bags—too much for two women to carry. Each Saturday morning, I loaded their bags into Dad's 1957 Ford Country Squire station wagon, and Dad delivered both people and bags to their home on Fourth Avenue. I went along to help get the bags into the house. Each time Dad and I entered the Anderson home, we held our breath. The house wreaked with the smell of urine. The wallpaper was dingy and stained. The wooden floor was soft and saggy in many places making it necessary to walk carefully on it.

After we left the Anderson house, we hurried to get back to the store. Dad did not like leaving Mom alone on such a busy day.

"Jim," said Dad as he turned off Fourth Avenue onto Clay Street. "I'm going to have to hire some more help. Weekends are just too busy for the three of us, and Myrtle doesn't like to work on Saturday."

"Dad," I responded, "I don't mind working all day on Saturday."

"Son, you're almost doing that now. I hate to admit that your momma is right, but I need to hire another meat cutter who can work a few days a week, especially Saturday."

After parking in the side lot, Dad and I hurried into the store. Three or four customers were patiently waiting at the meat counter. Dad briskly walked back to serve them.

"Jimmy," Mom said. "I hate to do this to you, but you need to run this bag over to the Andersons."

"Oh, man," I sighed as I looked into the forgotten bag which contained a few canned goods and a five-pound bag of sugar. If there was one thing that I did not want to do, it was to go back into Mrs. Anderson's house.

"Hurry back, Jim," ordered Mom. "We're busy and we need you to stay a little longer today." She hesitated, took a breath, and gave a sympathetic smile. "Sorry."

When I arrived at the Anderson house, I knocked on the door. Miss Mattie answered the door and took the bag of groceries. Relieved at not having to enter the house, I briskly walked up Fourth Avenue and turned onto Clay Street toward the store. As I was walking up Clay, I passed the Gibson house. Margie and Allie were sitting in the swing on the front porch staring into space with their usual blank look.

"Hey, Margie. Hey, Allie," I said with a smile.

Margie continued in her trance while Allie gave a little wave accompanied by a tiny smile.

"Margie!!" thundered a stern male voice from inside the house. "You and Allie get in here!"

The girls immediately vacated the swing. The screened door slammed behind them as they entered the house. The same male voice thundered again, "Who are you talking to?"

"They're not talking to anybody, Ricky!" The loud and forceful voice was that of Mrs. Gibson. "It's just the little boy from down at the store. Leave Margie and Allie alone!"

As I stood in the street in front of the house, quiet followed.

After I stood there for a few seconds, I continued my walk back to the store.

***

Days at school were awesome. I loved my classes and I especially enjoyed seeing Judy in algebra class and in the library. After a couple of weeks of school, something occurred in the library on Monday that filled me with ecstasy...............and agony.

"Jimmy," called Mrs. Brown. "Come here, please."

I had been sitting quietly at my table with Bucky, so I knew that I wasn't in any trouble.

"Yes, Ma'am," I said as I approached her desk.

"Judy Garner is in the reference section trying to get Friday's library cards alphabetized. She needs to finish before the end of the period. Would you mind helping her?"

Would I mind helping her!?! Was Mrs. Brown serious?

"No, Ma'am. Be glad to," I said as calmly as I could.

Slightly weak in the knees, I made my way over to the reference section of the library where Judy sat at a table organizing library cards.

"Hey," I said as I took a seat across the table from her. "Mrs. Brown told me to help you with all these cards."

"Great," she said. "I'm afraid that we might run out of time." As she spoke, she looked at me with those beautiful blue eyes, and I could not help but smile.

"I have already alphabetized the A's and B's," she went on. "You take the C's through the J's, and I'll take the rest."

"Sounds good to me," I said.

We immediately started separating the cards into stacks. As I was working, I looked across the table at Judy every few seconds. She was working intensely at her task when she looked up at me. The brow over her beautiful eyes were raised creating a wrinkled forehead and a look of annoyance.

"What are you looking at?" she inquired with some hostility.

"I'm looking at you," I said with a slight chuckle. "We have over a half hour until the bell rings. The two of us will finish these cards with time to spare." As she continued with her look of annoyance, I continued. "We've got plenty of time. Why are you in such a hurry?"

"Because I want to get done with this!" she snapped.

"Okay," I murmured meekly. Something was bothering Judy, and I was hoping that it wasn't me.

We completed our task with over ten minutes left in the period. Upon completion, Judy gathered the cards, put them on her cart, and – without saying a word – took the cart and parked it next to Mrs. Brown's desk. I continued to watch her as she quickly glanced in my direction while taking her assigned seat in the main section of the library.

Bewildered, I returned to my table.

***

"Hey, Horsehead," quipped Bucky. "What's eating you?"

As Bucky and I were walking home from school, I could not get my thoughts away from Judy. Was it something I did? Was it something that I didn't do? I was perplexed and bothered.

"Horsehead," Bucky said. "Are you listening to me?"

"Sorry about that," I explained. "I had my mind on something."

In an effort to change the subject, I asked, "Why don't you see if you can come over Wednesday night and watch the big game with me?"

"What big game?" asked Bucky with a puzzled look.

"The Yankees are playing the Orioles on TV. It's the 154th game of the season."

"So?"

"It's Roger Maris' last chance to break Babe Ruth's record."

Bucky liked baseball, and he knew that Mickey Mantle and Roger Maris had been making serious runs at Ruth's single season homerun record; however, he was unaware that the commissioner of baseball, Ford Frick, had decreed that the record would have to be broken within 154 games. The 1961 season contained 162 games, but Frick believed that the record would have to be tied or broken in the same number of games that Ruth played in 1927. Mantle or Maris would have to hit sixty homeruns to tie—sixty-one to break—Ruth's record and do it within 154 games.

It had become apparent that my hero, Mickey Mantle, would not be the one to catch or surpass Ruth. With fifty-three homeruns, Mantle had not participated in a game during the entire week. Mantle had developed a heavy cold and was not expected to return to the line-up until the following Sunday. With fifty-eight homers, Maris had an opportunity. Failing to homer on Tuesday, the 153rd game, he would have to hit two homers to tie the record or three to break it in game 154 on Wednesday night. Breaking the record would require him to hit three homeruns—a long shot: however, Maris was capable of hitting two homers to tie it. During the season, he had hit two homeruns in a single game on numerous occasions. The ABC television network would be carrying the telecast nationally from Baltimore, and I planned to be watching the 6:00 p.m. telecast locally on Channel 8.

As I turned to enter the store, Bucky peeled off toward his house. Maybe he would be able to escape his baby-sitting duties and join me for the big game. Of course, I had to make sure that I could escape any store-keeping duties.

"Hey, Mom," I said as I entered the store brandishing a big smile. The store was almost empty. Only a few kids were at the front counter buying penny-candy. I joined Mom behind the counter and helped serve the kids.

After the kids left the store—and before Mom could go up into the apartment to prepare dinner—I put my arm around her and said, "I've got a big favor to ask."

She removed my arm from her shoulders and put her hands on her hips. With a suspicious look, she asked, "Okay, what is it?"

"Well," I said, "the Yankees are playing the Orioles on TV Wednesday night at 6:00. It's a really big game, and I would really like to see it."

"So, you want me to come back down Wednesday night before 6:00? Is that it?"

"Yes, Ma'am," I said with a slight aura of pleading. "I want to invite Bucky to watch it with me."

"Well," she chuckled, "I guess you are worth a baseball game."

***

As I crossed the threshold into algebra class the next morning, I saw that Judy had not yet arrived. I took my usual seat behind her desk and waited. The tardy bell rang—and no Judy. Checking the roll, Mr. Robertson marked her as absent. I was concerned. Judy never missed school. She had received perfect attendance certificates every year. Something was wrong. The anxiety that she had shown in the library the previous day probably had little to do with me…………, but what? My concern increased when she was absent again on the following day, Wednesday.

***

Worried about Judy, I suffered a sinking feeling as Bucky and I walked home from school. As we passed Sixth Avenue, we encountered Silas and asked him to join us for the game.

After we had watched a scoreless first inning, Silas started shaking his head as he sat in Dad's rocking chair.

"What's with you?" I asked.

"I just can't believe that I'm sitting here with a couple of crackers watching a bunch of other crackers play baseball on television," he retorted with a chuckle.

"Well," Bucky said, "you've got to believe it……because you are!"

With that, I chimed in, "All of those players aren't crackers. The catcher for the Yankees is Elston Howard, a colored guy and a great player."

"Yeah," smirked Silas. "One player out of nine. For a nigga to play in the major leagues," he went on, "he *has* to be a great player.

Silas had a point. Even in 1961, for a Black man to make a major league roster, he could not be just a good player; he had to be a great player.

After making an out in the first inning, Maris came to bat in the third inning against the Oriole's ace pitcher, Milt Pappas. Bucky, Silas, and I paused our conversation as we intently stared at the black and white television screen. We watched as the left-handed hitting Maris swung and drove the baseball into the right field stands for his fifty-ninth homerun of the season.

"Hey, man," said Silas. "He just needs one more to tie the Babe."

"There are six more innings to play," I declared. "He could do it."

We continued to watch the game with anticipation, but our hopes faded as Maris failed in his next at-bat. All season long I had hoped that Mickey Mantle would be the one to break Ruth's record. Mantle was my favorite baseball player, and he was the true Yankee super-star. He had been my hero since Uncle Henry and Aunt Elise had given me a Mickey Mantle tee shirt on my ninth birthday. Even so, I found myself pulling for Roger Maris.

Maris was a quiet man without a lot of flash. He even appeared to be embarrassed by all the attention paid to him during the season. Even though Mantle was my hero, I had developed a great admiration for Maris.

Bucky, Silas, and I took deep breaths as Maris stepped to the plate in the seventh inning. In a nine-inning game, this could be Maris' last opportunity to tie Ruth. Milt Pappas went into his wind-up and fired a pitch that seemed to have a lot of extra effort into it. Maris swung and drove the ball deep toward the right field stands. As the three of us jumped to our feet, the ball curved foul. Shaking our heads, we sat back down. That would be as close as Maris would get to Ruth's record. On the next pitch, he popped out to the first baseman. He got another opportunity in the ninth inning but grounded out on a checked swing. The Yankees went on to win the game clinching the American League pennant placing them into yet another World Series, but Roger Maris had failed to tie or break Ruth's record in 154 games. The 1961 season had eight more games. This gave Maris a chance to set a 162-game single season record. I was pulling for him.

***

Judy missed school again on Thursday. When I entered algebra class on Friday, Judy was already seated in her usual front-row seat. With some trepidation, I took my seat behind her. I did not know what to say, so I said nothing.

"Hey," she said as she turned to face me.

"Hey, yourself," I said.

"Listen, Jimmy," she said with a sigh. "I'm sorry that I was mean to you in the library the other day. I was upset with my parents, and that had nothing to do with you. You know I like you. Can we still be friends?"

"Sure, Judy," I said with a grin.

I could not help but wonder what had upset Judy, but I did not want to pry. If she wanted me to know, she would tell me.

"Are you going to help me in the library today?" she asked.

"Yeah, if Mrs. Brown will let me."

"Oh, she will."

***

As Judy and I sat in the reference section of the library alphabetizing library cards, Judy looked up at me.

"My brother was hit by a car Monday morning. He was taken to Baptist Hospital."

Glenn Garner was Judy's brother. He was a tenth grader at Hume Fogg Technical High School which was located in downtown Nashville on the corner of Eighth Avenue North and Broadway. After completing the ninth grade, students were allowed to transfer from the school to which they were zoned to Hume Fogg in order to receive a vocational education. Students had to provide their own transportation. Glenn walked from his home on Tenth Avenue to Buchanan Street where he boarded the city bus for his journey downtown. He was crossing Buchanan Street when he was struck by the car.

"Is he okay?" I inquired.

"He is now. He broke a couple of ribs and has a lot of bumps and bruises. He's been in the hospital since Monday but came home yesterday morning."

"So that's why you were so upset that day," I said.

"Well, I was upset that Glenn was hurt, but I was more upset that my parents insisted that I go on to school. I was worried about Glenn and was angry with my parents. I'm afraid that I took it out on you……. I'm sorry."

***

Saturday morning found Mom working the front counter and Dad working the meat counter. I was sitting behind the meat counter feverishly looking through the week's newspapers for a suitable "current event" to summarize and turn into civics class on Monday. I had kept all the *Nashville Tennessean* issues for the week. Thursday's paper had a big story about Roger Maris failing to break Ruth's record, but I decided that Mrs. Jolly would want a different kind of article. Tuesday's paper featured a front-page story about the Secretary General of the United Nations, Dag Hammarskjold, being killed in a plane crash in Africa on his way to the Congo. The article explained that he was going there to attempt to stem the growing tide of communism in that area. This article had promise. It was much better than Wednesday's story about Hurricane Esther ravaging the coast of North Carolina. As I was cutting out the Hammarskjold article, Mr. Patterson and Mr. Gates entered the store.

"Hey, Stony," said Mr. Patterson, chewing on an unlit cigar. "Have you seen the morning paper?"

"I did," answered Dad. "Did Paul have anything to do with that?"

"He sure did," interjected Mr. Gates. "Pat was afraid for him to go on one of them 'freedom rides,' but he did anyway. Man," he said turning to Mr. Patterson, "you have got to be proud of that boy."

"Hey, Dad," I interrupted. "Can I see the paper?"

Without saying anything, Dad just handed me the newspaper. The headline on the front page read: "I.C.C. Bans Interstate Bus Segregation." The article reported that segregation based on race could not occur in bus seating or in waiting rooms at bus terminals. Paul and the other "freedom riders" had prevailed with the help of Robert Kennedy, the Attorney General, who had filed a petition with the Interstate Commerce Commission on May 29.

Although this article was front-page news, I hesitated to use it as my current event. I was concerned because of the "nigger-lover" tag that Roger had been pinning on me. My hesitation was brief. Mr. Patterson and Mr. Gates were neighbors; Silas was my friend. To hell with Roger.

***

Roger Maris caught Babe Ruth on Tuesday, September 26, when he blasted his sixtieth home run of the season. On Sunday, October 1, he hit his sixty-first home run off Tracy Stallard of the Boston Red Sox. Maris had established a new single season record for home runs; however, his record was tarnished by his not achieving it in 154 games.

In any case, October of 1961 found Roger Maris catching Babe Ruth. October found me still chasing Judy.

Sonny Fields and Other Heroes

It was the first Friday in November. As we were walking home from school, Bucky and I could not help but notice the colorful beauty that shrouded Clay Street. October had bequeathed the many trees that lined our way with leaves of vibrant orange, red, and golden yellow. Such beauty demanded that even a couple of fourteen-year-old boys marvel. In fact, October had been a marvelous month. I had become Judy's part-time helper in the library, and the New York Yankees had won their nineteenth World Series. The Yanks had dispatched the Cincinnati Reds in five games. The only downer was that Mickey Mantle had played very sparingly due to an injury. Other than that, October had been a "red letter" month. It had also been a good month for Dad. He had hired a meat-cutter who gave him much needed relief from the grueling hours at the store.

Sonny Fields was a short man who was heavy-set with a huge belly hanging over his belt. His salt-and-pepper hair was kept in a very short crew cut. He always wore tan workpants and a white V-neck tee shirt. Sonny's right eye was obviously an artificial glass eye that was in a constant squint. Dad had scheduled Sonny to work four days per week: Wednesday, Thursday, and Friday from noon to 6 p.m. and Saturday from 9:00 a.m. until 7:00 p.m.

As Bucky and I approached the store, we saw Sonny's gray 1950 Studebaker occupying one of the parking spaces in front of the store steps. Studebaker was an odd-looking car with a small, rounded grill which came to a point causing the front of the car to resemble a rocket ship. I thought the car to be quite ugly, but Sonny had let it be known that he was a Studebaker man.

As usual, Bucky and I went our separate ways. Bucky went home to face the chore of baby-sitting with the twins, and I entered the store to relieve Mom at the front counter. As I entered the store, she was sitting on a stool behind the counter. Dad and Sonny were standing behind the meat counter at the rear of the store engaging in conversation. Both men were joking and laughing. The store was empty of customers.

"Hey, Mom," I said. "I'm gonna get a cold drink and then take over."

"Take your time," she said.

On the way to the drink box at the rear of the store, I walked by the showcase of meat that Dad and Sonny had spent the entire day preparing. As I peered through the glass into the meat case, I saw the fruits of their work: sliced bacon, pork chops, minute steaks, whole and cut chicken, ground beef, ham hocks, and chunks of white pork that our customers referred to as "fat back." On the shelf above the main area within the meat case were loaves of cheeses and lunch meats ready to be sliced to the customers' order: American cheese, cheddar cheese, liver cheese, hot and mild souse meat, boiled ham, and – of course – bologna. The arrangement was beautiful.

"Looks good," I said as I proceeded to the drink box.

Dad acknowledged with a nod and a wink of his eye. Sonny nodded – and would have winked if he had had more than one eye.

***

With the addition of Sonny, Saturdays at the store had become much more manageable. Both Dad and Sonny worked at the meat counter while Mom and I handled the check-out. When the Anderson's needed to be delivered to their home with their weekly groceries, Sonny's presence allowed Dad and me to do so without the fear of leaving Mom alone in the store.

"I should have hired more help a long time ago," said Dad as we were returning to the store from the Anderson home. "When Sonny comes to work on Wednesdays at noon, maybe I will take a break—at least, that's what your momma wants me to do."

"Yeah," I agreed. "How do you like Sonny, Dad?"

"Sonny is a good worker and a likeable guy. I like him – and more importantly—our customers like him. He is a good fit." After a little hesitation, Dad chuckled, "Even if he does drive an ugly car."

***

Each Monday was "current events day" in my 6th period Civics class. Mrs. Jolly collected all the articles and summaries from the students and took her seat behind her desk.

"Okay, students," said Mrs. Jolly. "I have a special assignment for you this week. Saturday is November 11. Does anyone know the significance of that date?"

As I looked around the room, I saw a few hands go up.

"Helen," Mrs. Jolly said as she looked at Helen Blackwell.

"It's Veterans Day," answered Helen.

"That's right. It is Veterans Day. It's a day set aside each year to honor those who have served in our armed forces. The special assignment I have for you is about Veterans Day. I want each of you to write an essay on Veterans Day. I want you to include the purpose of the day, the historical background of the day, and –most of all—what Veterans Day means to you, personally."

Mrs. Jolly paused a moment to allow her eyes to scan the room. With the pause, Bucky raised his hand.

"How long does it have to be?" he asked.

"Length doesn't matter that much, but I would say one handwritten page, at least. It can certainly be longer, but I am interested in an essay that shows that you have put some serious thought into what you have written. This topic is something that I want you to really think about." After a brief pause, she emphasized, "What does Veterans Day mean to you-- *personally*?"

Mrs. Jolly went on to tell us that the essay would be due at the beginning of the period on Friday. Bucky and several other students raised their hands.

"Yes, Rex."

"Do we get out of school on Friday since the holiday is on Saturday?" asked Rex Cothern with a glimmer of hope in his eye.

"Sorry, Rex," smiled Mrs. Jolly. "Nashville schools do not close for Veterans Day, but I appreciate your concern."

***

At the beginning of 5th period the following day, Coach Pinkston slowly walked up the steps into the upper bleachers of the gymnasium where the students had assembled for Physical Education roll call. When Mr. Pinkston called the name of each student, the student was supposed to answer as "dressed" if he was wearing the required blue shorts and white tee shirt. If not, he was to answer as "not dressed." In addition, if the student had taken a shower following the previous P.E. class, he was to answer as "shower." If he had not taken a shower, he was to answer, "no shower." As Coach Pinkston went down the roll, each student answered, "dressed, shower."

After the roll was completed, Coach Pinkston tossed a couple of footballs to us and told us to report to the practice field. We chose up teams and played touch-football the entire period. I enjoyed P.E. on Tuesdays and Thursdays where I had gained a reputation as one who could throw a football with some accuracy; however, I enjoyed the alternate days being Judy's library helper a lot more.

Toward the end of class, Coach Pinkston blew a whistle, and we jogged back into the P.E. locker room. My locker was located by a window at the end of a row of lockers. I had left my towel hanging on the locker door with my loafers and clothes inside the locker. After I removed my gym clothing, I wrapped myself in my towel and headed to the showers. There was a series of pegs next to the shower room where we hung our towels. The shower was a large room with shower heads coming out of the walls. There were no partitions, and I used to feel a little strange taking a shower with a bunch of other naked guys; however, I had gotten over it. Like the other guys, I just didn't even think about it anymore. It was just part of school.

As I returned to my locker to dress for my next class, I noticed something disturbing. My jeans, shirt, and underwear had been removed from my locker and lay scattered on the floor along the row of lockers. No other locker had been disturbed.

"Did anybody see who did this?" I asked as I picked up the clothes. The other guys in that area just shook their heads. I looked at Bucky who also had a puzzled look. I checked the pockets of my jeans and found that the dollar bill that I had taken to school was still there. Nothing had been taken. I decided not to report it to Coach Pinkston; after all, no one seemed to know anything about it. I just dressed and went to my next class.

***

"Hey, Horsehead," said Bucky as he entered the store. There were no customers in the store, and I was sitting on the stool behind the check-out counter reading a Superman comic book and waiting for Mom to return from the apartment.

"Grasshopper," I said. "Are you free?"

"Yeah, for a while," he smiled. "When are you getting off?"

As he was asking that question, I saw Mom walking in the back door which led from the apartment stairs.

"Right now!" I said. I wanted to talk to Bucky and get his thoughts on what had happened in the P.E. locker room earlier that day. After Mom relieved me at the cash register, Bucky and I walked back to the drink box where I retrieved a Double Cola and Bucky chose an RC. As we approached Mom at the front counter, I pulled 21-cents from my pocket and put it on the counter.

"Hey, Mom. We're gonna go sit in Dad's car," I announced.

"Okay. Just be back by closing time," she said.

Bucky and I walked out to the side parking lot and crawled into Dad's '50 DeSoto. The car was parked facing the Fifth Avenue and Clay Street intersection which provided a great view of people coming and going from the store.

"I've been thinking about finding my clothes on the floor in P.E. today," I said. "My clothes were the only ones. No other lockers were messed with."

"I've been thinking about that, too," said Bucky. "I can think of only one person who might want to pick on you."

"Roger?" I asked.

"Yep," he replied.

"Me, too, but I'm not really sure that it was him."

"Who else, Horsehead?"

That was a really good question. I could think of no one else who would want to target me.

"Well, until I am sure, there is nothing to do......" I hesitated. "I kind of dread going to P.E. on Thursday."

"Yeah. He's bigger than....." Bucky suddenly stopped talking and stared down Clay Street. I looked in that direction and saw the Gibson girls, Margie and Allie, walking toward the store.

"Well," continued Bucky. "There goes Weird and Weirder."

I gave a little laugh, but immediately felt bad that I had.

"Margie never says anything," I said. "I've tried to get her to talk, but she just won't," I continued. "Allie will say something sometimes, but not a lot. Margie is in my English class and does her work, but she never raises her hand or says anything. She gets to class early and sits on the back row. She puts her head on the desk until Mrs. Acuff starts class." I took a pause and a deep breath. "Weird is right."

"Hey, look!" ordered Bucky with some excitement. "There's Ellen McNabb."

Ellen was Buzz's older sister, a year older than me, but still in an eighth-grade homeroom. In those days, you had to repeat any course that you did not pass. A student could be taking tenth grade English, ninth grade science, and eighth grade social studies. The student would be assigned to a median grade homeroom. Ellen was obviously one of those students.

"Do you know her?" I asked.

"Not very well," he said, "but I've heard stuff."

"Like what?"

Bucky didn't answer. He just stared at Ellen as she walked up the steps toward the entrance to the store. I could not help but notice that Ellen was wearing some tight peddle pusher pants and a very tight-fitting blouse.

"Like what?" I reiterated. "What have you heard?"

"Bones told me that she will do it for a Pepsi," he said with a snicker.

I just looked at him, and we both broke into a very juvenile laugh.

***

"Hey, Mom," I said as I entered the store the following Wednesday afternoon.

"How was school?" she asked.

"It was okay. I'm gonna run upstairs right quick and grab an encyclopedia and be right back," I said.

"No problem," said Mom with a smile. "Take your time."

I went upstairs into our apartment. I found Dad lying on the couch in the living room. With Sonny manning the meat counter, Dad was taking Wednesday afternoons to rest. I grabbed the "V" volume from my set of Funk & Wagnalls Encyclopedia. I had had this set for a while. Long before my parents opened our grocery store, Mom had purchased one volume per week from the A&P Store at Ninth Avenue and Buchanan Street. She had paid three dollars per volume. Just about everyone in Kalb Hollow owned a set of Funk & Wagnalls.

Upon entering the store to relieve Mom, I stopped at the drink box and retrieved a Double Cola. Sipping from the bottle, I made my way behind the front counter where I rang up a ten-cent sale and dropped a dime into the cash drawer.

"Thanks for waiting," I said. "I've got it."

As I watched Mom leave the store, a group of lower

elementary-aged children entered and immediately stopped in front of the candy case.

"Two of deez," said a skinny little Black boy as he laid two pennies on the counter.

As ordered, I reached into the candy case and presented him with two Hershey Kisses.

One by one, each child made a selection and placed their pennies on the counter. When all were served, they left the store happily giggling as the door closed behind them.

"It doesn't take much to make them happy, does it?" exclaimed Sonny as he moved to the front of the empty store and stared out of the window.

"Not a lot," I said as I opened the encyclopedia to "Veterans Day" and started reading.

"What ya doing there, Jimmy?" asked Sonny as he turned away from the window.

"I'm reading up on Veterans Day," I responded. "I'm writing a report for civics class. It's supposed to tell about Veterans Day and what it means to me."

"Yeah," said Sonny. "Veterans Day is this Saturday." After a pause, Sonny gave a sarcastic smile. "We would have a holiday if we weren't in the grocery business."

Sonny was right. The store only closed two days per year: Thanksgiving and Christmas. We closed early on New Year's Day, Memorial Day, Independence Day, and Labor Day. Except for those days, Stone's Shop and Save Market was a grind.

"It's not a holiday from school, either" I complained.

"Nashville schools aren't closed for Veterans Day, so I get to go to school this Friday. In fact, that's when this report is due."

Suddenly, the door opened, and Tommy entered the store wearing his work boots and hard hat.

"Hey, Jim," he said as he walked directly to the drink box in the rear of store. He returned with a Dr. Pepper and placed a dime on the counter.

"Hey, Tommy," I said. "Have you had a chance to meet Sonny?"

"Nice to meet ya, Sonny," said Tommy extending his hand.

"Tommy is working downtown on the new auditorium," I declared.

"Hey," said Sonny addressing Tommy. "I understand that we're going to have an ice hockey team when the auditorium is completed,"

"Ice hockey?" asked Tommy in some disbelief. "I don't see ice hockey being a big thing in Nashville."

"I don't either, but that's what I heard," said Sonny. "That building will be used for a lot of things—concerts, meetings, and a bunch of other stuff. Who knows……? They might even bring the Harlem Globetrotters here."

"Yeah," Tommy chuckled. "Hey Sport," turning his attention to me. "What are you doing with the Funk and Wagnalls?"

"Working on a report for civics class that's due Friday."

"He's gotta tell what Veterans Day means to him," chimed Sonny.

"Well, what does it mean to ya?" chided Tommy.

"I have no idea," I said. "But I'll think of something."

"I'm an army veteran, Jimmy," said Sonny. "I can tell you what that means to me."

"Oh?" Tommy and I said almost simultaneously.

"To me, it means pride," exclaimed Sonny. "The pride I have in fighting for my country."

"When were you in the army?" asked Tommy.

"From 1941 to 1944," said Sonny. "That's when I lost my eye."

Tommy and I glanced at each other, then turned our attention back to Sonny.

"I served in the 5th Army under General Mark Clark in Italy," Sonny continued. "I was wounded in January of 1944 near a town called Cassino. A shell fragment put my eye out."

At that moment the door opened, and Mr. Gates walked in.

"Hey, Little Stony. You got any pork chops back there?" he asked gesturing to the meat counter.

"I can have you some in a New York minute," interjected Sonny. "Come on back."

As Sonny and Mr. Gates walked to the back meat counter, Tommy put his empty Dr. Pepper bottle on the counter and left the store. As I put the bottle into the basket near the drink box, Mom emerged from the apartment to take over at the checkout counter. When she arrived at the front counter, Mom noticed the encyclopedia.

"What are you working on?" she asked.

I explained the Civics assignment to her and told her about Sonny's experience.

"If you'll hang around a few minutes," she said as she took her place behind the counter, "I'll tell you about some of your relatives and what Veterans Day might mean to them. I can definitely tell you what it means to me."

"Yeah, Mom. I need all the help I can get."

***

The following day at school seemed particularly long. I was dreading P.E. class. When Coach Pinkston blew the whistle ending class, I ran into the locker room and showered as fast as I could. I wanted to return to my locker before anyone could tamper with my clothes again. I enjoyed a sigh of relief as I approached my locker from the shower. No clothing was lying on the floor; however, the relief was short-lived. When I opened my locker, I found that my Fruit-of-the-Loom underwear was soaking wet. Since I was the first student out of the shower, no one else was near the locker. I believed Roger to be the culprit, but I was not totally sure.

"Who else?" said Bucky as we walked home from school. "Nobody else would pick on you like that."

All I could do was hang my head. I just couldn't let this go on.

"What are you going to do?" asked Bucky.

"I wish I knew."

***

"Hey, Dad," I said. It was Saturday morning and Dad and I were returning to the store from the Anderson delivery. "I need to talk to you about something."

"Okay," said Dad.

"I may be getting into some trouble at school this week," I said.

"Why do you say that, Son?"

I explained what had been going on in P.E. class, and Dad listened intently.

"I am going to face who I am pretty sure is doing it and have it out with him," I said. "I know you and Mom don't want me fighting or getting into trouble at school, but I've got to do something."

"Have you told the coach?"

"No, Dad. I really don't know what to tell him. Since I am not completely sure of who's doing it, I don't see what Coach could do?"

"Well, Son. You're right. Your mother and I don't want you getting into trouble at school, but I don't want you to let anybody run over you either." After a hesitation, Dad asked, "Who do you think is messing with you?"

"Roger."

"Roger Newell?" Dad asked.

"Yeah. Roger Newell," I said with a sigh.

"That complicates things, Jim. Roger is Kate's boy."

"I know, Dad."

Kate Newell, Roger's mom, was my mother's cousin. She and Mom were not particularly close, but Mom was very close to Kate's mother, Mom's Aunt Alice. Roger and his mom lived with Aunt Alice on Ninth Avenue near the Little League field. Aunt Alice had practically raised him.

"Son, if things get ugly between you and Roger, it could upset things between your mother and Alice," said Dad. "Why don't you talk this over with your mom and see what she thinks?"

"Okay. I will."

After the store closed, Mom completed her nightly paperwork and cleared the register. On the way upstairs into the apartment, I explained the problem to her.

"Mom, I don't want to get into trouble at school, and I don't want to cause trouble between you and Aunt Alice. I just don't know what to do."

"It doesn't sound like that you are the one causing the trouble," said Mom.

"Yeah, but I don't know what to do?" I said.

"Well, I think it's pretty simple," Mom said.

"Really?"

"Yep. Just buy a combination lock and put it on your P.E. locker," she said. "Wouldn't that solve the problem?"

"Maybe," I said with some hesitation. "I don't have P.E. again until Tuesday. I'll try it and see."

***

A discussion of our current event articles occurred each Monday in Mrs. Jolly's Civics class. After the discussion she collected our papers.

"Helen," she said to Helen Blackwell. "While I collect the current events, will you return these papers, please?"

"Yes, Ma'am," replied Helen.

Mrs. Jolly addressed the class, "The papers that Helen is returning to you are the Veteran's Day essays that you turned

117

in last Friday. I really enjoyed reading them." After a pause, she looked directly at Rex Cothern. "Almost all of them were very good."

Rex was a terror on the football field, but he was not known for any academic prowess.

I glanced at the papers as they were returned and most of the students had an "A" marked at the top of the page. I looked at my paper when Helen returned it to me. I also received an "A".

"I am proud of the thought that was put into these essays," said Mrs. Jolly. "There is one paper that I would like to be read aloud because I think it reflects the essence of why we celebrate those people who served our country." After pausing and visually scanning the room, she looked at me. "Jim Stone, would you mind coming up to the front of the class and read your essay?"

Oh, crap! Double crap! I hated standing in front of a class. It made me nervous and self-conscience. I had rather walk through hell with gasoline underwear!

"Well, Jimmy," she said with a smile.

I took a deep breath and replied, "Yes, Mam."

As I moved to the front of the class, I could feel my face burning red with embarrassment. As I faced the class, I felt my knees quivering. Most of the students were looking at me and waiting for me to start reading. Some of them—like Helen and Claudia—had the look of pity on their faces. Bucky was struggling not to snicker. I just wanted to get it over with, so I started reading:

"Veteran's Day is a federal holiday in the United States. It is observed every year on November 11 to honor those Americans who have served in the armed forces. Veteran's Day was originally called Armistice Day, and it was to memorialize the end of the fighting of World War I on November 11, 1918. Armistice Day was celebrated by most European countries immediately following the end of World War I but did not become a federal holiday in the United States until 1926 when it became a law passed by Congress and signed by President Calvin Coolidge. In 1954, a few years after the end of the Second World War, Congress passed a bill that was signed by President Dwight Eisenhower that changed Armistice Day to Veteran's Day. Each November 11, parades and ceremonies to honor veterans are held in cities and towns across the nation."

"What does Veteran's Day mean to me? I wrestled with that question. To be honest, I had never thought much about it; however, after talking with friends and family, I know what it means to me now. It means one word: sacrifice. Military service requires sacrifice. Those who have served in the armed forces have sacrificed their time, postponed careers, and lost time with family and friends in order to secure the blessings enjoyed in a free nation. Many of our veterans have sacrificed more than time. Sonny Fields is a man who works in a neighborhood grocery. He is a World War II veteran who served in the 5th U.S. Army during the invasion of Italy in 1945. He was struck in the face by a shell fragment and sacrificed his right eye. Richard Roughton drives a cab for Checker Cab Company. He is my mom's brother. Uncle Richard is also a veteran of World War II. He served in an

engineering battalion of the 3rd U.S. Army under General George Patton. Having entered Germany in early 1945, the truck in which he was driving struck a land mine. The explosion destroyed the truck and left Uncle Richard with serious abdominal injuries. I have always been a little bit afraid of Uncle Richard. He comes across as a mean and unfriendly person; however, he lives in constant pain and has undergone 16 surgeries since 1945. He is presently scheduled for a 17th. Today, there are thousands of veterans who have similar stories to that of Sonny Fields and Richard Roughton. There are also thousands of people who served in the armed forces who never became veterans. Dewey Morgan served in the 1st Army during World War II as an infantryman. He was the husband of my mom's sister. In September of 1944, Uncle Dewy was killed in France. His sacrifice included his wife and a 2-year-old son who has grown up without a father. J.R. White, my mom's cousin, was 19 years of age when he was killed in the Pacific war on an island called Iwo Jima. Those people who sacrificed their lives and did not live to become veterans are honored on Memorial Day, the last Monday of May."

"It is fitting that Veterans Day—as well as Memorial Day—be filled with parades and speeches. It is fitting that those who served our country be honored for their courage and sacrifices."

At the conclusion of my reading, one could hear a pin drop in the classroom. All the students were sitting quietly in their desks. Some were staring into nowhere; others had their heads down. The students in this class were baby boomers: the children of World War II with a faint memory of the Korean War. Every child in this class had been touched by war in some way. Each one had a parent, uncle, aunt, or other family member who had displayed the courage and sacrifice to serve in the defense of our country. Although it was unknown to them at the time, several of these students would soon be called upon to make such sacrifices themselves.

***

A New Game

The employment of Sonny gave Dad a much-needed rest during the week and some much-needed help on Saturdays. It also provided a boon for me; on Saturday afternoons I was free to hang out with my buddies, climb the cliffs, and roam the bottoms. Sometimes I just went upstairs and watched college football on TV. I had recently become a fan of college football. While checking out the sports page in the *Nashville Tennessean* on a Sunday afternoon in mid-September, I had become intrigued by a color picture. The picture was an action-shot that had been taken the previous Saturday during a local college football game. One of the teams in the picture had magnificently beautiful uniforms. The pants were a flat gold color with a very wide black stripe down the outside of each leg. The solid black jerseys were adorned with bright gold numerals, and the helmets were bright gold with black numbers on each side of the helmet. It was those black and gold uniforms that caused me to become a die-hard fan of Vanderbilt University football – a long suffering fan. Week after week, the Commodores lost game after game; however, I could not get past those magnificent football uniforms. Although the Commodores did not play well, they looked great!

Actually, the 1961 season began in promising fashion. The Commodores began that season with a 16-6 victory at the University of West Virginia. They followed that up the next week with a convincing 21-0 win over the Georgia Bulldogs in Athens, Georgia. Hopes were high for the next contest as the Commodores faced the Crimson Tide of the University of Alabama. It was the first Saturday in October. As usual, I helped Dad open the store at 6:30 a.m. As I counted the money into the cash drawer, I could hardly wait for the 1 p.m. kick-off.

The morning drug along. Time seemed to crawl. The Andersons ran late that day as well, so it wasn't until after 12:30 that Dad and I returned from delivering the Andersons and their groceries. I quickly exited Dad's '57 Country Squire and hurried into the store. Sonny was with customers at the meat counter, and Mom had just finished with a check-out.

"Hey, Mom," I said. "Is it okay for me to go?"

"Sure," she said.

With that I ascended the back stairs and entered the apartment foyer where the radio was located. The AM radio dial was already on 650, WSM radio. Famous for broadcasting the Grand Ole Opry, WSM also anchored the Commodore Radio Network. The legendary Larry Munson handled the play-by-play of Vanderbilt football. Listening to a Munson broadcast was the next-best thing to being at the game. He was phenomenal as he created word pictures in the listener's mind.

He was a true artist as a sports broadcaster; however, not even Larry Munson could paint anything positive for Vandy fans as the Tide embarrassed the Commodores, 35-6. Vanderbilt did not recover. They lost the next seven games and ended the season with a 2-8 record. A series of losing seasons had begun.

As Larry Munson wrapped up the Alabama broadcast, I heard a knock at the apartment door. It was Silas. He had a football tucked under his arm and he stood on the landing at the top of the steps outside the door.

"Hey, Jimmy," he said. "Can you come out and throw the ball around?"

"Okay," I responded. "I can throw it if you can catch it."

We scampered down the long flight of steps onto the parking lot at the side of the store. We stood about fifteen yards apart as we threw the football back and forth.

"Hit me with a long one," Silas exclaimed as he turned and ran full speed toward the pony field. I took a few steps back and hurled the football as far as I could. Silas, racing toward the pony field, caught the pass in stride over his right shoulder.

"Wow," I shouted. "Nice catch!"

Excitedly, Silas turned and ran back toward the parking lot.

"Man!!" he exclaimed. "You can handle that football!"

"Yes, he can," someone shouted from behind me. It was Bucky.

"Jimmy believes he's Johnny Unitas," chided Bucky.

Somewhat out of breath, Silas ran up to Bucky and me.

"Man! We've got to get a game up!" exclaimed Silas.

"I would love to get a game up," exclaimed Bucky, "but there is only three of us."

"We can get more guys," Silas replied. "You can get Bones and Buzz, and I know some more guys who will play."

"We need a place to play," said Bucky.

"We can play two-hand-touch right here on the pavement," I added.

"Nah, Horsehead," Bucky responded. We need a place to play tackle football."

"I know a place," said Silas. "The outfield down at Morgan Park is perfect!"

"Well, all-right!" exclaimed Bucky. "Let's get some guys and head down there!"

"There is a problem," interjected Silas. "The Gray-Y teams play there on Saturdays."

Gray-Y was elementary school football sponsored by the YMCA. Fifth and sixth grade teams from various elementary schools in North Nashville played each other on Saturdays. Gray-Y used the park on Saturdays from late mornings until late afternoons.

"We could play there tomorrow after church," said Silas. "Gray-Y has lined off left field of the baseball diamond into a fifty-yard football field. It's perfect!"

"Hey, Bucky. Can you get away tomorrow?" I asked.

"Yeah. Pretty sure I can. Let's line up some guys and meet down there at 2 o'clock tomorrow."

***

Bucky, Bones, Buzz and I enjoyed a sunny Sunday afternoon walk down Fourth Avenue. As we approached Morgan Park, I saw Silas and three other guys on the field. Just as Silas had said, left field had chalk lines every five yards creating a fifty-yard football field.

"Hey," declared Buzz. "There's Silas and three other niggers."

With that, Bones lightly slapped Buzz on the back of the head.

"You've got to watch your mouth down here," warned Bones.

"Don't be stupid, Buzz," chimed Bucky.

"Hey, Silas!" I yelled excitedly as we stepped onto the field.

Silas and I made introductions as the two groups studied each other closely. Alvin was about my height. He was light skinned with a little fluff around his middle. Isaac was almost as tall as Bucky: he was lean but extremely muscular for a fourteen-year-old. Jacob was Isaac's younger brother. About the size of Bones, he was trim, but not skinny. As we threw the football around, it became obvious that Isaac and Jacob were gifted athletes.

With Isaac and Bucky as captains, we divided into two racially integrated teams of four. We had no court order to integrate; each captain just wanted to put together the better team. One thing became very obvious after we started the game; Isaac was the best player on the field. He was a fast runner and, like Silas, could catch a football on a dead run. He also showed himself to be a tackling machine. He made tackles from one side of the field to the other. I was taken down several times by Isaac during the afternoon. It hurt. This guy was something special!

It was a great afternoon. We played until the sun dropped below the horizon, and darkness forced us to go our separate ways.

And so it began. Sunday after Sunday we met at Morgan Park to play football and have the time of our lives.

∗∗∗

A Very Blue Hawaii

There was much for which to be thankful on that Thanksgiving Day of 1961. The store was closed; Mom and Dad could enjoy a full day of rest and relaxation from the rigorous efforts needed to operate the store. We were thankful for the much-needed relief that the employment of Sonny Fields afforded Dad. I was especially thankful for combination locks. Since locking my gym locker, my belongings had not been vandalized, and I was able to avoid a confrontation with Roger—at least, for the time being.

When I awoke that Thanksgiving morning, I glanced at my unset alarm clock. It was 8:10 a.m. That was later than I had slept in months. I roused myself from my bed, slipped on my pants, and journeyed into the living room. Dad was sitting in his rocking chair reading the morning newspaper with his dime-store reading glasses perched on the bridge of his nose.

"Hey, Bud," he said. "There's some biscuits and gravy waiting for you in the kitchen."

Thanksgiving Day had started: good food, rest and relaxation, and time with family. Mom, Dad, and I spent the morning and early afternoon watching the Macy's Thanksgiving Day Parade followed by watching the Green Bay Packers defeat the Detroit Lions in their annual Thanksgiving Day matchup. Mom had prepared a great Thanksgiving meal. Immediately after watching the Packers take care of the Lions, Mom, Dad, and I sat down at the kitchen table to have chicken and dressing, cranberry sauce, green beans, mashed potatoes, and hot rolls. My Mom was amazing. She worked in the store, kept our apartment immaculately clean, washed and ironed our clothing, and prepared a hot evening meal every day. There was no way she would let Thanksgiving be celebrated without a very special feast.

After helping Mom with the dishes, she and I joined Dad in the living room. He had already fallen asleep in his rocking chair. Mom took a seat on the couch with her *True Story* magazine. I sat down in the big easy-chair and was about to drift off when the phone rang.

"Hello," said Mom. "He's right here. Hold on."

As Mom passed the phone to me, she said, "Its Fran."

"Hey, Cuz," said Fran. "Aunt Elise is taking Henry Jr. and me to the movies tomorrow. Wanna go?"

"Yeah. What's playing?" I asked.

"*Blue Hawaii*," she said. "It's an Elvis movie."

"I like Elvis. I have to work until noon tomorrow, though.

"So, we'll pick you up at 12:30."

"I'll be ready."

***

"I'll pick you up right here in three hours. Be waiting," said Aunt Elise as Henry Jr., Fran, and I exited her 1959 Ford Galaxy. She let us out right in front of the *Tennessee Theatre*. There were three other movie theatres on Church Street in downtown Nashville, but none could compare to the *Tennessee;* it was a movie palace. Entering the huge lobby, we were walking on extremely plush maroon colored carpeting. To our right was the long concession bar that spanned the length of the lobby ending near the entrance of the main auditorium. To our left was a long, wide, winding stairway that led up to the spacious balcony. The carpeted steps were adorned by a beautiful brass railing. In the center of the lobby's high ceiling hung an elaborate chandelier. The *Tennessee Theatre* was more than a movie theatre; it was an experience.

In 1961, admission into the theatre was sixty-five cents. The cost of a bag of popcorn was ten cents as was the cost of a Coca Cola. At that time, one could enjoy a great movie, admire the grandeur of the theater, partake in popcorn and Coke, —all for less than a dollar. Amazing!

We decided to forgo the concession bar and go directly into the main auditorium. We found seats and sat down just as the newsreel had started. There was a lot more to going to the movies in the early sixties than just previews and the main feature film. The movie experience started with a newsreel from

Movietone News which highlighted recent significant news events. The newsreel was followed by a cartoon which featured characters like Porgy Pig, Bugs Bunny, and Daffy Duck. The cartoon was often followed by a short comedy which featured comics like The Three Stooges, Laurel and Hardy, and Abbott and Costello. The previews of coming attractions preceded the feature film. Immediately following the feature, Movietone News reappeared and the cycle of entertainment repeated. One did not have a particular time to enter the theatre. You just purchased a ticket and found a seat. If the feature had already started, you just remained to watch it again. You could remain in a movie palace for hours and watch the movie as many times as you desired. Those were the days!!

Just as the cartoon was beginning, Fran and I decided to go to the concession bar for popcorn and Coke. We left Henry Jr. to save our seats. As Fran and I approached the concession bar, we could see that few people were in the lines; therefore, we looked forward to getting back to our seats in time for the comedy short. We took our place in one of the lines, and that is when I saw her! It was Judy! She was being served at the front of the next line. Lee Whitaker was standing with her. I saw her smile as he handed her a popcorn and Coke. I was struck dumb. As she turned away from the line with Lee, our eyes met. I tried to hide my shock, but Judy's look of surprise instantly changed to an extremely irritated look. As she and Lee walked by, she gave me a disdainful stare.

"Who is *that?*" asked Fran.

"Oh, they're a couple of people I know from school," I

responded while trying to hide the gut-wrenching that was going on inside me.

Damn!! The love of my life had a boyfriend.

"If looks could kill, Jimmy, you would be dead," said Fran noticing Judy's demeanor.

Actually, I felt dead. I am sure that *Blue Hawaii* was a wonderful movie, but I hardly remember any of it. During the entire movie, my mind was fixed on Judy and Lee. I felt disappointment, sadness, hurt, and anger. I had been gut-punched and I didn't know what to do about it.

***

The next day was Saturday. Dad and I opened the store as usual. As I was counting the money into the cash drawer, Dad walked up from the meat counter.

"Hey, Bud. Are you okay?" he inquired.

"Yeah, Dad. I'm fine," I said. "Just too much Thanksgiving, I guess."

"Well, all right," said Dad after a brief hesitation. "If you say so."

At 6:30 on the dot, I unlocked the door and turned the sign on the window from "closed" to "open." Moments later, my first customers entered the store – The Gibson sisters. Weird and Weirder.

The girls grabbed a box of Kellogg's Corn Flakes and a quart of milk and presented them to me at the check-out counter. Margie wore the usual blank expression, but not Allie. She was looking at me with an intensely puzzled look as if to say,

"What's eating you?" or "Do you have a problem?" Was my mood so dark that even Allie Gibson noticed? I realized that I had to buck up and cheer up even if I had to fake it. And fake it I did—all day long.

***

The weekly Sunday afternoon football game at Morgan Park temporarily took my mind off my failing love life, but Monday morning brought a sense of dread. I knew that I would see Judy in algebra class and the library. I did not know what to expect or how to react. I was bothered by the disdainful look that she had given me at the theatre, and I did not understand her being upset with me. I was the one who was being dumped and kicked to the curb in favor of Lee Whitaker.

As I worked the front counter at the store and checked out the early morning customers, I could not escape that feeling of dread. As the last of a long line of customers left the store, Bucky entered.

"Ready to go, Horsehead?" asked Bucky.

"As soon as Miss Myrtle gets here," I said. "In fact, that's her now."

"Hey, Mr. Jim," said Miss Myrtle closing the door behind her. "You can go on to school. I'm here."

"Yes, Ma'am." It still bothered me that she called me "Mr. Jim."

As Bucky and I walked up Clay Street toward North High School, neither of us said anything until we were walking by the white stone wall in front of St. Cecelia Convent.

"Hey, Horsehead," said Bucky. "What's eating you? You haven't said a word since we left the store."

"I'm fine," I responded.

"No, you're not," chirped Bucky. "Now, let me see.................. Did your daddy gave you more hours of work? .... No, that's not it!........He cut your pay?.........No! That's not it either?..........I know!!! It's your love life—Judy Garner."

"What about Judy Garner, Grasshopper?" I asked in an unfriendly tone.

"Well," he hesitated. "Since you guys are sweet one each other...."

I immediately interrupted. "What do you mean 'sweet on each other'?"

"Come on, Horsehead. You can't keep your eyes off her in the cafeteria or the library. Everybody notices it," he chided. "She hasn't broken your heart, has she?" he asked in what I believed to be a sarcastic and condescending manner.

I did not respond, and, sensing that he had hit a nerve, Bucky got quiet also. We walked the last few blocks to school in complete silence. As we entered the front door of North High School, Bucky put his hand on my shoulder and said, "I'm sorry, man. I didn't mean to make you mad."

✱✱✱

After leaving second period science, I hurried to algebra class. I took my usual seat behind Judy's regular desk. I didn't know what to expect. I didn't know what to say, and I didn't know what to do; therefore, I decided to say nothing and play it by ear.

As usual, Judy entered the class with her friends, Claudia and Rella. Judy left her friends and walked toward her seat looking downward refusing to allow her eyes to meet mine. She took her seat and immediately faced the front of the classroom without saying a single word. As I stared at the back of her head, my emotions changed from sadness and confusion into anger. I was convinced that Judy was making it clear that she was no longer interested in me.

Later that day in the library, Mrs. Brown assigned me to help Judy with library cards. Feeling very uncomfortable, I worked with Judy, but no words passed between us.

And so it was. Day after day. November turned to December, and Judy and I did not speak. I was perplexed, angry, and sad. I could not understand the reason that I was being ignored; however, I did understand one thing: Judy was done with me, and I had to get over her.

The upcoming winter loomed as being long, cold, and hard.

Chapter 3

Winter/Spring, 1962

The Reckoning

New Year's Day of 1962 was cold and blustery with light snowfall. The Store's closing at noon allowed me to hang out with Bucky in the afternoon. Enduring a cold wind, we sat on a huge rock at the edge of the cliffs overlooking the bottoms. Actually, the cliffs were the steep wall of an abandoned rock quarry. At the foot of the cliffs was a large expanse of gravel surrounding a relatively small pond of water known as the Blue Hole. Local legend had it that the Blue Hole had no bottom. Bucky and I knew that to be ridiculous, but the pond was known to be extremely deep—too deep for a couple of guys who did not swim.

"I wonder how many dead bodies have been thrown into the Blue Hole," mused Bucky.

"I don't know," I replied, "but I know one I'd like to throw in there."

"Yeah. I know," said Bucky. "Roger is such a bastard."

After I chuckled in agreement, Bucky got quiet. After a long and thoughtful pause, Bucky said something that concerned me.

135

"Jimmy," he said. He hesitated and stared into space. Since he called me by my name instead of "Horsehead," I knew something was really eating him.

"Jimmy," he continued, "one of these days I might just throw myself into the Blue Hole."

"What?.........What are you talking about?" I asked.

"I'm talking about my life!" he said emphatically, visibly upset. "I love the twins, but I shouldn't have to watch them all the time. I shouldn't have to do housework as much as I do. There is no time for me to do what I want to do. And I shouldn't need you to pay my way into the movies."

Just a couple of days earlier, Bucky and I had gone to see *The Comancheros* at the Tennessee Theatre. I had slipped Bucky a dollar which paid his admission and concessions.

"C'mon, Grasshopper," I said. "You know that I don't mind helping you out."

"I know, but it's the principle of the thing. I'm the only guy that still takes a lunch to school. Hell, while you are in the cafeteria line with everyone else, I'm alone at a table opening my brown bag. Sometimes, momma gives me just enough money to buy milk," he complained.

I didn't know what to say, so I said nothing.

"Hell, Horsehead," he continued, "I'm not going to throw myself into the Blue Hole, but I'll tell you what I am going to do. As soon as I can, I'm leaving home."

"Really?" I chided.

"Yes. Really!" he said emphatically. "When I'm sixteen, I'm getting a part-time job. When I'm seventeen, I'm quitting school and working full-time so I can save enough money to get out on my own!"

I still did not know what to say. I hoped that he was just venting. I agreed that he had too much responsibility with the kids and chores. I also agreed that a part-time job would allow him to have his own money; however, I disagreed with his quitting school. Nevertheless, I remained quiet. After a pause, I attempted to change the subject.

"Man. It's getting cold," I said. "Let's get outa here."

We abandoned our rock and headed across the pony field.

"When are you going to stop using the lock on your gym locker?" Bucky asked.

"I don't know," I replied. "I'd love to stop using it. The other guys look at me like I'm from another planet, but I don't know what else to do."

"Why don't you just have it out with Roger. Punch him in his ugly nose."

"Because I don't Know that it's him," I said. "I need to know it's him before I can do anything."

We walked a few more steps, and Bucky stopped dead in his tracks.

"Horsehead," he said with some glee. "We're gonna prove it's him. I've got an idea."

***

"I thought it was you!!!" I yelled at the top of my voice.

In front of my gym locker stood a surprised Roger dropping my Fruit-of-the-Looms on the locker room floor.

It was Tuesday, January 2nd, the first day back from Christmas vacation. While playing basketball in the gym during P.E. class, Bucky and I had kept our eyes on Roger. When we saw him slip back into the locker room, we followed him. While hiding around a corner, we saw him open my locker. When we saw him pull an article of clothing from the locker, that's when I jumped around the corner and yelled.

Roger picked up my underwear and slung them back into the locker.

"What are you going to do about it?" Roger asked in a menacing tone.

"Well, Roger," I said matter of factly, "first, I'm gonna tell Coach Pinkston what you've been doing. Then I'll go down to the principal's office and have a talk with Mr. Arrington."

Roger just stood there staring at me with a stupid looking smirk.

"After school today," I continued, "I'm going down on Ninth Avenue and see Aunt Alice."

"Tell anybody you want, Stone," said Roger angrily. "It's your word against mine."

"Not hardly," shouted Bucky as he emerged from around the corner of a row of lockers. "It's your word against *ours!*"

As Roger slammed the locker door, we were interrupted by the sound of the P.E. class entering the locker room.

"Tell you what, Roger," I said calmly, "there's a way that I can let you off the hook.......let by-gones be by-gones."

Bucky turned and gave me a dumb-founded look.

With guys coming into our part of the locker room,

I said, "Can't talk about it now. See you in the library tomorrow……………….Right now, I need to take a shower, so get away from my locker."

***

"Horsehead," said Bucky as we began our walk home. "You know that broom stick that holds up the window near your P.E. locker?" Without giving me time to answer, he continued emphatically, "Hell, you should have grabbed that stick and beat the cold shit out of Roger. I can't believe you let him off with that 'by-gones be by-gones' crap!"

"You don't understand, Man!" I shot back. "Roger and I are related – third cousins, I believe! He lives with his grandmother who is my mom's aunt….and they are best friends!"

"So…," said Bucky.

"So," I said, "Dad told me to be really careful how I deal with Roger and to talk to Mom before I do something that could cause a problem between Mom and Aunt Alice. Heck, Grasshopper, it was Mom's idea for me to put a lock on my locker."

After a thoughtful pause, Bucky said, "Well, what are you going to do?"

"When Silas gets home from school," I said, "I'm going to walk over and ask him a question."

***

I got a favorable answer from Silas. I knew that I would. Just a couple of weeks prior, Silas had the idea of my arranging a

139

football game between our Morgan Park group and Roger and his posse. I had run the idea past Roger, and he emphatically told me that he would not play football or anything else with a "bunch of niggers or nigger-lovers." I believed that my threats to expose Roger's locker room nonsense would change his mind.

As Bucky and I walked to school the following morning, Bucky was a bit bewildered.

"Do you mean to tell me that you're gonna let that bastard off the hook with a football game?" Bucky asked emphatically.

"Absolutely," I said. "I've told you why I can't fight him. A football game is the next best thing. It will give me a chance to knock his butt off. Silas wants a piece of him, too."

"Hell! I do, too," said Bucky, "but he might not agree to play."

"We'll see," I said.

***

He did agree. Roger knew that I had him in a vice. It took him a couple of days to check with Melvin, Jew Baby, and the rest of his guys, but the game was on!!! It was set for Sunday afternoon, January 14, at 2:00p.m.—rain, sleet, or snow.

***

True Colors

It was Friday evening, January 12. It was two days before the game that we had dubbed as the Kalb Hollow Bowl. I was working as sack boy while Mom worked the register. It had been mid-term exam week at school. Each morning, Monday through Wednesday, we had exams in two subjects. School had been dismissed at noon on those days, and there was no school Thursday and Friday. Much of those two days had been spent at Morgan Park practicing for the Kalb Hollow Bowl. Silas had been particularly intense about the game—as had I.

Just before closing time, the phone rang.

"Stone's Shop and Save," I answered.

"Jimmy Stone!" a familiar voice laughingly yelled into the phone. "We're gonna kick your butt."

It was Steve.

"Is that so?" I asked with a chuckle. "How many players have you got?"

"Right now, we have six," he said, "but we could have eight."

"There's eight of us, but if you only have six," I continued, "we'll play six at a time."

"That's okay," said Steve. "I was just kidding about kicking your butt, but my brother ain't kidding. Roger is going to target you, so be ready."

"Don't worry about me. See you at 2:00 on Sunday at Morgan Park. Be there!!!"

***

The Kalb Hollow Bowl enjoyed an afternoon that was perfect for football—bright sunshine, cool but not cold, and a very slight breeze. Bucky, Bones, Buzz, and I arrived at Morgan Park a little before 1:30. Silas, Isaac, Jacob, and Alvin were already there. We had met at Morgan Park the previous Friday and created a few "backyard" football plays. We were ready.

"Hey, Jimmy Stone!" came a voice from someone walking toward the park on Fourth Avenue. It was Steve. Roger and the rest of his guys were close behind. Roger had come up with eight players, so the teams had even numbers.

"We're gonna kick your butt, Jimmy Stone," laughed Steve as he stepped onto the field.

"Somebody's butt is gonna be kicked. It might be yours!" I yelled back.

Steve and I slapped hands as we met in the middle of the field. We were joined by both teams. After going over the previously agreed rules, Buzz flipped a coin high into the air.

"Heads," shouted Roger.

The coin landed, bounced twice, and rested with "heads" showing.

"We will receive," said Roger without hesitation.

Under the rules, the kicking team could decide how to kick off. The kicking team could place-kick, punt, or throw the football. We decided that I would throw the football. Roger and his team spread out on their side of the field to receive the ball.

"Throw it as high as you can," instructed Isaac. "That'll give us time to get down the field and cover."

"Okay," I said, "and I'm going to throw it toward Roger."

I backed up ten yards or so in order to get a running start. I threw the football as high and far as I could toward Roger. As the ball spiraled upward, Roger moved forward and camped under the ball. He failed to catch the ball cleanly. It went through his arms, hit the ground, and bounced back into his grasp. Just as Roger secured the football, he looked up to see Isaac streaking down upon him. Roger screamed!! Yes!! That's right!! Roger screamed like a girl!!!

Screaming did him no good. Isaac, running at full speed, planted his shoulder squarely into Roger's chest. Roger went flying backward while the ball went hurtling upward. As Roger landed on his back with a thud, the football hit the ground and bounded toward our goal line. Bone scooped up the football and carried it across the goal line for our first touchdown.

Although it continued for over an hour, the game was decided with Roger's scream. His being intimidated to such an extent took the fight out of most of his team. Steve and Melvin played hard but to no avail. When the game ended, my Morgan Park guys boasted a 66-0 victory.

During the game, Roger was quiet. No one heard his usual mouthing and ordering. He was clearly intimidated and clearly embarrassed. He said nothing to his team-mates, and his team-mates said nothing to him. Roger had shown his true colors, a coward with a big mouth.

***

For the remainder of our time at North High School and beyond, Roger and I rarely spoke. He did not like me, and I certainly did not like him. I knew that he was a cowardly bully, and he knew that I knew it. That was that.

***

Spring Fling

A Sunday afternoon in mid-April found Bucky and I sitting under the sycamore tree in the pony field. There wasn't much else to do on a Sunday afternoon after the football games at Morgan Park had come to an end. As we chewed on blades of grass and smelled the newly sprouted wild onions, Bucky gave me a goofy look.

"What's your problem, Grasshopper?" I asked.

"I don't have a problem, but you do," he said.

"Well, I don't know of any problem," I replied.

"Oh, yes you do," chuckled Bucky, "and her name is Judy Garner."

I rested the back of my head against the sycamore tree, took a deep breath, and rolled my eyes.

"I'm over her," I insisted.

"I don't think so, Horsehead," Bucky said with a smirky laugh. "If you are over her, you wouldn't be looking at her all the time." After a pause, he continued, "You can't keep your eyes off her in the library or in the cafeteria." He paused again and continued, "Hell, Horsehead, I'm embarrassed by the way you look at her. Its pitiful!"

"Well, you won't be embarrassed much longer," I retorted. "I'll admit that I'm not completely over her, but I'm working on it. I've joined the club."

"The club? What club?" asked Bucky.

"I was watching *The Little Rascals* on T.V. the other day, and

Spanky, Alfalfa, and Buckwheat started the 'He-man Woman-Haters Club.' I joined," I said laughingly.

"Hey! I saw that too, but that club didn't do much for Alfalfa," smirked Bucky.

"I don't care," I insisted. "From now on, I'm a he-man woman-hater!"

Bucky and I enjoyed a laugh and resumed chewing on blades of grass and enjoying the aroma of wild onions. After several minutes, Bucky broke the silence with a serious comment.

"Why don't you just ask her what the problem is? Ask her why she is ignoring you."

"Look, Grasshopper, I don't want to talk to her," I said emphatically. "I want to be free of her!"

With that, Bucky fully reclined on the ground at the base of the tree with his arms behind his head. He thoughtfully peered up through the sycamore branches as they gently swayed with the breeze.

"Let me tell you something," he said as he raised himself to a sitting position. "You are not going to be free of her until you can get your mind off her. You need to stop wondering why she dumped you. Just ask her, damn it! Ask her why she dumped you.!"

"I know why!" I replied with some emotion. "She likes Lee Whitaker."

"Do you really know that?" he asked. "Have you seen them together at school?"

I thought for a moment. "No, but I saw them together at the movies."

"That was months ago," he replied. "There may be nothing to that."

"Then why is she ignoring me and refusing to speak to me?" I asked.

"That's what you need to find out, Dum-Dum," he chided.

With that, Bucky assumed his former position, put his arms behind his head, and renewed his interest in the swaying branches and rustling leaves of the sycamore tree. I rested the back of my head against the tree and closed my eyes. I needed a break from this conversation.

"Say, Horsehead," said Bucky as he sat up once again. "Ask Judy to go to the Friday night dance with you."

I responded by looking at Bucky as though he was crazy.

"I mean it, Horsehead," Bucky continued. "You'd go wouldn't you?"

"She is not going to go to the dance with me because I'm not going to ask her……. You must be crazy, Grasshopper," I said with some irritation.

"Even if she refused, she would probably give you a reason…………..You'd find out what the problem is," he reasoned.

"Look, man. I just don't want to talk to her," I insisted, "and besides, she's probably already going to the dance with Lee."

"Well, that's possible," he relented. After a thoughtful moment, he continued, "Just go to the dance by yourself. You can scope it out. If Lee and her are there together, then you know the deal. If not, then she's mad at you about something else."

"You might be right," I said, "but I'm not going to ask her to the Spring Fling, and I'm not going by myself either." After a moment of hesitation, I stood up and said, "But –right now— I'm going home."

***

As Bucky and I approached the store on our walk home the following day, we saw a police cruiser parked in the front parking area. After Bucky and I went our separate ways, I entered the store. Officer Marcum was standing at the meat counter in the rear of the store talking with Dad. Mr. Marcum often stopped at the store for a soft drink and a chat. Mr. Marcum was over six feet tall and very lean with jet-black hair except for some gray on the temples. He was wearing the uniform of the Nashville Police Department: navy blue pants and a short-sleeved white shirt with an NPD insignia on each sleeve. A silver-colored badge gleamed from the left side of his chest.

Marcum and Dad were approximately the same age and had been friends for decades. In addition to visiting a few times per week, he drove by the store several times each day. He believed that the visibility of the police was an important deterrent to crime. Mom had told me that there had been some significant history between Marcum and Dad, but she never elaborated.

As I was retrieving my daily Double Cola from the drink box at the rear of the store, I could not help overhearing their conversation. They were discussing the upcoming referendum in June regarding the merging of the Nashville city government with the Davidson County government into a single government for both city and county. Currently, there was a Nashville mayor and city council and a Davidson County administrator and legislature. There was a Nashville Police Department and a County Sheriff's Department. Nashville had its school system and Davidson County had a separate school system. Should the referendum pass the June vote, the two political entities would be merged into one which would consolidate government and services under the banner of Metropolitan Government of Nashville and Davidson County—Metro Government for short. A couple of years earlier, a similar referendum had failed.

"I think it's going to pass this time, James," said Marcum.

"I'm definitely voting for it this time," said Dad. "If it doesn't pass, city taxes will have to go up."

"Yeah, that's right," Marcum agreed. "So many people are moving out of Nashville and into the county. Subdivisions are going up everywhere. Just over the city limits, houses in Bordeaux Hills are selling as fast as they can be built. Those buyers are mainly White people from Kalb Hollow. The same is true for the Parkwood subdivision out Dickerson Road. Nashville's tax base is moving to the suburbs. That referendum has got to pass this time."

"Hey, Mr. Marcum," I said as I made my way to relieve Mom at the front counter.

"Hi, Jim," said Marcum. "Well, James," turning to Dad, "I guess I better get back on patrol."

As Dad and Marcum were walking toward the front of the store, Tommy Martin entered wearing his work clothes, hard hat, and boots.

"Hello there, Mr. Marcum," said Tommy.

"Hey, Tommy," Marcum responded. "How's the new auditorium coming along?"

"Slow," said Tommy as he moved toward the drink box and his afternoon Dr. Pepper. "We're working six days a week trying to keep on schedule."

As I moved behind the front counter, Tommy emerged from the back of the store with his Dr. Pepper and put a dime on the counter.

"I'm bushed," he said with a groan. "See ya."

After Tommy exited the store, Marcum turned to Dad, "Well, James. There goes the Martin family enforcer."

"What are you talking about, Marc?" asked Dad.

James, Fred Martin is one of the meanest drunks I have ever had to deal with," said Marcum. "I can't count the Friday nights I've had to arrest him for beating up his wife." After a pause, Marcum continued, "Didn't do any good though. Mrs. Martin always refused to press charges."

"So, what about Tommy?" I interrupted.

"A year or so ago," Marcum explained, "I arrived at the Martin house after the people across the street from them had called in a disturbance. Well, I knew what it was about." Mr. Marcum hesitated with a chuckle. "When I got to the Martin house, I found Fred sitting at the top of his front steps with his hands cupped over his face. Blood was streaming between his fingers."

"Don't tell me!" Mom interjected.

"Yes," Marcum went on. "Tommy had come to his mother's defense and broke Fred's nose."

"Wow," said Dad.

"Yep," said Marcum. "Tommy hurries home every Friday night to keep his dad in line."

"Damn shame," said Dad.

"So, that's why Tommy stays in that nasty house," said Mom.

"That's right, Bess," replied Marcum, "and he's likely to stay there as long as his mom needs him to protect her." After a pause, he said, "Well, I've loafed around here long enough. I've got to get back to work."

***

By the time that school dismissed on Wednesday, I had decided to go to the dance on Friday night. Bucky was right. If I was going to free my mind of Judy, I needed to know why she had been ignoring me. I had to know if it was Lee –or me.

As Bucky and I were passing St. Cecilia Convent on our way home, a thought entered my mind.

"Hey, Buck," I said, "why don't you go with me Friday night?"

"C'mon, Horsehead," said Bucky, "I can't go. They want us to wear a coat and tie, and I don't have one."

"Just wear some dress pants and a shirt," I insisted. "They won't care."

"I don't have any dress pants," said Bucky, "and I'm not going to show up in Levi's."

I could see that Bucky was getting upset, so I decided to drop the subject.

"Well, okay," I said. "I'm not real sure that I can go. I might be needed at the store Friday night."

After Bucky and I went our separate ways, I entered the store and found Mom checking a customer. Sonny was working with some people at the meat counter. It was Wednesday, so Dad was upstairs resting.

"Hey, Mom," I said. "Can I talk to you a minute?"

"Sure, Jim. What's on your mind?"

"It's about Friday night," I said gingerly. "I'd kinda like to go to the school dance Friday night. It's for ninth and tenth graders."

"What's the time frame?" she asked.

"It's from 7:00 until 9:00, but I'll probably leave early."

"Are you going with somebody or are you going stag?" she asked.

"I'm going by myself, and I'll be home before 9:00," I said.

"Sure. Have a good time and be home by 9:30."

***

I was glad that Dad gave me a ride to the dance. It was a warm night and walking the six blocks from the store to the school while wearing my Sunday-go-to-meeting gray suit would have been very uncomfortable. As I exited the station wagon, Dad said that he would pick me up at 9.

"Don't worry about it, Dad," I said. "I'll probably leave earlier than that. I'll just walk home."

As I entered the gymnasium, I saw the student body president, Danny Hall, spinning records while acting as disc jockey. Several couples were on the floor dancing to a Chubby Checker record. Many others were sitting in the folding chairs that lined the walls of the gym. Others were standing in groups talking. Several teachers, the principal, the assistant principal, and a few parents were acting as chaperones.

While surveying the dance floor looking for Judy or Lee, I saw big Rex Cothern doing the peppermint twist with tiny Helen Blackwell. It was a funny site, but they were obviously having a good time. I also saw Lee Whitaker. He was dancing with Joan Wheeler, a tenth grader. I started walking around the edges of the dance floor hoping to see Judy. After walking across one end of the floor, I saw her sitting at the far corner of the gym talking with some of her girlfriends. I quickly took a seat that had a good view of them. I started to feel like a stalker, but I was determined to talk to Judy as soon as she was alone. During the wait, I saw Lee dance with a couple of other girls. I could not help but take that as a good sign.

I waited and watched as Judy talked and laughed with her friends. It seemed like an eternity before Judy rose from her seat and walked over to the record table. This was my chance. "It's now or never," I said to myself. I nervously strolled over to her.

"Hi, Judy," I said with a quiver in my voice. "Can I talk to you a minute?"

"Oh, I guess so," she said coolly. "I saw you sitting over there by yourself. Where's your girlfriend?"

"My girlfriend?" I responded with a puzzled expression.

"Yes, your girlfriend," she said with some harshness. She paused and continued, "She's very pretty."

"Judy, I don't have a girlfriend. I don't even know what you're talking about," I said emphatically.

"Look, Jimmy," she said. "I don't care if you have a girlfriend, I'm just glad that she's pretty." Did you enjoy the movie?"

"What movie?" I was beginning to get angry.

"The Elvis movie. *Blue Hawaii*." Wasn't it great?" she said with a sarcastic tone.

"You're talking about Fran," I said.

"Oh, is that her name?"

"Yeah. That's her name…………and she's my cousin," I insisted.

"So, you took your cousin to the movies?" she asked in a tone of unbelief.

"Actually, Fran took me to the movies along with my other cousin, Henry. My aunt dropped us and picked us up after the show."

Judy just looked at me. She showed no expression. She just looked at me.

"Look," I said, "I was just wondering why you stopped speaking to me—why you have ignored me for months."

After a pause and no response from Judy, I decided to end the conversation which was going nowhere.

"Well," I said. "Good night."

I briskly walked away, left the gym, and began my long walk

home. I had not mentioned Judy's being with Lee at the movie. I just didn't care. Walking home that night, I was sad, but not suffering any real sense of loss. In fact, I felt free. Maybe I really had become a he-man woman hater. I hoped so.

Chapter 4
Summer/Fall, 1962

The Professor

The church on Osage Street had less than fifty members. Since the congregation could not support a fulltime minister, each Sunday morning featured a guest preacher. Billy Brewington only spoke at our church four or five times per year, but he was always interesting—even for a near fifteen-year-old boy. He believed in a literal interpretation of the Bible and preached it in such a way that held the attention of the congregants; however, he was not a fire and brimstone preacher like Brother Cullom. Billy Brewington's sermons were always connected to the "golden rule" and believed that when a person served his fellow man, he was serving God. Such was his sermon on this second Sunday of June 1962. The school year had ended the previous Friday, and I was eager for summer vacation. I planned to meet Bucky and Silas right after church; however, my thoughts moved away from such things when Brother Brewington ended his sermon with a question: "If you met your Maker today, would He be proud of the life you have lived?"

Even for one my age, that question demanded some introspection. I considered myself to be a good person. I didn't tell lies or cheat, and I believed myself to be honest. I would never take anything that didn't belong to me. I had always tried to treat others the way I wanted to be treated. I didn't cuss or use profane language; however, I knew there was a problem. Although I never used bad language around others, I often cussed in private when I became frustrated. I also had started noticing girls and looking at them in a way that Brother Cullom would call "a lustful manner." As Brother Brewington was closing his sermon, I thought: "Is God proud of the life I am living?" I concluded that He probably was not.

My introspection came to an end when the congregation stood and sang *Just as I Am*. At the conclusion of the hymn, Brother Brewington went back to the microphone.

"I want to say one more thing before we dismiss." He paused and slowly surveyed the congregation with a serious expression. "Go!!" he said as the serious expression faded into a smile, "and sin no more!...........or, at least, try to cut back a little."

***

On the way from church to the store, Dad and I stopped at Bud's Hardware at Fourteenth and Buchanan Street to pick up a quart of red paint. I had agreed to handle some small grocery deliveries with my bike; however, my twenty-four-inch Western Flyer was old and in need of paint.

"You can paint the bike tomorrow after Myrtle comes in," said Dad as we got back into his green and white '55 Chevy.

"Son," he continued. "This is the car I'm going to use to teach you to drive."

"I thought you would use the station wagon," I said.

"The station wagon has an automatic transmission," he said. "I want you to learn how to drive a standard shift like this car. If you can use a clutch and know how to shift gears, you will be able to drive anything."

That was fine with me. I just wanted to learn how to drive and get my driver's license. I would turn sixteen-years-old in a year, so I had a year to learn how to drive a standard shift.

As we moved down Buchanan Street, my mind turned to something else.

"Hey, Dad," I said. "Can I ask you a question?"

"Sure, Bud. What's on your mind?"

"How do you know Mr. Marcum?" I asked.

Dad did not answer immediately. He took a deep breath and stared at the road ahead.

"Mom said that y'all had some history," I continued. "I was just wondering."

"Didn't your momma tell you?" Dad asked.

"No," I replied. "She just said that there was some history."

"Well, Son," he said. "Marc and I have a lot of history. When we were little kids, we lived on opposite sides of a duplex over on Third Avenue. We were playmates."

"Really?" I said.

"Yeah," Dad said with a smile. "Me, your Uncle Bill, Marc, and his sister played cowboys just about every day." Dad broke into a laugh. "We always made Marc's little sister, Brenda, to be the bad guy."

"Are you and Mr. Marcum the same age?" I asked.

"Yep," Dad replied. "We started to school together at Elliott School."

"Hey, Dad," I said. "Is that the school over on Jefferson Street that has one door for boys and another door for girls?"

"That's the one," laughed Dad. "Boys and girls had to use different doors to enter and leave the school. Things were different back then."

"Mom said that you went all the way through school—in the front door and out the back."

"Yeah, Son," Dad said without a chuckle. "Your momma thinks that's funny." After an uncomfortable pause, Dad continued, "You know that I didn't finish the second grade."

"Yeah. I know," I said.

I really did know. Although Dad had learned how to read well and was very proficient with numbers, he had never learned how to write in cursive. He had to print everything, and he did not do that very well.

"I believe it was just after Christmas in 1917 that my daddy, your grandfather, fell off a building that he was painting. He broke his back." After a pause, Dad continued, "I remember that like it was yesterday. Daddy lost a lot of use of his legs. He couldn't really walk; he just shuffled along slowly for short distances. He spent most of his time in his rocking chair groaning every time he moved."

Dad went on to explain that my grandmother found a job

at Standard Candy Company on Second Avenue leaving my semi-invalid grandfather to babysit with Dad's four-year-old sister, my Aunt Paulene. Dad and Uncle Bill stopped going to school to help care for my grandfather and Aunt Paulene. They also scouted the area for odd jobs to help with the family's finances. Uncle Bill was a couple of years older than Dad. That enabled him to get a job working two days a week at the Oasis Market on Third Avenue and Taylor Street. He earned twenty-five-cents per day sweeping, cleaning, and putting up stock. At eight-years-old, Dad just hustled for any odd job he could find.

"Say, Dad," I interrupted, "what about Mr. Marcum. Did you stay friends?"

"Sure," said Dad. "We continued to live on opposite sides of the duplex for several more years. Marc got out of bed every morning and went to school. Me and Bill got up and went wherever we thought we could make a dime."

With that, we pulled into the front parking area of the store.

"Actually, Jim," said Dad, "Marc did me a really big favor that definitely changed my life. He's the best friend I ever had, but that story will have to wait. We've got to get into the store and help your momma."

＊＊＊

I discovered that painting metal with a brush was not easy. It was impossible not to leave brush marks. Dad had told me that I would need to apply two coats of paint to my Western Flyer, maybe three. I had established a workstation under a big shade tree next to the garage behind the side parking lot.

159

Dad and I had opened the store at 6:30 a.m., and I worked at the front counter until I was relieved by Miss Myrtle at noon. I retrieved my Western Flyer from the garage and set up shop under the big tree.

I learned something else about painting that day: oil-based paint did not dry quickly. After waiting under the tree for over an hour, I decided to return the bike to the garage and resume painting it later that day. As I was leaving the garage, I saw a tall husky guy walking toward me from the direction of the store.

"Hello," he said. "Are you Jimmy?"

"Yeah," I answered with an inquisitive look.

"My name is David Devers. We just moved into a house up the street. The lady in the store said that I should meet you."

"Sure, David," I said. "Which house do you live in?"

"The big white house two doors up the street," he replied.

"I'm painting my bike, but the first coat is taking a long time to dry. I'll need to put on another coat."

"That won't be today," said David. "It'll have to dry over-night."

"Really?" I said.

"Yep," he replied. "Would you want to come and sit on my front porch and listen to the radio?"

"Well………. sure," I said gingerly. "Let's get something to drink first."

We entered the store and walked back to the drink box. David pulled out an RC and I extracted my usual Double Cola.

"Man, those Double Colas are strong," David declared.

"Yeah," I agreed. "My friend, Bucky, says that drinking

Double Cola will put hair on your chest. I need all the help I can get."

As we walked toward the front counter, David reached into his pocket.

"Keep your money," I said. "This one is on me."

I put two dimes and a penny on the counter as Miss Myrtle smiled and said, "Thanks, Mr. Jim."

Sipping our drinks, David and I walked up to his house.

"They call me 'Professor'," declared David.

That did not surprise me at all. He was half-a-head taller than me: he had a huge head with bushy brown hair, and he wore geeky horned rim glasses. His shirt was tucked into his jeans and buttoned all the way up to his neck. In his shirt pocket was a pocket liner filled with ballpoint pens. This guy was certainly different.

"I'll just call you 'Prof' if that's all right," I said with a chuckle.

"That's fine with me," smiled Prof.

There were two big rocking chairs on Prof's porch. On a small table between the chairs was a little Philco radio plugged into an outlet next to the front door.

"I listen to WKDA," said Prof.

"Yeah, great," I said. "Me too."

There were two top 40 pop radio stations in Nashville at that time. WKDA, 1240 on the AM dial was one of them. The other was WMAK, 1300 AM. Both stations were good, but I liked the DJ's on WKDA better. Prof did too.

I found Prof to be easy going and talkative. As we listened

to WKDA pump out pop hit after hit, I learned that Prof was a year younger than I. He lived with his mom along with his older brother and his brother's wife. Daniel, his brother, was twelve years older than Prof. Their Dad had died a few years ago while Daniel was serving in Germany. While stationed there, he met Hilda. Their marriage had produced a little girl who had just celebrated her second birthday. Prof's mom worked in the sewing room at Horace Small Manufacturing Company on Charlotte Avenue. The company produced apparel for women. Daniel worked as the warehouse manager at Tennessee Wholesale Drugs on First Avenue near Broadway in downtown Nashville. Hilda stayed at home with the baby and Prof. I got the feeling that Prof and Hilda did not get along very well.

After we had talked and listened to music for over two hours, I decided to return to the store.

"Well, Prof," I said as I rose from the rocking chair, "I better go. I think I'll check and see if the paint's dry."

"Check all you want to," he laughed, "but it's still wet."

***

When Dad and I opened the store the following morning, the usual group of customers were waiting for the doors to open. In rapid succession, Pall Mall, Winston, Salem, Chesterfield, Camel, and Lucky Strike cigarettes left the building. As the last of the early group was leaving, the Martin girls came in for a dime's worth of bologna. When the store cleared of customers, Dad joined me at the front counter.

"When Myrtle comes in, I want you to make a couple of signs before you get back to painting," he said.

"Sure, Dad," I replied. "What kind of signs?"

"I want a couple of signs put in the front windows that says we will do free delivery on Monday through Thursday from 12:00 until 2:00," he said. "Can you handle that?"

"Yep. No problem," I bragged.

As Dad started walking back to the meat counter, Allie Gibson entered the store.

"Hey, Allie," I said cheerfully. "How are you?"

"Fine," she said quietly. "Can I get a pound of bacon?"

"Sure," I said. "Just go back and tell Dad. He'll fix you up."

Along with the bacon, Allie put a loaf of bread and half gallon of milk on the counter.

"That'll be a dollar and six cents," I said.

Allie gave me two dollars. I gave her the change and bagged the purchases. She had her usual blank look, but it was unusual for Margie not to be with her. They were always together.

"Is Margie okay?" I asked with some concern.

Allie lifted her head, and I could see that she had been crying. I also noticed some redness on her face below her eye.

"No," she said sadly.

With that, she immediately turned and quickly exited the store.

***

"Hi there, Mr. Jim," said Miss Myrtle as she entered the store at 12:00 noon. She was always on time. "Have you got big plans today?"

"Yes, Ma'am," I replied. "I'm gonna make two signs and finish painting my bike."

Less than a half-hour later, I had completed both signs. As I was taping the last one to the window over the potato bin, I saw a police car drive by the store. I couldn't see the driver, but it was probably Mr. Marcum.

"Hey, Dad," I said as I walked back to the meat counter. "Are you going to tell me how you and Mr. Marcum became best friends?"

"Son," he replied, "I don't think I'm his best friend, but he's mine."

"C'mon, Dad," I pleaded. "Tell me."

"Jim, have you ever done something that you're ashamed of?" asked Dad.

"Well…………sure," I replied.

"I'm not going to ask you what it was because things like that are hard to talk about," said Dad in a serious tone. "I'm very ashamed of some things I did when I was young." After a pause, he continued, "If it hadn't been for Marc, I probably would have kept on doing them. In a way, he saved my life."

"What did you do?" I asked.

"Well, Son," Dad went on, "Marc and I lived on opposite sides of the duplex on Third Avenue for a long time. We grew up there. When I was fifteen, I got a job at the Red Ace gas station down on Eighth and Jefferson. That would have been the winter of 1923. I worked six days a week for $11. Bill had already gone to work herding cattle and pigs into the slaughterhouse down at the stockyards on Second Avenue. With Momma, Bill, and me working, we were doing okay. We could afford more room than we had on Third Avenue, so Momma found a bigger house over on Heiman Street."

"What about Mr. Marcum, Dad?" I asked.

"Well, Marc was still going to school. On his way to Hume Fogg, he walked by the gas station every morning, but that's about the only time I saw him."

Dad took a deep breath. "It was right after moving into the house on Heiman that Daddy died. Paulene was only 9 or 10, so Momma didn't feel right about leaving her at home alone. She decided to quit working and tend to Paulene. With Bill and me working, we did okay until that summer when Bill married your Aunt Agnes and moved to Louisville. That was a good move for them because Bill got a really good job with the L&N Railroad. It wasn't good for Momma because I was the only one working. Things got real tight."

Dad was interrupted by a customer at the meat counter. I opened the drink box and retrieved a Double Cola.

"I'll be out front, Dad," I said.

I left a dime on the counter with Miss Myrtle and moved onto the front porch steps and sat down to wait for Dad. Across the street on the corner of Fifth and Clay, Mrs. Gates was tending her flowers. It was late spring, and she had the most beautiful yard in the neighborhood. As I was watching Mrs. Gates water her flowers, Dad sat down on the steps beside me.

"Marc finished high school," said Dad as he lit a Lucky Strike. "That was 1926, about the same time that I made a really bad decision."

I must have given Dad a strange look. He put his hand on my shoulder and continued.

"The owner of the Red Ace station, Mr. Craven, asked me if I would like to make some extra money by helping him two nights a week. Of course, I needed the money, so I agreed to drive his pick-up truck to a place near Ashland City and bring several crates to the station. He told me that I would pick up the crates every Tuesday and Friday night. He said he would pay me $5 for each trip."

Dad stopped talking and stared down Fifth Avenue.

"Son," he said, "an extra $10 a week was a lot of money back then, but when something sounds too good to be true, it probably is." Dad paused and shook his head. "When I got down to Ashland City that first night, two guys loaded the truck with wooden boxes filled with Mason Jars. Each jar was filled with moonshine whiskey."

"Did you take them to the gas station?" I asked.

"Yes, I did, Son," he said. "I felt like I had to. I really needed the money."

"How long did you do this?" I asked.

"A little more than four years," he replied. "I knew it was illegal, but I felt that I couldn't pass up the money."

I didn't know what to say or how to feel. I was a bit disappointed that Dad had done something wrong, but I also was old enough to understand why he did it.

After we had sat quietly for a few moments, Dad continued, "I contributed some of the extra money to Momma's household expenses and saved the rest." Dad chuckled and looked at me with a smile. "I hid my savings in a coffee can buried under the house."

"What did you do with it, Dad?" I asked.

"I bought my first car with it," he said. "I paid $60 for a 1921 Ford, did a little work on it, and sold it for $140. With that money, I bought two more and sold them. That's how this little sideline of buying and selling cars started."

"Is that car business the reason that you left the gas station?" I asked.

"No, Son," he replied, "but I wish I had. Mr. Craven came to me again during the summer of 1931 and asked me if I wanted to help him on Saturday nights."

"To make more moonshine runs?" I asked.

"No, but it was something else that was against the law, and I was stupid enough to do it," he declared.

Dad went on to tell me that Mr. Craven had been using a storage building behind the station to operate a small-time gambling operation on Saturday nights. Crap games were the order of the day, and a patron would occasionally become unruly, and a fight would break out. Dad was six feet tall and a muscular 23-year-old. Craven paid him another $5 to be the bouncer.

"Wow, Dad. Did you ever have to throw anybody out?" I asked.

"Sometimes," he said. "Probably one guy too many.

Somebody must have got mad enough to report the game to the police. Just a week or two before Christmas, the police raided the game." Dad hesitated, slowly shook his head, and continued, "A police car and a police van showed up with a search warrant and arrested everyone at the game. Counting me and Craven, there must have been fourteen or fifteen guys."

Dad stopped telling his story and looked down. When he looked up, he had a tear in his eye. I had never seen my dad this emotional.

"There were too many of us to get everybody into the police van, so a couple more police cars showed up. I was standing by the door to the storage building. One of the officers came out of the shadows and told the sergeant that he would take me. That officer was Marcum."

"Dad," I interrupted, "did Mr. Marcum take you to jail?"

"No, he didn't," said Dad. "As we drove away, he offered me a deal. He told me that if I would quit working at the Red Ace station and not do anything else that was against the law, he would take me home and not downtown." After a long pause, Dad continued, "I gave Marc my word and I have kept it. With no education, I have had a lot of hard and dirty jobs since then, but nothing illegal."

I did not know what to say or how to respond. I don't think Dad expected a response. He told me all of this for a reason.

"A man with little education is real limited, Son," he went on. "I didn't have any education. Neither did my daddy. I want you to get an education. I want you to finish high school and go on to college." Dad paused. "I don't want you to be the last one hired and the first one laid off. Poor and desperate people will do desperate things. Don't ever be desperate."

Dad turned and looked at me with his emotional heaviness changing into a smile.

"Something good came out of all that, Jim," he said in a more cheerful manner. "Marc helped me get a job down at Werthan Bag Company. That's where I met your momma."

He turned and put his hand on my shoulder.

"Well," he said, "you need to finish painting that bike."

***

I had almost finished painting the Western Flyer when Prof joined me under the big tree. He was wearing jeans, tennis shoes, and a white tee shirt.

"Hey, Prof," I said. "What happened to that button-down shirt and all of those ballpoint pens?"

"Well, I decided that if we were going to climb down those cliffs, I had better dress for it," he said.

After taking the bike into the garage, Prof and I headed across the pony field toward the cliffs. I planned to take Prof down the cliffs, show him the Blue Hole, and explore the bottoms; however, those plans came to an abrupt halt. When Prof and I reached the cliffs overlooking the Blue Hole, a black '58 Chevy was parked about fifty feet to the left of the Blue Hole. It was parked facing the opposite direction from where we were standing. We could see a man's elbow resting through the driver-side window.

"Do you think that guy is down there by himself?" asked Prof.

"Don't know," I said. "Let's move around to where we can see better."

Feeling adventurous, we quietly moved around the circular rim of the cliffs until we gained a driver-side view of the car. We assumed a prone position behind a small mound of gravel. We could see a man and a woman in the front seat.

"How did they get down there?" whispered Prof.

"There's a road," I said quietly. "Eighth Avenue continues across Clay Street and leads to the bottoms. It goes beside St. Cecelia and becomes a gravel road. It ends down there."

"Wonder what they're doing down there," whispered Prof.

We didn't have to wait very long for that to be revealed. The man got out of the car and walked to the trunk. He looked to be in his forties. He was a husky guy with tattoos running down both arms. We watched as he opened the trunk and removed two bottles of beer from an ice cooler. After closing the trunk, he resumed his place in the front seat of the car.

After several minutes of watching the occupants of the car drink and chat, our spirit of adventure turned to boredom.

"Hey, Prof," I said. "Let's climb down and I'll show you the bottoms."

"Wait!" whispered Prof excitedly. "She's opening her door."

The woman exited the passenger side of the car. For a moment, I thought that it must be her turn to get the beer. I was wrong. She walked to the rear of the car and positioned herself with her back to us. We watched as she kicked off her shoes and removed the red shorts that she was wearing, placing them on the trunk of the car. Prof and I gave each other a startled look, but immediately refocused our attention on the lady who removed her panties which she also placed on the trunk of the car.

"Wow!" whispered Prof.

I did not respond. Neither Prof nor I had ever gazed upon the naked backside of a full-grown woman. As we continued to gaze upon this stunning site, she abruptly turned and faced our direction.

"Wow!" whispered Prof.

Suddenly, the woman assumed a squatting position and started to pee.

"Oh, man," giggled Prof.

Neither of us could control our giggling. Prof rolled over on his back and faced the sky. He ceased trying to control himself.

"Now," said Prof in an excited voice, "I can die happy!"

I laughed so hard that tears came to my eyes. I looked at Prof who was laughing just as hard.

"Hey, Jimmy," he laughed. "I thought you brought me here to show me the bottoms. You only showed me one!"

The couple in the car must have heard our laughing. We heard the car start and drive away.

It had been an afternoon to remember!

***

Bucky's eyes became as big as saucers as I relayed to him the adventure that Prof and I had enjoyed that afternoon. Bucky had joined me on the steps of the store a little after dark, and I immediately shared the experience.

"Who is this Prof?" asked Bucky.

"He just moved into the big white house up the street," I said pointing to the second house from the store. "He's an okay guy. His name is David, but he said that everybody calls him 'Professor.' I just call him 'Prof.' The name seems to fit. The first time I met him he was wearing a shirt buttoned all the way up to his neck, and he had a bunch of ballpoint pens in his shirt pocket."

"Damn," chuckled Bucky. "Is this guy normal?"

"Oh, yeah," I said. "He's a little different, that's all. He's pretty smart and really into electronics. He was telling me how transistors work, but I had no idea what he was talking about."

Suddenly, a voice came out of the darkness, "Hey, Jim."

As the shadowy figure moved into the light, we saw Prof approaching us sporting a big smile.

"Hey, Prof," I answered. "This is Bucky, the guy I told you about."

After the introductions were complete, we decided to retire to Dad's DeSoto.

"Bucky, did Jim tell you about the time we had today?" asked Prof as he slid into the backseat.

"Oh, yes!" said Bucky. "He couldn't wait to tell me what I had missed."

We sat in the DeSoto talking and watching people enter and leave the store. We must have talked and laughed for over an hour when Bucky sat straight up.

"Damn," exclaimed Bucky. "Will you look at that?!"

Walking across the parking lot toward the store was Ellen McNabb. She was wearing cut-off jeans that were extremely short and tight. Her red halter top was very tight and low cut, leaving little to our imagination. As she approached the steps of the store, she looked toward the DeSoto and caught us staring at her. She smiled and gave us a provocative wave.

"Oh," said Prof. "I think I'm really going to like living in this neighborhood."

***

The Sting

The summer of 1962 was speeding away. Aside from working in the store, I had spent my days on Prof's front porch listening to the radio, climbing the cliffs, and exploring the bottoms. Bucky, Prof, Bones, Buzz, and I spent an afternoon or two each week playing baseball at Morgan Park with Silas, Isaac, Jacob, and Alvin. Much to Dad's liking, the June referendum combining the Nashville city government and the Davidson County government had passed. The election for Metro mayor and the Metro council was scheduled for November with Metropolitan government commencing the following April. Dad, Mr. Patterson, Mr. Gates, and almost everyone around the store were supporting Nashville's city mayor, Ben West, for Metro mayor. His major opponent would be a Davidson County judge, Beverly Briley. Dad said that even if Mayor West was not running, it would be difficult for him to vote for a guy named "Beverly."

A Thursday morning in late July found me at the front counter reading a *Superman* comic book when the big C.B. Ragland truck pulled up in front of the store. Chewing on the usual unlit cigar, Mr. Patterson effortlessly moved sixteen boxes of canned goods and other grocery items into the store. After Mr. Patterson left, Mom relieved me of counter duties so that I could help Dad and Sonny put stock on the shelves in preparation for the weekend. With the three of us working, we finished within a couple of hours.

"Go ahead, Jimmy," said Mom. "I'll stay until Myrtle gets here."

"Deal!" I said.

I immediately left the store and walked up the street where I found Prof sitting on his front porch listening to WKDA. I made myself comfortable in one of the porch chairs and joined Prof in listening to Ray Charles singing *I Can't Stop Loving You*. I noticed the morning newspaper lying in one of the chairs. I retrieved it and turned to the sports page. The Yankees had won their third straight game and were in first place in the American League. While checking the National League standings, I saw Bucky entering Prof's gate.

"Is this all you bastards have got to do?" chuckled Bucky as he seated himself in the porch swing.

"I thought you were babysitting today," I said.

"Nope. I caught a break," he said. "Dad is off work today and tomorrow, so I'm on parole."

Prof had picked up the entertainment section of the paper and saw something that perked his interest.

"Hey," he said, "there's a movie opening today at the Loews that we ought to go see."

"What is it?" I asked.

"It's called *Dr. No*, and it's a spy movie," replied Prof.

"Okay," I said. "What else is playing?"

Prof handed me the entertainment section so I could see for myself.

"Hey," I said with some excitement. "There's a Randolph Scott western playing at the Paramount." Next to John Wayne, Randolph Scott was my favorite cowboy.

"C'mon, Jim," interrupted Prof. "I'm tired of westerns. That's all you see on TV. Let's see *Dr. No*.

"Yeah. Okay," I said. Prof was right. Television in 1962 was inundated with westerns: *Gunsmoke, Bonanza, Have Gun Will Travel, Cheyenne,* and *Tales of Wells Fargo* – just to name a few.

"Hold up, Horsehead," said Bucky. "You know the score on me with anything that costs money."

"Yeah. Don't worry, Grasshopper. I got you covered," I replied.

Turning to Prof, I asked, "How are you fixed for money?"

"I'm okay," he said. "I've got a couple of bucks."

"Let's meet at the store at noon tomorrow," I suggested. "We'll walk downtown and ride the bus back."

The agreement was made, so we just settled back and listened to WKDA.

***

By walking downtown, each of us saved seventeen cents in bus fare. It was an easy walk. Loews Theatre was located on Church Street at Sixth Avenue. From the store, we walked straight down Fifth Avenue to Church. The street was called Church Street for a reason. At the turn of the twentieth century, there had been at least one church on every corner from Second Avenue to Eighth Avenue. The only church remaining on the street was The Downtown Presbyterian Church which was located on the southeast corner of Church Street and Fifth Avenue. The original building was built in 1812. In its day, the church had some very well-known people as members including Andrew and Rachel Jackson. On the steps of the church in 1815, General Jackson was awarded a ceremonial sword by the congregation for his service in the War of 1812. The original building was destroyed by fire. The current building was erected in 1852.

As we walked down Fifth Avenue, we crossed streets that were named after U.S. Presidents: Buchanan Street, Garfield Street, Taylor Street, Madison Street, and Jefferson Street. After crossing Garfield Street, the Morgan Park playground, community center, and public swimming pool were on our left. The Werthan Bag Corporation was on our right. Werthan opened in 1908 making burlap and cotton bags. My mom and dad met in the early 1930's while working in the cotton mill where raw cotton was made into cloth. In 1952, Werthan converted to the manufacture of paper bags.

As we approached Monroe Street, a Jewish-owned clothing store came into view on the far-left corner of Fifth Avenue and

Monroe. Schatten's Dry Goods had been there for years. Mr. Schatten was short and thin with a full head of gray hair. He was always exquisitely dressed and very personable.

"Dad said that Mr. Schatten disowned his only daughter," I said as we passed his store.

"What do you mean, 'disowned' her?" asked Bucky.

"Well........." I said, "he doesn't speak to her. She's not allowed to visit, and he's cut her out of the will."

"Does your dad know why?" asked Prof.

"Yeah," I replied. "He disowned her for marrying a gentile."

"For what?" asked Bucky.

"For marrying a gentile," I said.

"What the hell is a gentile, Horsehead?" Bucky asked inquisitively.

"Do you mean to tell me that you don't know what a gentile is?" I asked sarcastically.

"Well, do you?" asked Bucky.

"Grasshopper, you are a gentile," I replied. "So is Prof. So am I. A gentile is anyone who is not a Jew."

"So, what's the big deal about a Jew marrying a gentile?" asked Prof.

"Hey, I don't know," I replied. "It's a Jewish thing, I guess."

We arrived at the corner of Fifth Avenue and Jefferson Street. Jefferson was a very busy street. A few blocks away was the Jefferson Street Bridge which connected North Nashville and East Nashville across the Cumberland River. There were many businesses on Jefferson Street: convenience stores, a barber college, hardware stores, clothing stores, and others.

Most were owned by African Americans. Fisk University was located on Jefferson Street at Eighteenth Avenue. Fisk was one of the oldest all-Black colleges in the country. It was founded in 1866 as a school for the children of former slaves. It had a world-renowned choral group called the Fisk Jubilee Singers. The group had performed at many venues including a performance in London for Queen Victoria. In addition, Fisk University had an excellent academic reputation.

We stood on the corner of Fifth and Jefferson waiting for the traffic light to stop traffic or for a break in the traffic so we could cross the busy street. As we waited, a white Chevy Nova came down Fifth Avenue and stopped beside us.

"Hey," shouted the driver as he peered through the open window on the passenger side. "Do you boys want to have some fun?"

"No, Sir," said Prof as Bucky and I gave each other a puzzled look. "We've got business downtown."

At that moment, the traffic light changed stopping the Jefferson Street traffic. We quickly scurried across Jefferson Street.

"What was that about?" I asked as we continued our journey downtown.

"That guy was a pimp," said Prof.

"A what?" I asked.

"Horsehead," shouted Bucky, "are you gonna tell me you don't know what a pimp is?"

"I know what it is," I insisted.

"Hey, Bucky," interrupted Prof with a laugh. "This could've been your lucky day if you had any money!"

"Very funny," replied Bucky.

***

Exiting the Lowe's Theatre and walking up Sixth Avenue toward the bus shelters, *Dr. No* was all that we could talk about. We were struck by the suave and debonair character, James Bond. He had a license to kill and a way with the women. We were also struck by Ursula Andress, the first of the "Bond Girls."

"Thanks to her," chuckled Bucky, "that movie had some really good parts."

All three of us broke into an immature laugh agreeing that we were fortunate in choosing Ursula Andress over Randolph Scott.

The bus shelters were located on Sixth Avenue between Union Street and Deaderick Street. The shelters were the hub of the Nashville bus system. Across Sixth Avenue from the shelters was the iconic Andrew Jackson Hotel. Neither the shelters nor the hotel is there today. The former bus shelters are now the home of Legislative Plaza. The hotel site is now home to the Tennessee Performing Arts Center.

We boarded the St. Cecelia bus which transported us down Fifth Avenue to the Clay Street stop. Deboarding the bus across Clay Street from the store, we went our separate ways. As I entered the store to take over the front counter from Mom, Silas was leaving with a small bag of items.

"Guess what, Jimmy," said Silas in an excited tone.

"What?" I said.,

"You know that big field across Clay Street from the St. Cecelia Convent?" he asked.

"Yeah," I said.

"A carnival is setting up there. It looks like a big one," he exclaimed.

"Well, all right," I replied. "Do you know when its opening?"

'Nope," he said, "but probably next week."

***

Business was always slow on Mondays. With few customers, the time seemed to crawl. I spent most of the morning reading comic books and listening to WKDA. Silas came into the store about 11:30 with his baseball and glove. He, Prof, and I had spent Sunday afternoon watching the carnival being set up in the field across from St. Cecelia. We learned that the carnival was to open on Wednesday night and close the following Monday. We had watched as a large Ferris Wheel was erected. I had always been afraid of heights, so I avoided Ferris wheels. There were several other rides being erected as well as bumper cars and games. We were really looking forward to Wednesday night.

"Hey, man," said Silas as he laid his glove and ball on the ice cream freezer near the front counter. "You wanna throw some ball?"

Silas and I often went into the backyard of the store and played "strike-out." It was a simple game in which there was a pitcher and a catcher. The catcher served as umpire calling balls and strikes. When the pitcher struck out three make-believe batters or walked four, the pitcher and catcher exchanged places.

"Yeah," I replied, "just as soon as Miss Myrtle gets here."

As Silas and I were talking, a young man came into the store and proceeded to the meat counter. He was somewhat short and stocky with fiery red hair and a million freckles. Silas and I recognized him as one of the carnival workers. After a few minutes, he approached the front counter with twenty-cents-worth of lunch meat, a small box of Premium saltines, a nickel bag of chips, and a Nehi orange.

"That'll be fifty-two cents," I said as I started bagging his purchases.

I took his money and put it into the cash drawer.

"And forty-eight-cents is your change. Thank you and come back," I said with a smile.

The young man stared at the forty-eight-cents. He slowly looked up with a look of annoyance.

"Hey, look," he said. "I gave you a ten-dollar-bill."

I turned to look at the ledge over the cash drawer. I immediately realized that I had not handled the money properly. I had put his bill into the cash drawer instead of on the ledge.

"I'm pretty sure that you gave me a one-dollar-bill," I said.

"Look. I gave you a ten, and you owe me nine dollars," he said emphatically.

I didn't know what to do. Maybe he did give me a ten, and maybe he didn't. Being a little distraught, I took a deep breath and retrieved nine dollars from the cash drawer and gave it to him. Pocketing the money, he turned and briskly exited the store. I looked at Silas.

"Did you happen to see?" I asked.

"Naw, man," replied Silas. "I wasn't paying any attention."

"Well," I said. "I'll find out tonight when Mom balances the register. I hope he really did give me a ten-dollar-bill and the register isn't short."

***

After Miss Myrtle relieved me at the counter, Silas and I proceeded to the backyard to play "strike-out." Silas pitched first and struck out his three make-believe batters. My turn to pitch did not go well.

"Man! What's wrong with you?" shouted Silas. You've walked three batters and haven't struck out any!"

"I'm just a little off today," I said.

'No, man! You're a lot off," declared Silas. "You need to get those nine dollars off your mind."

"Yeah," I said.

After an hour or so, we were joined by Prof. We decided to climb down the cliffs and hang out in the bottoms. As supper time approached, Silas and Prof went home, and I went into the store to take over counter duties. Over the next three hours I waited on several customers and tried to read a comic book; however, my mind was on nine dollars and not on the adventures of Superman.

At closing time, Mom came into the store to close the cash register. After Dad closed and locked the front door, Mom turned to me and said, "Jimmy, look in the slot and give me a reading.

Our cash register had a little slot that one could look into and see the amount of money that was received that day. The numbers in the slot were small and difficult for Mom to read.

"Okay, Mom," I said. We took in $83.19." It had been a very slow day.

Mom started counting the money in the cash register. We opened the store each morning with $90.00 in the register. After receiving $83.19, she should finish her count with $173.19. Sometimes the register ended the day a few cents short or a few cents over; however, a large shortage would lead to questions. I held my breath as Mom continued counting. Dad had returned to the meat count in the rear of the store. He was busy cleaning knives and meat cleavers and putting them away.

When Mom finished counting, she took a deep sigh and turned to me, "Jimmy, we are nine dollars short. Do you know anything about this?"

"Yes, Ma'am. I do., "I replied.

As I started telling Mom the cause of the shortage, she stopped me.

"I think your dad needs to hear this, too," she said.

Turning toward the meat counter, she shouted, "James, you need to come up here."

After Dad came to the front counter, I related the event that led to the register being short.

"I know that I messed up," I said apologetically. "I don't

know why I put the money into the drawer instead of waiting until I had given the guy his change."

"I know why," interrupted Dad. "I remember that boy coming in here. You were busy talking with Silas instead of paying attention to what you were doing!"

"I know, Dad, and it will not happen again," I promised.

"Well, James," said Mom. "What do you want to do?"

"Jim," said Dad, "people in business have to pay for their mistakes. What do you think should happen?"

I realized where this was going.

"Whatever you say, Dad," I replied.

"We could let him work it off," interjected Mom.

"That wouldn't get the nine dollars back," said Dad. Turning to me, he continued, "What do you want to do, Jim?"

"It's not what I want to do, Dad," I said. "It's what I should do."

I had a stash of savings in a cigar box in my room.

"I'll be right back with nine dollars," I said.

"Okay, Son. Hurry back," said Dad as Mom gave him a harsh look of annoyance.

***

The following Wednesday was historic. I overcame my fear of heights and rode the Ferris Wheel. After Mom had relieved me of my store duties at 7:00 p.m., I went to the carnival accompanied by Bucky, Silas, Isaiah, and Prof. Before leaving the store, I had slipped a couple of dollars to Bucky. I did not want to embarrass him by paying his way on the rides.

"I'm proud of ya," said Bucky as we de-boarded the Ferris Wheel.

"Hey, I'm proud of myself," I replied. "It really wasn't that scary."

The four of us walked around for a few minutes. I had felt a little nervous since arriving at the carnival because I saw no Black people except Silas and Isaiah. I was relieved after we rode the Ferris Wheel and a couple of other rides with no problem. Obviously, green was the only color that interested the carnival people.

"Hey," said Prof, "there's the Tilt-a-Whirl. Let's get on that!"

"Okay," said Isaiah.

"Wait a minute, guys" exclaimed Silas. "I get sick to my stomach every time I ride the Tilt-a-Whirl. Yawl go ahead, though. I'll wait here."

Bucky, Prof, Isaiah, and I abandoned Silas and climbed aboard the ride. It was the fastest Tilt-a-Whirl I had ever experienced. It jerked us around for several minutes – a nice long ride. As we skipped down the exit ramp, we joyfully agreed that we had to ride it again, but when we got to the end of the ramp, Silas was nowhere to be seen.

"Silas!" yelled Bucky. "Hey, Silas!"

"Where could that dude be?" asked Isaiah rhetorically.

"Look," said Prof. "There he is!"

We looked in the direction that Prof was pointing and saw Silas running toward us.

"Hey, Jimmy," he shouted with some excitement. "This is your lucky day!!"

"What are you talking about?" I asked with a chuckle.

"There's a dunking machine down there," replied Silas.

"What's a dunking machine?" asked Prof.

"Oh, come on," said Bucky. "Do you mean to tell me that you don't know what a dunking machine is?"

"A dunking machine," explained Silas, "is where a guy sits on a little seat that's over a big tank of water. If you throw a baseball and it hits a target, the seat collapses and drops the dude into the water."

With that, Silas turned to me and said, "You're gonna love this, Jimmy!"

I had no idea what Silas meant, but we walked down to the dunking machine. A guy was sitting on a seat hovering over a huge vat of water. The target was a round red disk with a diameter of twelve inches or so.

Silas couldn't control his excitement as the said, "All you gotta do is hit that red disk with a baseball, and your best friend will fall into the water."

"My best friend?" I mused. With that, I took a closer look at the person on the dunking seat. He was a stocky guy with fiery red hair and a million freckles. I just looked at Silas and we broke into joyous laughter.

"This is going to be great!!" I exclaimed.

"You get to throw three baseballs for twenty-five cents," said Silas. "This is going to be the best quarter you ever spent!"

I gave a quarter to the attendant and went to the designated mark. The mark was about sixty feet from the target.

"Just pretend that you're Sandy Koufax and that target is my glove," said Silas. "Just rear back and let it rip!"

I did let it rip. A nano-second after the ball left my hand, the freckled thief hit the water. It was great!

"Man!" said Silas with excitement. "You've got two more throws!!"

As the four of us laughed and slapped hands, the red-headed punk climbed back onto the seat hovering above the water.

"Hey, I know you!" he shouted. "You're that turtle-nose looking kid from down at that funky little store."

With that, I threw the second ball, and he dropped into the tank again.

Silas, Bucky, Isaiah, and Prof erupted into exuberant laughter.

No sooner than the red-headed crook re-seated himself, the third baseball found the target.

"Three out of three!!" yelled Silas.

For my effort, the attendant awarded me with a large Mickey Mouse doll. I vowed to my buddies that I would cherish it always.

"See ya, Punk!" I shouted as we walked away with glee. We all agreed: revenge is best served cold—and wet!

***

Heartbreak

The summer of 1962 had passed quickly. On the morning after Labor Day Bucky, Prof, and I were making our trek toward North Nashville High School. We could not believe how fast summer vacation had gone by. It had been awesome: playing baseball at Morgan Park, playing "strike out" with Silas, climbing the cliffs, roaming the bottoms, going to movies, and listening to WKDA on Prof's porch. It had been great!

Although I had vowed to be a faithful member of the He-Man Woman Haters Club, I had started to backslide during the waning days of August. I had tried mightily, but I had not been able to keep Judy out of my mind.

"Hey, Prof," said Bucky as we approached the convent on Clay Street. "Do you know why Jimmy is so happy?"

"He likes school?" mused Prof.

"There's more to it than that," chuckled Bucky. "He'll get to see his woman!"

"Wow!" said Prof. Turning to me, he asked, "You got a woman!?!"

"Not really," I said sheepishly.

"He almost did," interjected Bucky with a laugh, "but she dumped him!"

I turned toward Bucky and gave him an angry stare. He immediately realized that he had touched a nerve. Prof realized it too. We completed our journey largely in silence.

***

I found myself in Mr. Potter's homeroom again along with Bucky. We were also together in the second period in Biology and in Physical Education the fifth period. We may have had more classes together, but I had opted to take Algebra II while

Bucky enrolled in General Math. I really did not enjoy algebra, but I had two good reasons for taking it. I intended to go on to college after high school, and two years of algebra may be required. More importantly, I knew that Judy would be taking Algebra II. Failing as a He-Man Woman Hater, I was hoping that Judy and I would have other classes together. Perhaps we would be in the library again. As I left homeroom and worked my way to English class, I was overflowing with warm anticipation.

I was in Mrs. Acuff's class again. Her tenth grade English class would be a great way to start the day. She was very business-like and firm, yet friendly. She was demanding, yet fair. Her class had always been interesting and enjoyable. Entering the classroom, I took the first seat in the first row –just like the previous year. Only a few students had entered. One of them was Margie Gibson. Again, she had taken a seat at the back of the room and had buried her head on the desk. As I sat in my seat watching students enter the room and quietly taking their seats, I was hoping that Judy would be one of them. The tardy bell rang, and Mrs. Acuff closed the door to begin class. No Judy. That was okay. Maybe she would be in biology class. If not, I knew that she would be in Mr. Robertson's third period algebra class.

Following second period biology class, I hurried to Mr. Robertson's room and claimed the same seat I had occupied the previous year. I expected – or hoped—that Judy would claim her same seat. As students filed into the classroom, I waited for Judy with growing anxiety. Amazingly, the students claimed the same seats that they had occupied the previous year. Rella and Claudia, Judy's best friends, entered and took their usual seats, but Judy was not with them. That was not unusual; Judy had often entered the classroom later than her friends. As I continued to wait, my anxiety accelerated. When the tardy bell rang, Mr. Robertson closed the door to begin class. No Judy. My heart sank. In calling the roll, Mr. Robertson did not call Judy's name. I glanced over toward Claudia and Rella. Both girls were looking at me. Claudia appeared to be giggling. I could only wonder what the hell was going on.

***

Entering the cafeteria following algebra class, I found Bucky sitting alone at his usual table at the front of the cafeteria. He had arrived there moments earlier and was reaching into the brown paper bag that contained his lunch. Deciding to forgo eating lunch, I immediately took a seat across the table from Bucky.

"Are you not eating today?" asked Bucky.

"I'm not hungry," I replied glumly.

"Uh oh," exclaimed Bucky. "Horsehead, you're always hungry. What's wrong?"

"I haven't seen Judy Garner today," I confided. "She wasn't in algebra class."

"She's probably just absent," said Bucky, "sick or something."

"Nope," I replied. "The teacher didn't call her name during roll call."

"Well, maybe she decided to skip algebra this year," retorted Bucky.

"No way, Grasshopper," I said. "She actually likes algebra."

Bucky turned his attention toward the back of the cafeteria, then turned and faced me.

"Rella and her other friends are sitting at that back table," he said. "Go back there and ask them where she is."

"No," I replied. "I don't really want to do that."

"Horsehead," said Bucky, "you're too bashful for your own good. Go on back there."

"Naw, Buck," I replied. "I just can't do it."

"The hell you can't!" he emphatically replied. "If you weren't so damn bashful, you would have asked her to go to the movies last year! You would have taken her to the spring dance!" Bucky hesitated, then exclaimed, "Hell, Man! What are you afraid of?!"

I really did not know how to answer, but I was getting really irritated with Bucky's insistence.

"Well, Grasshopper," I finally replied. "What are you afraid of?"

"What are you talking about?" he responded.

"I'm talking about Mary Beth Warner. I know you like her!" I said emphatically. "I haven't seen you ask her to the movies, the dance, or even talk to her!"

Bucky and I just stared at each other. I knew that it was I who had touched a nerve this time. I sensed that I needed to back up on this conversation.

"Look, Grasshopper," I said. "No one can blame you for liking Mary Beth. She's really pretty."

"Pretty?!" Bucky shot back loudly. "She's gorgeous! She's

more than gorgeous!" He hesitated and then continued, "She's absolutely stacked—built like a brick house."

Bucky was right. Mary Beth Warren was a petite little blond. She was barely five feet tall but had curves in all the right places. When Mary Beth Warren walked by, she commanded attention.

After a brief pause, Bucky continued, "Look, Horsehead, I can't take Mary Beth or any other girl to the movies or anywhere else. I don't have two nickels to rub together." He gave me an exasperated look and sadly said, "I can only go to the movies because you pay my way."

I knew Bucky was right. I was hindered by being overly shy. He was hindered by being broke.

"Yeah. I understand," I relented.

"You can understand," he argued, "but that has nothing to do with Judy." After another pause, he continued, "If you don't go back there and ask about Judy, I will."

"Come on, Man," I pleaded. "Don't do that."

With that, Bucky pushed back from the table and stood up.

"Okay, Grasshopper," I said with some trepidation. "I'll go."

I gingerly made my way back to the rear of the cafeteria. As I approached the table, I could feel my face glowing red and my legs quivering.

"Well, look who's here," said Claudia sarcastically. "Let me guess. You want to know where Judy is."

"Oh, stop it, Claudia," order Rella. Turning to me, she continued, "Judy has transferred to Hume Fogg to take secretarial courses."

I was speechless. I could only stand there.

"Jimmy," continued Rella, "you know where she lives. Just stop by and see her. I know that she would be glad to see you."

"Okay, maybe I will," I said. "Thanks, Rella."

***

Judy lived on Tenth Avenue. I knew exactly where she lived; however, I did not go to see her. Although Bucky and Prof constantly encouraged me to do so, I was just too shy. Maybe I feared rejection. Life is full of disappointments; this one was self-imposed. At any event, I never saw Judy again. She was the first girl that I had ever really loved. Thankfully, she would not be the last.

***

Un-Civil Rights

September is a beautiful month in Nashville. September of 1962 was no different: warm sunny days, cooler nights, and college football on Saturdays. My favorite team was the Vanderbilt Commodores; however, since the Commodores often lost, I needed a back-up team. My second favorite team was a football powerhouse, a team that had won the National Championship in 1960 and finished as the number five team in America in 1961 sporting nine wins, one loss, and one tie. That team was the Rebels of the University of Mississippi, fondly known as Ole Miss. Both Vandy and Ole Miss would start their respective seasons on Saturday, September 22. The Commodores would open at the University of West Virginia while Ole Miss would begin its season in Memphis against the Tigers of Memphis State University. I could hardly wait.

On Tuesday, September 11, I helped Dad open the store at 6:30 a.m. By 7:00 a.m. the initial rush of customers had exited the store. As usual, I hurried to the front porch to fetch the morning newspaper, the *Nashville Tennessean*. Before leaving for school, I enjoyed turning to the sports page to check on the Yankees and the other baseball scores. At this time of year, there was usually an article reporting on pre-season football practice at Vanderbilt. Occasionally, there was an article featuring Ole Miss; however, on this particular morning, a front-page story grabbed my immediate attention. The headline referenced the University of Mississippi, the Supreme Court, and a man named James Meredith.

According to the newspaper, Meredith was a Black man who had been attending Jackson State College in Jackson, Mississippi. Meredith had applied for admittance to all-White Ole Miss in January 1961. After being initially accepted, Ole Miss reversed its decision and denied his admission. According to sources, he was denied when his race was discovered. Aided by lawyers from the National Association for the Advancement of Colored Peoples (NAACP), Meredith sued the university in order to gain admittance. Although he lost his suit in the lower courts, the Supreme Court of the United States ordered the university and the state of Mississippi to allow his admittance.

Before I could finish the article, Miss Myrtle arrived to take over the front counter and allow me to go to school.

"Good morning, Mr. Jim," she said cheerfully.

"Good morning," I said trying to match her cheerfulness.

"Your two buddies are waiting for you on the porch," she said. "Have a good day at school and try to learn something every chance you get."

***

Entering the store after school that afternoon, I found Mom working at the front counter. Dad, Mr. Gates, and Officer Marcum were standing in front of the meat counter engaging in conversation.

"Hey, Mom," I said. "I'm gonna get a cold drink and be right back."

"Take your time," she replied, "and find out what those three are talking about back there."

I took my time selecting my daily Double Cola while I eavesdropped.

"This could get real interesting," said Mr. Gates. "The governor down there, Ross Barnett, said he didn't care what the Supreme Court said."

"It's going to get more than interesting, Herman," said Mr. Marcum. "I don't understand why that boy would want to go where he's not welcome."

"Well," replied Mr. Gates, "he's not a boy. James Meredith is twenty-nine years old. He served in the Air Force for nine years. He's a Korean War veteran, and he's from Mississippi.

Don't you think he's earned the right to attend the University of Mississippi?"

"Of course, he has," replied Marcum. "I'm just saying that he's putting himself in some serious danger. There are already demonstrations happening on the Ole Miss campus. The Klan will probably get involved and things could quickly turn violent. I just don't understand the point."

"I do, Marc," retorted Gates. "He's making the same point that Rosa Parks made down in Montgomery when she decided to sit at the front of a bus—the same point that Paul Patterson and those other students made by sitting at those lunch counters in downtown Nashville. Meredith just wants the same right a White guy has."

"I don't disagree with that, Herman," said Marcum," but............. that's Mississippi."

"Hey, Stony," said Gates turning toward Dad. "You've been awful quiet. What are you thinking?"

"I'm thinking that Meredith has the right to go to Ole Miss," said Dad, "but I'm also thinking that things are going to get real ugly down in Oxford."

Following a few thoughtful moments, Marcum turned to Dad and asked, "Why is your boy taking so long getting that Double Cola?"

"Because," laughed Dad, "his momma sent him back here to find out what we're talking about."

✳✳✳

The James Meredith controversy was widely reported on television, radio, and newspapers during mid-September. The controversy had become a war of words between Mississippi Governor Ross Barnett and the U.S. Attorney General, Robert Kennedy. Barnett was blatantly violating a court order by refusing to allow Meredith admittance into Ole Miss. The Attorney General, the President's brother, was continually warning Barnett that he could face heavy fines and possible imprisonment for failing to obey a court order. Things began to come to a head on Saturday, September 29, when a belligerent Ross Barnett delivered a fiery speech at the halftime of the Ole Miss – Kentucky football game in Oxford. On Sunday, September 30, the governor was ordered to admit Meredith by 1:00 p.m. on October 1 or be subjected to daily fines of $10,000. Later that day, Barnett agreed to allow Meredith's enrollment. That's when all hell broke out on the Ole Miss campus as well as downtown Oxford.

I was surprised at how little had been said at school regarding the Meredith controversy. Mr. Price, my World History teacher, only mentioned it briefly. He was more interested in the history of ancient Mesopotamia. Except for conversations between Dad and Mr. Gates, nothing was said in the store. While Silas and I were pitching baseball, I had asked him if Paul was going down to Ole Miss and take part in the demonstrations. After his answer was a simple "no," the subject was dropped.

Arriving at the store following attending school on Monday, October 1, I found that the *Nashville Benner,* Nashville's evening newspaper, had not yet arrived.

"Hey, Mom. Have you heard any news about that Ole Miss thing?" I asked.

'No," she said. "I'm sure something will be in the paper. Its running late today."

With that, she left the front counter to me and went upstairs to prepare supper.

It was a typical Monday. Business was slow, so I was able to complete my English homework between customers. A little after 6:00 p.m., I heard something lightly strike the front of the screened door. It was the late edition of the *Nashville Benner.* The front-page headline was breath-taking: "Ole Miss Enrolls Meredith After Riots kill 2, Injures 75." The article read as follows:

OXFORD, Miss., Oct. 1, 1962 (UPI)—Negro James Meredith registered today at the University of Mississippi and began classes on a campus littered with the debris of a major riot that took two lives and injured at least 75 persons.

About 400 U.S. deputy marshals and 1,000 federal troops guarded the campus as the 29-year-old Negro cracked the segregation barriers of the 114-year-old school.

The campus was brought under military control early today, but the rioting spread to downtown Oxford and at least one soldier was hurt in a barrage of rocks, timbers and pop bottles before the crowd was dispersed with tear gas and reinforcements were brought in. Shots were fired over the heads of the rioters.

Meredith, whose determination to desegregate Ole Miss brought about a conflict that threatened to rock the Union, walked solemnly to an American Colonial History class to shouts of "Nigger, Nigger" and "Was it worth two deaths?"

The campus itself looked like a battleground. It was littered with burned-out automobiles, tear gas canisters and broken glass and echoed to the cadence of marching troops, including the Mississippi National Guard which President Kennedy summoned yesterday.

Army troops began moving onto the campus at midnight, three hours after the riot began, but it was not until 6 a.m. that the last stubborn segregationists were routed.

Before dawn a military force of 2,600 was on or near the Oxford campus. Troops were converging from all directions on the Northern Mississippi town which had been the home of the late Nobel-prize winner author, William Faulkner.

Twelve marshals were either wounded or injured, three of them seriously, and five soldiers were hurt. Most of the wounds were caused by bricks and blows with lengths of pipe. But there were some gunshot wounds. Many of the rioters apparently were students from Mississippi State College at Starkville. A massive demonstration was conducted there yesterday afternoon including marches through the Negro section of Starkville and the burning in effigy of President Kennedy.

In the downtown area, troops under command of Brig. Gen. Charles Billingslea dispersed bands of marauding demonstrators. Rioters hurled firebombs at Army vehicles and chased cars containing Negroes.

Some of the demonstrators were routed with tear gas and fixed bayonets. Several of the infantrymen were Negroes, who gritted their teeth as crowds taunted them and told them to go to Cuba or back to New Jersey. One Negro soldier was hit on the neck with a bottle.

Truckload after truckload of troops poured into Courthouse Square where soldiers had pinned down some of the rioters. Ten helicopters circled overhead spotting crowds which were reforming in alleys for another attack on the troops. Officials announced the arrest of 108 persons. Among those arrested was Melvin Bruce, 24, of Decatur, Ga., a supporter of the American Nazi Party. He was charged with being a sniper who had been firing on marshals and soldiers during the eight hours of rioting.

The rioting began as President Kennedy, in a televised address, was appealing to Mississippians to comply with the federal law even though they did not agree with it.

Meredith, 29, a Negro veteran of the Korean War who thrice had been denied entry to the campus by Gov. Ross Barnett and Lt. Gov. Paul B. Johnson was escorted secretly into the university by a motorcade of U.S. marshals and bedded down for the night at a dormitory which was put under heavy guard.

Shortly before 10 p.m. the word flashed around campus that Meredith was there. And, even as Kennedy spoke, the riot began.

Reading this article, I felt ashamed—ashamed of people reacting so violently to a nine-year military veteran applying to be admitted to a state university in his home state. I felt it odd that a Black man was good enough to serve in the Korean War with White people, but he was not good enough to attend college with White people. Over the next several days, it was clear that the events in Oxford, Mississippi had little effect on life in Nashville. People continued to come and go from the store without any mention of the Ole Miss riot. The Sunday afternoon football games at Morgan Park continued with no mention. I agreed with Dad; people were just not comfortable talking about it. The order of the day appeared to be "live and let live."

***

The Russians Are Coming

Bucky did not realize how lucky he was to be taking biology. The classroom included four rows of four tables. Each table seated two people. On the first day of classes, I arrived in the classroom before Bucky and proceeded to claim the first table in the fourth row. That table was directly across from the teacher's desk. After Bucky entered the classroom and sat down beside me, he questioned my table selection given the close proximity to the teacher. I assured him that it made no difference where we sat. Having been in Mr. Hale's General Science class the previous year, I knew he would spend very little time in the classroom. His method of operation was to call the roll, write the daily assignment on the chalk board, and leave the classroom. He usually returned with only a few minutes left in the period. Mr. Hale never taught a class or administered a test. At the end of a six-week grading period, he spent a class session calling each student up to his desk where he checked their notebooks for completed assignments and assigned a grade according. Mr. Hale was a man of medium height and weight with brown curly hair and chestnut-colored eyes. His brown horn-rimmed glasses and knee length lab coat gave him the aura of a scientist. His appearance and mannerisms were actually quite intimidating. When the students completed their daily assignment, we usually were allowed to quietly talk for the remainder of the period.

Bucky was lucky to be taking biology for another reason. The table directly behind our table was claimed by Bucky's secret squeeze, Mary Beth Warren. She was joined at the table by Lee Whittaker. I had no hard feelings toward Lee regarding Judy, but I was unsure how Bucky would feel about Lee sharing a table with Mary Beth. At any event, both Lee and Bucky had great taste in women.

***

As September gave way to October, I found myself looking forward to days at school; however, I had mixed feelings on Thursday, October 4. The first game of the World Series would be played that afternoon in New York. Again, the Yankees were American League champions and would face the National League champs, the San Francisco Giants. The series looked to be epic. The power-laden New York Yankees featuring homer-hammering Mickey Mantle and Roger Maris against the powerful San Francisco Giants featuring the vastly talented Willie Mays, Orlando Cepeda, and Felipe Alou. It would be a series for the ages.

"Hey, Horsehead," said Bucky as we trekked from the store toward school. "I thought you might be sick today."

"Why would you think that?" I asked.

"I thought you might stay home and watch the baseball game on TV," he replied.

"I'd like to, but I'm not doing well in algebra and can't afford to miss," I said.

"I thought I might take algebra next year," interjected Prof, "but I'm a little scared of it, especially since you're finding it so hard."

"Not me," said Bucky. "I'm quitting school as soon as I turn seventeen. Until then, I'm only taking what I have to take."

Neither Prof nor I argued with Bucky. It would not change his mind. Besides, maybe being in biology class with Mary Beth Warren would do the trick.

***

Time flies when you're having fun. October was flying. On October 7, the long-awaited Municipal Auditorium opened in downtown Nashville. Constructed by Nashville Bridge Company, Municipal Auditorium was the only multi-use center in the South with air conditioning. Tommy had informed me that Nashville's hockey team, the Dixie Flyers, would debut at the auditorium on Saturday, October 27. The New York Yankees had added another World Series championship to their resume by defeating the San Francisco Giants in seven games. The nationally ranked Ole Miss football team continued to be undefeated. Unfortunately, my Vanderbilt Commodores were still winless.

On Monday, October 22, Mr. Hale wrote the day's

assignment on the chalk board and left the classroom. As usual, the students broke into conversation as soon as the assignment was completed. Bucky and I turned to face Lee and Mary Beth. I had gotten over Lee's past flirtations with Judy. The four of us really enjoyed talking and laughing. Mary Beth had her purse placed on their table between she and Lee. Lee picked it up and started fumbling with it.

"Hey, Mary Beth," said Lee playfully. "What have you got in here? Let me see: lipstick, compact, Kleenex, ………….. what's this?"

Lee had removed a very small cellophane package from the purse. "Trojan" appeared on the label. Lee, Bucky, and I just stared at it. Suddenly, Lee realized that he was holding a condom and quickly slammed it back into the purse. Mary Beth did not react. She simply moved her purse to the other side of the table out of Lee's reach. Thankfully, this awkward moment was interrupted by Mr. Hale entering the classroom. Bucky and I immediately turned and faced the front of the room. Mr. Hale gave Bucky and I a puzzled look.

"Jim, are you guys all right?" he asked.

"Yes, Sir," I answered. At that moment, the bell rang to dismiss class.

***

Mom, Dad, and I were late closing the store that evening. Several customers were still in the store at 8:00 p.m. Since Monday was a slow day, that was unusual. It was almost 8:30 before I could close and lock the door so Mom could begin counting money and closing the register. It was almost 9:00 before we entered the upstairs apartment. As usual, Mom and Dad had retired to bed by 10:00, but not me. I stayed up late every Monday night during football season. Following the 10 o'clock news, channel 5 replayed the video of the previous Sunday's NFL game featuring the Chicago Bears. The starting quarterback for the Bears was Bill Wade, a native Nashvillian and former All-American at Vanderbilt University. Wade had been the NFL's number one draft choice in 1952. His popularity in Nashville provided the Monday night replays with a substantial television audience.

After Mom and Dad retired, I moved from the couch and comfortably settled into Mom's easy chair. I did not mind sitting through the news. In fact, I enjoyed keeping up with current events. The newscast on this particular night was alarming and downright scary. The lead story was regarding a national television address that President Kennedy had delivered earlier that evening. The news anchor gave a stunning summary of the president's speech.

On October 14, an American U-2 spy plane made a high-altitude pass over the island nation of Cuba and photographed Soviet SS-4 medium range missiles being assembled for installation. The president declared that Soviet nuclear missiles in Cuba, just ninety miles from Florida, were unacceptable. From Cuba, SS-4 missiles could reach every city in the eastern United States, Mexico, and Central America. In response to the presence of these missiles in Cuba, President Kennedy announced a quarantine of that island nation. The quarantine would be enforced by a naval blockade in which the U.S. Navy would stop and search any ship from any nation bound for Cuba. The blockade would prohibit the delivery of any military weaponry. The quarantine would go into effect immediately. After viewing a brief clip from the president's speech, it was clear that he meant business. It was also clear—even to a fifteen-year-old—that the Cold War could become very hot.

The next morning, I left the check-out counter and darted onto the store porch to retrieve the morning newspaper as soon as I heard it hit the porch. Unrolling the newspaper, I found an ominous headline: "Pentagon Orders Sinking of Blockade Runners." The article reported that U.S. air and sea patrols had been dispatched to track vessels moving toward Cuba and report. American warships were ordered to stop and search any ship entering the quarantine area. The White House and the Defense Department said that any Soviet ship that refused to stop would be sunk. The article also reported that the president had warned the Soviets that any Cuban attack in the Western Hemisphere would bring instant retaliation upon Russian cities.

"Hey, Dad," I called to the back of the store. "Be sure and read the front page today."

"Always do, Jim," he replied.

I could tell that Dad did not yet know what was happening regarding the Cuba situation. On the walk to school with Bucky and Prof, I discovered that they were also unaware. After I filled them in on the situation, Prof showed concern, but Bucky did not seem to take it seriously.

"Hey, Horsehead," said Bucky. "Do you know what to do during a nuclear attack?"

"Well," I replied, "I guess we do the 'duck and cover' that we practiced in elementary school."

"Nah, that won't do you a bit of good," declared Bucky.

"Do you know?" asked Prof.

"Absolutely," replied Bucky. "You just tuck your head between your legs and kiss your ass goodbye."

Bucky broke into a hilarious laugh, but Prof and I just looked at each other.

"Not funny," said Prof.

***

Amazingly, nothing was said at school that day regarding the missile crisis. The day passed in typical fashion; however, the next day was very different. The *Tennessean* story on Wednesday proved as ominous as the story the previous day. The headline read: "U.S. Gives Showdown Order." In a news conference the previous day, Secretary of Defense Robert McNamara announced that twenty-five Russian vessels were moving toward Cuba. He had gone on to say that he had ordered the U.S. Navy to stop and search any ship that entered the quarantine area and to sink any ship that resisted.

The store was empty. I wanted Dad to see this article. Hurriedly, I made my way to the meat counter.

"Hey, Dad," I said. "You've got to read this now."

Dad took the paper, put on his glasses, and started reading. He stopped reading and looked at me.

"Son," he said, "these Russian ships are expected to enter Cuban waters twenty-four hours from **yesterday.** That means **today.**"

Dad took a breath as he refocused on the newspaper article.

"It also says here that Russia has put its military on full alert," he said.

Dad took a deep breath and adopted an even more serious expression.

"Maybe you ought to stay home today," he said.

At that moment, Miss Myrtle entered the store to free me to go to school.

"Dad," I said, "I think I'll just go to school.

My dad was obviously concerned. Both of us realized that the world was nearing the brink of war.

Dad hesitated, but then relented, "Okay, Jim. If something should happen, be sure and do what the teachers tell you."

"Okay, Dad," I said.

On the walk to school, Bucky was not nearly as light-hearted as he had been the previous day. He, as well as Prof, had listened to the reports on local television that morning. Those reports were sobering.

Homeroom was different that morning. An unusual number of students were absent. At the end of the recitation of the Lord's Prayer, the student body president added a prayer for peace. At the completion of the morning devotional, Mr. Potter turned on a radio, and we listened to live events as reported by NBC. The atmosphere in homeroom that morning was surreal.

Except for a few students being absent, English class was

quite normal. Mrs. Acuff was not going to allow a possible nuclear war to hinder her students in their study of Shakespeare's *Julius Caesar.*

When I entered biology class, things were very different. Mr. Hale was sitting at his desk with his chair turned toward a television that he had set up at the front of the classroom. After the tardy bell rang, Mr. Hale called the roll; however, he did not write an assignment on the board and leave the classroom.

"All right, class," he said. "We're going to spend this class period keeping tabs on what's going on down near Cuba."

With that, he turned and increased the volume on the T.V. I immediately recognized the voice of CBS newsman, Walter Cronkite. A camera from a CBS helicopter gave us a bird's eye view of a U.S. destroyer which had come alongside a Soviet cargo ship that had entered the quarantine zone. Cronkite informed the viewers that the cargo ship had stopped and allowed U.S. naval personnel to conduct a search. Since no weaponry was found, the ship was allowed to proceed toward Cuba.

Suddenly, the scene shifted to another camera in another helicopter. The camera was trained on two Soviet cargo ships being buzzed by a couple of U.S. fighter jets. As we intensely watched this scene, the camera revealed a U.S. warship coming into view. Cronkite informed his viewers that these ships were a mere ten miles from the quarantine area. The Soviet ships were steaming ahead showing no signs of stopping.

The clock on the classroom wall revealed only a couple of minutes left in the class period. As I prepared to exit the class by gathering my books and notebook, Mr. Hale silenced the T.V. volume.

"Before you leave, I want to tell you something," said Mr. Hale. He paused several moments before continuing, "If you are not right with God, you need to get right."

The bell rang, and the students silently exited the classroom.

***

When I returned to the store that afternoon, Dad was upstairs resting leaving the meat counter to Sonny.

"Hey, Jim," said Sonny as I was making my way toward my afternoon Double Cola. "Some news just broke."

"What news?" I asked.

"Khruschev has agreed to keep ships out of the interception area. That sounds like a step in the right direction.

"Yeah," I said hopefully. "Hey, Sonny. What do you think is going to happen?"

"Well, Jim, I think I'm right about this," he said. Both Kennedy and Khruschev experienced World War II. They know that war is a terrible thing, and that a nuclear war would be catastrophic for both sides." After a brief hesitation, Sonny continued, "I think they'll find a way out of this.............. they have to."

***

They did. After a few more very tense days, an agreement was reached that defused the situation. The *Tennessean* on Monday morning, October 29, delivered a huge sigh of relief:

"JFK Lauds Nikita Offer to Pull Cuba Rockets." In exchange for removing nuclear weaponry from Cuba, the United States pledged not to invade Cuba. The Secretary General of the United Nations, U -Thant, agreed to oversee the removal of weaponry from Cuba.

It took several months to remove the launchers and missiles from Cuba. By the following Spring, the weaponry was out of Cuba. A military confrontation was avoided.

***

The following Thursday afternoon, I arrived from school to find Dad, Sonny, and Mr. Gates having a conversation in the back of the store.

"Be right back, Mom," I said as I passed the front counter on my way to the drink box. As I retrieved my Double Cola, I could not help but eavesdrop.

"Aren't you glad that I killed your vote?" said Mr. Gates.

"What's that?" Dad asked.

"I know you voted for Nixon," chuckled Gates. "My vote for Kennedy killed your vote. Now, aren't you glad?"

"Herman," said Dad. "I think Nixon would have been a good president, but I will say that Kennedy has done a good job."

"Do you think Nixon would have handled the missile thing as good as Kennedy did?" asked Gates.

"Look," said Dad. "Kennedy is a good president. He stood up to Khruschev. He is fighting organized crime. He's trying to get Congress to pass a tax cut. But there is something else:

he's done something that recent Democrat presidents have not done."

"What would that be?" asked Mr. Gates.

"Let me tell him, Mr. Stone," interjected Sonny.

Dad nodded.

"Mr. Gates," said Sonny, "President Kennedy avoided getting us into a war. In the past, Democrats have failed to do that."

"What do you mean by that, Sonny?" asked Mr. Gates.

"Just look at the last fifty years or so," said Sonny. "Woodrow Wilson was President during World War I, Roosevelt in World War II, and it was Truman who ordered troops into Korea. All Democrat presidents."

"Look, guys," chimed Dad. "It's not always the party or the person. Things just have a way of getting out of control. President Kennedy didn't let that happen. He stood strong and let the Russians know that he meant business, but he was willing to talk and make a deal. He was willing to give a little to get a little and avoid war."

"Well, Stony," declared Mr. Gates, "I bet you vote for Kennedy in '64."

"You might be right, Herman," said Dad. "But there's one thing for sure. I don't want us to elect some fool that's gonna get us into another war."

Chapter 5
Fall-Winter, 1963-4

State Fair

Summer vacation of 1963 passed quickly but was very eventful! Shortly after his sixteenth birthday, Bucky secured a job as a busboy at the Bayou Restaurant, a seafood establishment on Commerce Street in downtown Nashville. A sixteen-year-old was allowed to work twenty hours per week. Bucky worked each Wednesday, Thursday, Friday, and Saturday from 5:00 p.m. until 9:00 p.m. He was paid one dollar per hour plus tips. On his days off he, Prof, and I climbed the cliffs, roamed the bottoms, listened to WKDA on Prof's porch, went to the movies, and just hung out. I could tell that Bucky was very proud of being able to buy his own snacks and pay his own way into the movies. Since he was working, his babysitting and other household chores were passed to his eleven-year-old sister, Cheryl. His days off were actually days off.

The summer of 1963 was also eventful for Dad and me. Dad had finally sold the 1958 Mercury station wagon that had taken up space in the store's side parking lot for almost two years. As for me, I passed my driving test shortly after my June birthday. The hours that Dad had supervised my driving the streets of Kalb Hollow had paid off; I had made friends with the clutch on Dad's '55 Chevy. The state trooper who had administered the driving test was impressed that I took the exam using a car with a standard transmission. That was obviously a rarity.

On the evening following the first day of school Bucky, Prof, and I were talking and joking while sitting in Dad's '50 DeSoto. Bucky and I were a bit disappointed at not having more classes together. We were not even in the same homeroom.

"Hell, Horsehead," declared Bucky. "It's your fault."

"How is it his fault?" asked Prof pointedly.

"Because he's taking all those hard-ass subjects," Bucky shot back. "Horsehead has turned into a first-class goody-goody."

"Are you serious?" I asked sarcastically.

"Damn right!" Bucky replied.

"Hey, Jimmy," asked Prof, "what's he talking about?"

"He's talking about Spanish and geometry," I said.

"That's right, I am," exclaimed Bucky. "Another thing, Prof. He's taking a typing class."

"Look, Grasshopper," I said, "I don't know if you are serious or not, but you know I want to go to college. A lot of colleges require two years of foreign language. Knowing how to use a typewriter will be handy too."

"What do you want to do when you get out of school, Jim?" asked Prof.

"I want to major in history in college. I might want to teach at some point, but I really want to be an officer in the navy."

"What's being in the navy got to do with going to college?" asked Bucky.

"There's two ways to become a naval officer, Grasshopper," I said. "One is to go to a college that has Naval R.O.T.C.; the other is to get into Officer Training School."

"What's R.O.T.C.?" asked Bucky.

"It stands for Reserve Officer Training Corps," I said. "If I take four years of naval R.O.T.C., I will become an officer after graduating. That's what I want to do."

"What college are you going to?" asked Prof.

"The only college around here that offers Naval R.O.T.C. is Vanderbilt. That's where I want to go," I declared.

"I don't think I want to go to college," said Prof thoughtfully, "but I will if I have to."

"What do you mean?" I asked.

"I want to work in electronics," said Prof. "I might want to work for a big electronics company, or I might just go into radio and television repair."

Prof was only a tenth grader, but he had already created a home-made radio. It did not work perfectly, but I was sure that Prof would perfect it. I did not know anything about TV tubes or radio transistors, but Prof certainly did.

"What about you, Buck?" asked Prof.

"Look," said Bucky. "I just want to quit school as soon as I turn seventeen and go to work full-time at the Bayou."

"That's crazy, Grasshopper," I said. "Do you want to be a busboy all your life?"

"Hell, no, Horsehead," said Bucky. "When I go full-time,

I can work my way up to waiter. Waiters and waitresses at the Bayou are making almost a hundred dollars a week in tips."

Prof and I knew it would be futile to argue with Bucky, so I changed the subject.

"I've got two classes with Margie Gibson, "I said. "History and English."

Bucky and Prof did not respond.

"She's weird, but she gets pretty good grades," I continued.

"Have you guys seen Silas lately" I asked.

"Yeah," said Prof. "I saw him in the store on Sunday morning. He's getting tall."

"He really is," I said. "Last year we were the same height, but he's over six-feet tall now."

"He and Isaac are playing football for Pearl this year," said Prof.

"Yeah, I know," I said. "They've been practicing twice a day all through August."

"Silas told me that his coach doesn't want them playing backyard football," said Prof.

"Man," said Bucky. "That means that they won't be playing Sunday afternoons this year."

"Yeah," said Prof, "but he told me that they would play after their season is over."

After a few moments of quiet, I changed the subject again.

"I'm looking forward to snow this winter," I suddenly declared.

"Really?" chimed Bucky.

"Yeah, really!" I said. "Do you remember all of those times that we walked to school with snow up to our ankles?"

"Yeah," chuckled Bucky.

"Well, those days are over," I said with a smile. "When it snows this winter, the schools will be closed, and we will stay home."

"Why are you saying that?" asked Bucky.

"Metropolitan schools," I said. "The county and city schools aren't separate anymore. The county and city governments merged back in April. That means that the school systems merged. When it snows, it won't be just the county schools that get out, the city schools will too. We'll get to stay home."

"I've just got one thing to say to that," said Bucky. "Let it snow; let it snow; let it snow!"

***

Monday, September 18, was Fair Day for the Metropolitan Public Schools. Schools were closed that day for students to have an opportunity to go to the Tennessee State Fair. The previous Friday each student had received a ticket for free admission on Fair Day. The fair would continue all week, but free admission was too good to pass up. Monday was one of Bucky's days off from the Bayou, so he, Prof, and I decided to go to the fair. We took the St. Cecelia bus to the bus shelter in downtown Nashville. We transferred to the Wedgewood Avenue bus which took us to the fairgrounds. We arrived about 10:00 a.m. and looked forward to a full day at the fair.

We immediately went to the midway where we enjoyed

some great rides: the Ferris Wheel, the tilt-a-whirl, the giant roller coaster, the haunted house, and others. We spent over an hour at the bumper cars. By mid-afternoon, we were hungry. We found a large food tent that served some great carnival food. We each enjoyed a foot-long hotdog with cheese, French fries, and a Coca Cola. It was great!

"Hey, guys," I said. "The last time I ate at the fair and then got on a ride, I got really sick. Let's go see some of the side shows."

We exited the food tent and walked to the end of the midway where there were several large tents. Each side show charged ten cents. We saw a bearded lady, an alligator man, a wild man from Borneo, and a creature from the Black Lagoon.

"Man, that creature was fake," declared Bucky.

"Yeah," chimed Prof. "All of them were probably fake." After a hesitation, he continued, "Let's go over to the games. Maybe we can win something."

"Sure," I said. "Let's go."

We walked past the saber-toothed tiger, the four-legged man, and the midget horse. Suddenly, Bucky stopped in his tracks.

"Hey," he said excitedly, "look at that!!"

Bucky pointed to a very large tent. The sign beside the entrance read, "Burlesque! Six Beautiful Ladies!! Admission $1.00"

"We have got to go in there!" declared Bucky.

"It costs a dollar," protested Prof. "We've got to save enough money for bus fare to get home."

"They're not going to let us in anyway," I said.

"I bet they will," said Bucky. "They'll take your dollar."

"Isn't a burlesque show where women take off their clothes?" I asked.

"Well, I hope so," said Bucky.

"Grasshopper," I said, "this may not be such a good idea."

"Damn, Horsehead," argued Bucky. "You've got to be such a goody-goody." Turning to Prof, Buck asked, "Professor, have you got a dollar for this?"

"Yep," said Prof pulling a dollar out of his pocket. "Let's go."

"I have a bad feeling about this," I said; however, I went along with them despite my ominous feelings.

The attendant at the entrance had no problem taking our money. Entering the tent, we found every seat taken. We joined a crowd of men standing behind and around the seating area which was facing a stage. I surveyed the crowd hoping I would not see anyone who might know me. I dreaded the thought of my parents or my friends at church knowing that I had attended a strip show.

Suddenly, the lights on the stage went up and music started playing. A lady danced onto the stage wearing a hat covered in large plume-like feathers. She was wrapped in what looked to be a red silk toga that was fastened over her left shoulder. As she danced seductively across the stage, she removed the plumage from her hat, and the feathers became two large fans, one for each hand. She moved to the middle of the stage and loosened her toga letting it fall to the floor. The crowd roared with approval. She used the fans to cover herself as she continued to dance. I surveyed the audience again. Young men, middle-aged men, and old men—all were staring intently at the seductive dancer. I glanced at Bucky who was staring intensely also. I looked at Prof and found him to be giggling.

"I can't believe this," said Prof gleefully.

"I can't either," I said sarcastically.

I felt extremely uncomfortable. I was standing in a tent watching a strip tease. I was on the verge of leaving the tent when the unthinkable happened.

I felt a hand gently resting on my left shoulder. Someone was behind me. I turned to see a man in a police uniform. Crap! Crap!! Double crap!!! It was worse than a policeman! it was Officer Marcum!

"Jimmy Stone," he said sternly, "get out of here right now, and I won't tell your parents."

I was stunned! Shocked! I just stood there.

"Right now!!" declared Mr. Marcum.

"Yes, Sir," I said. Turning to Bucky and Prof, I said, "Let's go, y'all."

I briskly moved through the crowd, exited the tent, and kept walking. I turned and saw Prof, but not Bucky. He was nowhere to be seen.

"He must've stayed in the tent," declared Prof.

"I guess so," I said. "I'm not waiting for him. Let's go to the bus stop. He'll find his way home."

***

An Infamous Day

The autumn of 1963 was not the best of times. Following the State Fair fiasco, things continued to go downhill. My beloved Vanderbilt Commodores football team continued to lose game after game. My New York Yankees were humiliated in the World Series by losing four straight games to the Los Angeles Dodgers allowing the Dodgers to snatch away the world championship.

"Great pitching always beats great hitting," gloated Mr. Gates. As soon as the last out was recorded in Game 4, Mr. Gates streaked across Clay Street and into the store to needle Dad.

More importantly, the Cold War seemed to be heating up. Communism was on the march, particularly in Southeast Asia. Over the previous year or two, a place called Viet Nam had been creeping into the news. Russian-backed communist insurgents called Viet Cong were attempting to overthrow the American-backed government of South Viet Nam. The U.S. had over a thousand troops in Viet Nam operating in an "advisory" capacity. Adhering to the "domino theory," the U.S. believed that if one nation fell under communist control, neighboring nations would fall in a domino effect. Under U.S. "containment" policy, the United States was drawing the line in Viet Nam just as it had in Korea a decade earlier. There seemed to be very little good news during the autumn of 1963.

Keeping with the tone of the news, November of 1963 was a gray and gloomy month. Clouds and rain dominated the weather. Friday, November 22, began as a cloudy day. It was a typical day at school; that is, until lunchtime. Standing in the cafeteria line, I heard someone say that George Washington had been shot. That made no sense to me, so I dismissed the comment until I sat down with Bucky at our usual table.

"Horsehead," said Bucky, "somebody said that President Kennedy has been shot."

"Are you sure?" I asked.

"No," replied Bucky, "but that's what Rex Cothern told me a few minutes ago."

After lunch, I entered my fourth period class. Mrs. Silver, my Spanish teacher, seemed to be unaware of any events; however, leaving Spanish class, I saw several students emerging from Mr. Price's history class. Mr. Price had set up a television in the front of his classroom. Many of the students were leaving his room with tears running down their cheeks. It was true!! I learned that President Kennedy had been shot in Dallas, Texas. This was surreal. It had only been the previous May 18 that JFK had visited Nashville and had made a speech at Vanderbilt University. Prof and I had gone downtown that Saturday and claimed a position along West End Avenue and saw President Kennedy as his motorcade passed on its way to Vanderbilt. As I looked at JFK, he was standing in the back of a black convertible and waving to the crowd that lined both sides of West End Avenue. His hair was flowing with a gentle breeze as he was joined by the First Lady in waving to the crowd. They were a magnificent looking couple.

By fifth period, everyone at North High School knew that the president had been shot and that he had been transported to a Dallas hospital. Mrs. Connelly, my typing teacher, acknowledged the event, but she said that the only thing we could do was to pray. After a moment of silent prayer, Mrs. Connelly gave us our daily typing task. What else could she do?

Approximately halfway through the class, there was a gentle knock on the classroom door. Sitting in the first row, I could clearly see the face of Rex Cothern peering through the little window in the door. His eyes were tearful. I watched as Rex slowly shook his head in a negative manner. He then placed an upside-down fist in front of his face with his thumb pointed downward. It was clear that President John F. Kennedy was dead.

***

Within a short time after JFK's death, Vice President Lyndon B. Johnson was sworn in as President of the United States. In less than twelve hours following the shooting Lee Harvey Oswald was arrested. A twenty-four-year-old from Fort Worth, Texas, Oswald was taken to the Dallas jail. It was widely reported that Oswald had visited the Soviet Union and had ties to Cuba and communism.

On Sunday, November 24, Oswald was to be transferred to another jail. The transfer was shown on national television. With the cameras rolling, Oswald emerged from the holding area and proceeded under guard toward a waiting vehicle. Suddenly, a man leaped from the onlooking crowd and shot Oswald from point-blank range. The assassin of President Kennedy had been assassinated by Jack Ruby, an owner of a Dallas strip club.

Two questions emerged that weekend. Did Oswald act

alone? For what reason did Jack Ruby take justice into his own hands?

∗∗∗

A Taste of Sin

As horrifying as the events of late November had been, life continued in Nashville, Tennessee. With the dawning of December, the growing spirit of Christmas was slowly removing the pall that had covered the people of Kalb Hollow—partially, at least. The dawn of December also brought colder weather. On an early December Monday, the near freezing temperature hastened the walk to school. As Bucky, Prof, and I walked up Clay Street toward school, Bucky reached into his coat pocket and pulled out a pack of Winston cigarettes. Extracting a cigarette from the pack, Bucky reached into his other pocket and displayed a lighter. As he lit up, he asked if Prof or I would like one.

"No, thanks," we answered almost in unison.

"When did you start smoking, Buck?" I asked.

"Just a few days ago," he said. "I didn't like it at first. It made my tongue burn, but I got used to it."

"Does it keep you warm while waiting for the bus when you get off work?" chided Prof.

"No, smart ass. I don't ride the bus home anymore," declared Bucky. "I hang around the restaurant until 10 o'clock and one of the waitresses drops me off on her way home."

"That's lucky," I said.

"It's more than lucky," said Bucky with a measure of glee. "She's a gorgeous woman, and that makes for a great trip."

"Is she prettier than Mary Beth Warren?" asked Prof.

"If you saw this girl," declared Bucky, "you would throw rocks at Mary Beth Warren!"

"I don't think so," I laughed.

"Let me tell you two bastards something," said Bucky with some excitement. "All the waitresses at The Bayou wear real short skirts—and I mean real short! It's part of their uniform. When Marcella—that's her name—gets into her car, her skirt rides up to the point where I can see the color of her panties!"

"You better be careful," said Prof. "If she catches you peeking, you might be back to riding the bus."

"She has caught me!" laughed Bucky. "She doesn't care!"

"Hey, Buck," I chided, "you might want to check her purse like Lee checked Mary Beth. Maybe she carries a rubber too."

"It doesn't matter," said Bucky. "Marcella is thirty-six years old and married." After a hesitation, Bucky continued, "But I can dream!!"

***

Metropolitan Nashville Public Schools close for a two-week Christmas vacation each year. The first day of vacation in 1963 was Monday, December 23. As Dad and I opened the store that morning, we were greeted by six inches of snow and temperatures in the 20's. It was a winter wonderland. I was excited by the fact that we would certainly have a white Christmas. The snow was not a surprise. It had been forecast a couple of days earlier which prompted our Kalb Hollow neighbors to stock up on groceries. The previous Saturday, items flew off the shelves as people prepared for serious winter conditions. Monday looked to be a slow day with icy conditions and most of our customers already stocked.

"It's too slick out there for Myrtle to get out today, Jim," said Dad. "I'm going to call her and tell her not to worry about coming to work today. You can work the front counter until your mom comes down at noon."

Luckily, the January editions of DC Comics had arrived. I spent the morning resting on a stool behind the front counter listening to WKDA and reading the adventures of Superman, Batman, and the Justice League of America. By the time that Mom came down from the apartment, we had sold very few items. When Mom relieved me at the front counter, I retired to the rear of the store, sat down on a stack of wooden soft drink cases, and resumed reading a comic book. I had been back there only a brief time when Bones and Buzz entered the store.

"Hey, Jimmy," said Bones as he walked toward me. "We're going down to the bottoms and see if the ponds have frozen. Wanna come?"

"Sure," I said. "Bucky and Prof might want to go too. Why don't you guys go see while I go upstairs and put on something warm?"

They agreed. I went upstairs and put on an extra pair of socks and some old rubber galoshes over my tennis shoes. I put on a sweater over a heavy shirt. I topped off with a jacket, stocking cap, and gloves. I didn't have a scarf, so I used a bath towel.

I went downstairs into the store and did not have to wait very long until I was joined by Bones, Buzz, Bucky, and Prof. All of us were feeling adventurous. We left the store and walked down to the pony field.

"Hey, guys," I said. "Don't we want to go down Fourth Avenue?"

"Naw," said Bones. "Let's climb down the cliffs. It'll be fun."

"It's awful slick and snowy to be climbing down those cliffs," I replied.

"You go on down Fourth Avenue," said Bucky. "We'll meet you at the bottom of the cliffs."

I hesitated. I was not comfortable with climbing down the cliffs in such icy conditions; however, a sixteen-year-old boy has a reputation to protect. I went along with them to the cliffs.

We trudged across the pony field with snow above our ankles. When we reached the edge of the cliffs, I looked down and saw that there was not as much snow as I had feared; however, the large rocks that we would be climbing over were glazed with ice.

"I don't know about this," I declared.

"It's okay," urged Bones. "Just take your time. Go slow."

With that, Bones and the others started down the icy escarpment. I stood at the edge and watched as they slowly worked their way down.

"Come on, Jimmy!" shouted Buzz.

I said to myself: "Here goes nothing."

I carefully placed my foot over the edge and very slowly moved downward. I had climbed approximately ten feet from the top when I found myself standing on a flat rock covered with ice. I looked around and could find no place to plant my next step. Somewhat panicked, I looked down the escarpment and saw that all my buddies had successful reached the bottom. I was afraid to continue. I was also hesitant to try to climb back up to the top.

"Come on, Jimmy," shouted Buzz. "We're waiting for you."

"I'm stuck," I shouted. "I have no place to go!"

"Yes, you do," came a voice from behind me.

I turned and saw Tommy. He had climbed down to where I was stuck.

"Take my hand," he said. "Just one step at a time."

With Tommy's help, I made it to the top of the cliffs.

"Thanks, Tommy," I said with much relief.

"Those guys are crazy," said Tommy. "This is much too dangerous."

I looked down to the bottom of the cliffs and shouted, "Y'all go on. I'm going back to the store. See you later."

"Let's go, Jim," said Tommy. "It's cold out here."

We trudged back across the pony field, shivering as we went.

"I got an interesting letter in the mail today," said Tommy as we made our way toward the store.

"Really?" I said.

"Yep," said Tommy. "It was from Selective Service."

"What's that?" I asked.

"It's the draft board," said Tommy. "It looks like I'll be a soldier pretty soon."

"Wow," I said.

"The letter ordered me to report to the First American Center downtown. That's where I'll get my army physical."

"When do you have to go down there?" I asked.

"January 6," replied Tommy. "You know," he went on, "you'll have to register at Selective Service when you turn eighteen."

"Yeah," I said as we entered the store.

We entered the store and found Mom behind the counter and Dad in the back. Otherwise, the store was empty.

Looking at me, Mom said, "I was wondering if you had enough sense to come out of the cold."

"Yeah, thanks to Tommy," I said. Turning to Tommy, I continued, "Hey Tommy, I think I owe you a Dr. Pepper."

***

Christmas Day fell on Wednesday in 1963. Indeed, it was a white Christmas. Nashville had experienced light snowfall on Christmas Eve that added a half-inch topping to the existing snow. The store was closed on Christmas Day. Mom, Dad, and I usually spent Christmas with Uncle Henry and Aunt Elise; however, Dad felt that the roads were too icy for a trip to the country. Staying at home provided a much-needed rest for Mom and Dad.

The remainder of Christmas week was sunny and slightly warmer. The roads were clear, but snow remained on the ground. Mom said that when snow refuses to melt, it was a sign that more snow would be coming.

Having my driver's license, Dad allowed me to drive myself to church on Sundays. The Sunday morning following Christmas was cold, but the sun was brightly shining. With the roads in good shape, I drove Dad's '55 Chevy to church. I was delighted that Brother Brewster was preaching that day.

"Our flesh speaks to us," said Brother Brewster. "It makes its wants and wishes known. The flesh wants us to do, say, and think things that bring it delight. In other words, our flesh wants us to sin. The Apostle Paul referred to it as our 'sinful nature.' Our sinful nature encourages us to please it."

Brother Brewster stopped speaking for a moment as his eyes scanned the congregation before continuing, "On the other hand, we have a spirit inside us that wants us to do, say, and think things that pleases God. It is a conflict between the good and the evil that rages inside each of us. It's like there are two dogs fighting inside us: an evil dog and a good dog. Eternally speaking, one of them is going to win the fight. Which one?"

Again, he stopped speaking and scanned the congregation.

"I know which one will win," he said. "It's the one that you feed." He hesitated before asking, "Which dog are you feeding?" After another brief pause, he continued, "If you tolerate envy, jealousy, or lustful thoughts, then you are feeding the evil dog— your own sinful nature. Looking at the wrong kind of movies or reading the wrong kind of books or magazines—more food for that evil dog. Having the wrong kind of friends—bad company is more evil dog food."

Bother Brewster stopped preaching briefly and took a deep breath.

"Feed the good dog," he said. "Attending church regularly is good food for the good dog. Spend your time with God-fearing people." He held up a Bible and said, "Read some passages out of this book every day. Pray every day. Look for ways to help others."

He stopped, smiled, and declared, "Fatten that good dog and put that evil dog on a diet."

***

The following Monday, Dad allowed me to drive the station wagon to make a delivery. When I returned, Bucky and Prof were standing near the front counter enjoying a soft drink and watching Miss Myrtle check out a customer.

"Hey, Jimmy," said Prof. "Let's go to my house. We can go down in the basement and listen to the radio."

"Sure," I said.

A few minutes later we were in Prof's basement. We were sitting on the concrete floor near the furnace listening to WKDA crank out the hits when Bucky broke into a joyous smile.

"I've got to tell you bastards something," he said. "I can't believe what happened to me Saturday night. I've got to tell somebody."

"I can tell that it must be something good," I said.

"No," said Bucky. "Not good—great!!!"

Bucky was almost shouting.

"Well, tell us," ordered Prof.

"Okay," said Bucky with glee. "When I got off work Saturday night, I waited for my ride with Marcella. When we got in the car, she told me that she needed to stop and check on the house of a friend who was out of town. The house was somewhere off Belmont Boulevard. When we got there, she wanted me to go in with her."

Suddenly, Bucky stopped talking and just broke into a joyous look.

"Well, is that it?" asked Prof.

"Hell, no," said Bucky. "This is the good part. Marcella unlocked the door, and we went inside. She turned on the lights and checked the kitchen and bathroom to make sure the pipes weren't frozen. After she came out of the bathroom, she told me that she didn't take me with her just to check the house."

"Wow," said Prof anticipating coming events in Bucky's story.

I did not say "wow," but I thought it.

"Marcella put her arms around my neck and kissed me!" said Bucky.

Prof and I glanced at each other. Prof's chin dropped. Mine probably did too.

"Marcella took my hand and led me into the bedroom." Bucky went on to tell Prof and I about what followed –and in great detail. As Bucky's narration continued, I could feel my teenage hormones starting to rage. I was envious of my friend as he told of his private sexual lesson he had received from a full-grown woman.

As I walked home, I could still feel the excitement of Bucky's story. As I walked up the outside steps leading to the apartment, Brother Brewster's good dog raised its head. I instinctively realized that something was very wrong about a thirty-six-year-old married woman seducing a sixteen-year-old boy; however, the bad dog was wishing it had been me.

***

A Winter Tragedy

New Year's Day—the first day of 1964—greeted Nashville with four to five inches of snow and temperatures in the teens. Store hours on New Year's Day were from 8 a.m. until noon. Dad and I worked at the store while Mom labored in the kitchen of our apartment preparing an afternoon meal. When Dad and I closed the store and went upstairs, we found chicken with cornbread dressing, macaroni and cheese, green beans, cranberry sauce, and black-eyed peas. On New Year's Day, black-eyed peas were required. The "wives' tale" said that one would receive a dollar in the new year for every black-eyed pea eaten on New Year's Day. We didn't really believe such tales, but we weren't taking any chances.

New Year's Day—except for Christmas—was my favorite holiday. It was college bowl game day!! Beginning with the Sugar Bowl at noon, the Cotton Bowl, Rose Bowl, and Orange Bowl followed in succession. I was particularly interested in the Sugar Bowl which provided a historic match-up. The Southeastern Conference Champion Ole Miss Rebels would face the powerful Crimson Tide of the University of Alabama.

Ole Miss was favored to win the game. Unfortunately for Alabama, the Tide's star quarterback, Joe Namath, would not be playing. He had broken an undisclosed team rule which prompted Coach Paul "Bear" Bryant to bench Namath for the Sugar Bowl.

The clash of the two college football powers was titanic; however, I was disappointed with the outcome. Alabama defeated Ole Miss by kicking four field goals to claim a 12-7 victory. Later in the day, Texas defeated Navy in the Cotton Bowl, and Illinois defeated Washington in the Rose Bowl. The Orange Bowl was played at night. I stayed up late to see Auburn fall to Nebraska.

It was after 10:30 p.m. before I got into bed. As I was drifting off to sleep, the sound of a siren zoomed past the store. A few seconds later, another siren screamed down Clay Street. Fully awakened, I went to my window where I could see blue and red lights of police cars flashing. The cars had stopped just past Bucky's house. Another police car, lights flashing and siren blaring, came up Fifth Avenue and turned right onto Clay Street to join the others.

By this time, Mom and Dad had come into my room. My window offered the best view, but we could only see the lights of police cars flashing in the darkness.

"Jim," said Dad, "isn't that about where those Gibson girls live?"

"They live right along there," I said, "but it could be another house."

We stood peering out the window when another vehicle

came roaring up Fifth Avenue with lights flashing and siren screaming. We watched as the Metro Emergency Vehicle turned onto Clay Street.

"Somebody's going to the hospital," said Mom.

"Or worse," said Dad.

"Hey, Dad," I said. "I'll put some clothes on and walk down to see what's going on."

"No, you won't," snapped Mom.

"Jim," said Dad, "It's too cold, too slick, and too dangerous. No telling what you might walk into down there."

"We'll find out what happened in the morning," said Mom. "We need to go to bed. 5:30 comes early."

***

When I awakened the next morning, it was a little past 5:30. Dad was already up and dressed. I found him sitting in his rocking chair in the living room watching the TV news on Channel 5.

"Anything on the news, Dad?" I asked.

"Very little, Son," replied Dad. "A man was shot and killed on Clay Street last night, and an arrest was made. No names or details were released until next-of-kin can be notified."

"Oh," I said.

"The sirens probably woke up the whole neighborhood," said Dad. "I'm sure that one of our customers will fill us in."

When Dad and I opened the store, the familiar group of customers were standing in the cold waiting to get cigarettes and snacks for their workday. It was January 2nd, and life was back to normal following the holidays. Unfortunately, none of our early morning customers knew any more about the shooting than Dad and me.

A little after 7:00 a.m., Tommy entered the store. Since he was not wearing his work clothes, I realized that he was not working.

"Morning, Jim," he said as he walked by the front counter toward the meat counter.

"You not working today?" asked Dad.

"No, Sir," replied Tommy. "We're off until Monday. Could I get a pound of boloney and ten slices of American cheese?"

"Sure," said Dad.

"I guess you heard about the shooting," said Tommy.

"All I know is what was on the morning news," said Dad. "There was a shooting on Clay Street, and somebody was killed."

"It was bad, Mr. Stone," said Tommy. "Let me tell you what I know."

I was overhearing the conversation. Since the store was empty of customers, I made my way to the meat counter.

"It wasn't at Bucky's house, was it?" I asked with concern.

"No," said Tommy. "When I heard the sirens, I was still awake. I walked up to where the police cars had parked." Tommy hesitated and looked intently at Dad. "Mr. Stone, Paula shot and killed Ricky."

"The Gibson's?" I asked.

"Yeah," said Tommy. "She shot him right in the chest with a shotgun."

Dad and I were stunned.

"Do you know why?" asked Dad.

"No, Sir," Tommy said. "All I know is that they took Ricky's body away in an ambulance. The police brought Paula out of the house in handcuffs. A police Chaplin showed up and talked to Allie and Margie for a while."

"Are Margie and Allie okay?" I asked.

"I don't know," replied Tommy. "While the Chaplin was still there, a car showed up and took the girls somewhere."

"That would be the welfare people," said Dad.

"It was strange, Mr. Stone," said Tommy. "When the girls were taken out of the house, Allie was crying, but Margie was stone-faced. It was like she was in a trance."

***

The next morning was Friday. It found Dad and Sonny preparing the meat case for the weekend. Mom was working the front counter while I prepared the vegetable bins with the produce that Dad and I had purchased at the Farmers' Market earlier that morning. While working the front bin, I saw a police car pull into the parking area in front of the store. Dressed for the cold weather, Mr. Marcum got out of the car and made his way into the store.

"Good morning, Bess," said Marcum. "I'm looking for an old fart named James Roy Stone. Have you seen him?"

"I have," laughed Mom. "You'll find him in his usual spot back there."

Dad popped his head up from behind the meat case and met Mr. Marcum with a warm smile.

"Hey, Marc," said Dad. "What's happening?"

"Not much," replied Marcum. "it's been a quiet morning. I bet you're curious about the incident the other night."

Sure am, Marc," said Dad. "What can you tell me?"

"The victim, Mr. Gibson, has a brother in town," said Marcum. "In fact, he's the only relative. He's having the body cremated and there will be no service."

"What about the girls?" asked Dad.

"Well, since their dad is dead and the mother is about to be indicted for murder," said Marcum, "Children's Services will try to place them in a foster home."

"What about the brother?" asked Dad.

"He's already said that he's not taking them," After a brief sigh, Marcum continued, "The Welfare Department will have a hard time finding a foster home. There's a shortage of foster parents, and most will not take teenage girls. These girls are probably headed for T.P.S."

Tennessee Preparatory School, better known as T.P.S., was a boarding school for children who were considered wards of the state. It was considered an excellent institution and graduated many young people who went on to become good and productive citizens. The school offered the same academic offerings and extra-curricular activities that were available in Tennessee's public schools.

"Marc," asked Dad, "do you know why Mrs. Gibson shot her husband?"

"Yeah, James," said Marcum. "It's nasty." He hesitated before continuing, "Is it okay for Jimmy to hear this?"

Dad hesitated and looked at me.

"It's okay, Marc," said Dad. "I think my boy knows that the world can be nasty."

"Well, this is very nasty," warned Marcum. "Ricky Gibson had been having sexual relations with his oldest daughter." Marcum stopped and took a deep breath. "It's been going on for a long time. It started when she was ten."

Dad couldn't believe his ears. His chin dropped to his chest, and he just slowly shook his head. My reaction was similar. What kind of man would do that?

"What about Allie?" I asked.

"She's okay physically," said Marcum. "Even though she was not molested by her father, she knew what was going on and was a witness to it." Marcum took a pause. Sighing, he looked at Dad and said, "The son-of-a-bitch deserved what he got."

***

It was the middle of January before the weather moderated sufficiently for schools to re-open. As Bucky, Prof, and I were walking home, there was something I could not get out of my mind. I had two classes with Margie Gibson. In those classes, I could not help but sadly notice Margie's empty seat. I was amazed that nobody else seemed to notice her absence. Was Margie so anonymous that no one noticed that she was not there?

***

Paula Gibson had her day in court in March 1964. She was originally charged with second degree murder; however, the District Attorney for Davidson County accepted a plea of manslaughter. She was sentenced to twelve years in prison. She would be eligible for parole in 1968.

Chapter 6
Spring-Summer, 1964

The Best Laid Plans

College Day occurred at North High School in mid-April 1964. Eleventh and twelfth graders who were interested in attending college could meet with representatives of various colleges and universities in the Middle Tennessee area. The meetings took place in the library where tables were arranged to accommodate the participating institutions: Belmont College, Trevecca Nazarene College, Peabody College, Vanderbilt University, Austin Peay State College, Middle Tennessee State College, and Tennessee Polytechnical Institute. There were two one-hour sessions; therefore, students could select to attend a session from two schools. My first session was with Mr. Jacobson from Vanderbilt. Including myself, only three students attended the first Vanderbilt session. It was only minutes into Mr. Jacobson's presentation that I realized that attending Vanderbilt could be a challenge for me. Mr. Jacobson provided a summary of the fields of study available at Vanderbilt as well as entrance requirements and cost. Entrance requirements were a concern.

A perspective student must have an acceptable score on the SAT test, and Vanderbilt usually did not accept applicants who had a high school final grade below a "B." I did not see the SAT as a problem, but I had earned a "D" in Algebra II. I was certainly willing to repeat that course in order to raise that grade; however, cost was a more serious problem. Tuition at Vanderbilt at that time was approximately $6500 per year—only slightly less than my family's income in 1964. I was bummed!

At the end of the presentation, Mr. Jacobson asked if there were any questions. I raised my hand.

"I'm interested in a career in the navy," I said. "Can a student get a Naval ROTC scholarship at Vanderbilt?"

"Yes," said Mr. Jacobson. "The U.S. Navy provides ROTC scholarships at Vanderbilt. The SAT requirement is the same for all students; however, the U.S. Navy only gives scholarships to those who major in a field related to math or science. That would be majors like engineering, medicine, mathematics, chemistry, physics, and the like."

My disappointment was probably apparent. Mr. Jacobson hesitated before asking, "Are there any other questions?"

***

As I was walking home that afternoon, I did not hide my disappointment.

"What the hell is wrong with you?" asked Bucky.

I explained my disappointment and frustration at not being able to attend Vanderbilt.

"I can probably overcome the grade problem by repeating

Algebra II, but I have no intention of majoring in science or math. Without the navy scholarship, Vandy is out."

"What now?" asked Prof.

"I will probably go to Middle Tennessee State College. There is no tuition there, only a registration fee. I saw the campus last year when the music group went down there. I can major in history. When I graduate, I'll try to get into Naval Officers Training School."

Although I could take an alternate path to become a naval officer, I was still disappointed that I could not attend Vanderbilt University.

***

The Spiral

On May 18, 1964, Bucky withdrew from North Nashville High School. Both Prof and I had pleaded with him to change his mind about quitting school, but he was determined to work full-time at the Bayou and move out on his own. He had already arranged his work schedule. He would work at the Bayou from 2:00 p.m. until 10:00 p.m. each Tuesday through Saturday.

By the time school ended that Monday, Bucky had already left the building. As Prof and I approached the store on our walk home, we found Bucky sitting on the edge of the store porch drinking an RC Cola and smoking a cigarette.

"Well, I guess you did it," I said.

"You're damn right I did," he said as smoke exited his

nostrils. "I'm gonna save as much money as I can and be out on my own within a couple of months."

"Where are you going to live?" I asked.

"I don't know right now, but I've got time to look around," he replied. "There's one thing for sure, it won't be over there," pointing to his house.

Bucky was bitter. He was angry at the unusual number of chores and baby-sitting that had been required of him. He was angry at not having any spending money. He was angry at being the only student of his age carrying a brown-bag lunch to school. Working at the Bayou on a part-time basis had freed him from most of his household chores and had provided some spending money. Working had also provided him with some self-respect. He saw full-time work providing him with freedom. At this point, Prof and I found it useless to try to reason with Bucky. The bitterness and anger emanating from him created a wall that shut out reason. Bucky was young and angry—and had a lot to learn.

***

The Sermon

During the second week of June, final exams occurred on Monday, Tuesday, and Wednesday. School was out of session on Thursday allowing teachers to finalize grades. Students reported on Friday to collect their final report cards. As Prof and I walked home with report cards in hand, I could not help thinking of Bucky. I thought back to all those times we had walked home together. It was difficult for me to believe that he had dropped out of school just one year before he could graduate. It was harder to believe that he had quit school for a low-paying job as a bus boy.

"What are you thinking about?" asked Prof as we walked by the big stone wall in front of the St. Cecelia convent.

"I'm thinking about how strange it feels to be walking home from school without Grasshopper," I replied.

"Bucky is a dumb ass," chuckled Prof.

"I don't know about that," I said, "but he has changed over the last few months. He's started smoking. He cusses all the time. He used to say a cussword every now and then, but now he puts one in almost every sentence that comes out of his mouth."

"Yeah," said Prof. "I wonder if he's still getting private lessons from that waitress. I would ask him, but it doesn't feel right."

"Yeah, I know," I said.

As we approached Sixth Avenue, we saw Silas getting off the bus that had delivered him from Pearl High School.

"Hey, Silas," I shouted. "Wait up."

Prof and I trotted over to Silas' bus stop. We were amazed at how Silas had grown.

"Hey, man," said Prof, "how tall are you now?"

"I'm six feet three inches," boasted Silas. "I'm a little taller than my dad."

"Are we gonna play some baseball this summer?" I asked.

"Probably not," replied Silas. "Dad got me a job working two days a week at C.B. Ragland. Most other days I'll be working out with Isaac getting ready for next season."

"Do you mean football?" asked Prof.

"Yeah," said Silas. "We're going to go down Fourth Avenue and run through the bottoms to the river and back. We're planning to do that four or five days a week. By August, we plan to be in top shape."

"Are you going pro or something," I chided.

"Nope," laughed Silas, "but I am getting letters from colleges. I hope to get a football scholarship."

"What schools?" I asked.

"Well, I got letters from Tennessee State A&I, Grambling, Jackson State, Purdue, Indiana, and Michigan State so far," he boasted.

Turning to Prof, I said, "Just think. We knew this guy before he became famous."

"Hey, Jimmy," inquired Silas with a serious look. "Where's Buck?"

"Bucky's not with us. He quit school a few weeks ago," I said.

Silas just shook his head. "That's crazy." He shook his head again before continuing, "Well, see you guys. Gotta go."

***

The following Sunday morning, I drove myself to church in Dad's '55 Chevy. Since I had made friends with the clutch, I found driving a standard shift to be fun. After parking in the church parking lot, I saw Brother Cullum working his way up the steps and into the church.

"Today is going to be real fun," I sarcastically said to myself.

Following the traditional three songs, prayer, and communion, Brother Cullum took his place behind the podium. As he scanned the congregation, I braced myself for a hellfire and brimstone sermon; however, something was different. His usual stern scowl was missing. In fact, it was replaced by a much softer expression highlighted by a bit of a smile.

"My message today is for all of you," he began, "but, in particular, my message is for the young people here at the Osage Street Church. This message is simple: bad company corrupts good character."

Brother Cullum again scanned the congregation making eye contact with most of the younger members.

"You won't find that exact quote in the Bible," he continued. "I'm not sure where it came from, and it really doesn't matter. What does matter is its truth."

Brother Cullum continued his sermon by explaining that people are influenced by the people with which they regularly associate.

"Young people," he went on, "Right now you are surrounded by people in this building who have sound values and good character. Now, young people, I am not saying that these people are perfect. We all sin and fall short of God's will; however, the people here at the Osage Street Church are good people." Brother Cullum stopped and took a few seconds before continuing, "I have a question for you. When you leave here today and go through the week, with what kind of people are you going to associate?" Again, he stopped and surveyed the congregation before continuing, "I have a quotation for you. I know that this gem came from Ben Franklin: 'If you lie down with dogs, you'll get up with fleas.'"

At that, there was a quiet chuckle from the congregation. Brother Cullum quickly surveyed the congregation before looking at the wooden clock on the wall.

"I see that it's approaching the noon hour; however, I have one more thing to say. Again, this is for everyone, but it is particularly for our young people. What I want to say is this: don't go along to get along." Following a brief pause, he said, "Let me say that again. Don't go along to get along. When you feel pressure from your friends to do something that you know is wrong, don't do it!" As he continued, his voice became louder and more emphatic. "There are times when you must stand up! Stand up for your beliefs! Stand up for your values! Stand up for your faith!" Brother Cullum paused and took a deep breath. "Don't let other people dictate how you live your life. Let Jesus dictate your life. If it's something that He would not do, say, or think, then you shouldn't either."

After Brother Cullum concluded his sermon, the congregation was led in a closing song and prayer. Exiting the church and driving home, I felt that Brother Cullum had been speaking directly to me. I remembered how I had "gone along to get along" at the state fair by attending that burlesque show. I remembered the embarrassment I had felt when Officer Marcum confronted me. I remembered "going along to get along" when I followed my buddies down the dangerous ice-covered cliffs and the embarrassment of being rescued by Tommy. I should have stood up.

✳✳✳

The Martian

James Bond was back! It was the second week in July and *Goldfinger* opened at the Loew's Theatre in downtown Nashville. It was the third Bond film. Bucky, Prof, and I had seen the first two, *Dr. No* and *From Russia with Love*. We were hooked on the adventures of the suave and debonair 007. We had to see *Goldfinger*.

We met at the store at noon on Monday, Bucky's day off. When Miss Myrtle entered the store to relieve me at the front counter, we hurried across the street to the bus stop. We exited the bus at the downtown bus shelter and walked to Loew's Theater on Church Street. Since it was a week-day afternoon, there was no line at the ticket window. When Bucky stepped to the window to purchase his ticket, he pulled a huge roll of five and ten-dollar bills from his front blue jean pocket.

"Hey, Grasshopper, why are you carrying so much money around with you?" I asked as we entered the lobby of the theater.

"I've got nowhere else to keep it," he said. "I can't leave it at home."

I accepted his answer, but I suspected that he just liked the feeling of having money.

The Bond girl in *Goldfinger* was Honor Blackmon. Although not the most beautiful of the Bond girls, Blackmon's character certainly had the most memorable name — Pussy Galore. We found the name to be tantalizingly risqué and hilarious.

On the return from the movie, we exited the bus in front of the store at Fifth and Clay. We immediately saw a young man sitting on the top step of the store's porch. Although he looked familiar, I did not know him; however, Bucky obviously knew him.

"Hey, Martian," Bucky shouted as we crossed Clay Street. "What's up?"

"Hey, Buck," came the reply.

As we approached the young man, I realized that I had seen him at school. I was taken by his slight build. He was slightly shorter than me, and he was extremely thin. He wore his light brown hair in a short crew cut which helped to emphasize his larger-than-normal ears. His thin face featured a sharply pointed nose.

"Martian, this is Jimmy and Prof," said Bucky. Turning to Prof and me, he continued, "This is Martian. He works with me at the Bayou."

"Good to meet you," I said. "Is that your real name?"

"No," said Martian. "My name is George Buford, but everybody calls me Martian."

"Why do they call you that?" asked Prof.

"Go ahead, Martian," interjected Bucky. "Show them."

Martian removed the shoe and sock from his right foot. He had an extra little toe – six toes on his right foot.

"Wow!" I said.

"The other foot is just like this one," said Martian.

"You have twelve toes!?!" exclaimed Prof.

"Yeah," said Martian, "and that ain't all."

With that, Martian stared right into my face and said, "Look me in the eyes, Jimmy."

"Dang," I said as I looked at his eyes. He had one blue eye and one brown eye.

As he put his sock and shoe back on his foot, he said, "That's why they call me Martian."

"Hey, ya'll," said Bucky. "Let's go up to Prof's and listen to some music."

"Let me check with Mom and see if I'm needed in the store," I said. "I'll be up there as soon as I can."

I was not needed at the store. When I arrived at Prof's porch, *it's a Hard Days Night* was playing on the radio while Bucky and Martian were telling Bayou stories.

"People come into the restaurant and eat some nasty looking stuff," said Martian.

"Yeah," said Bucky. "A lot of guys come into the Bayou after they get off work and order something called 'oysters on the half shell.' Its gross looking stuff."

"What is that?" asked Prof.

"It's just what it sounds like," said Martian. "It's raw oysters –maybe steamed a little – served on half of an oyster shell."

"Did you say "raw'?" I asked.

"Yep," said Bucky. "They are served by the dozen or half dozen."

"It's funky," said Martian. "Guys pick up the shell and let the oyster slide off the shell and into their mouth."

"Do they chew it?" asked Prof.

"Hell, no," said Bucky. "They just let them slide down their throat."

"Yuk!" I said. "Are you guys making this up?"

"No, man. I swear!" said Martian.

"There's two gay guys that come in every Friday night about 7 o'clock," said Bucky. "They sit at the bar and drink beer and eat oysters 'til closing time. They'll sit there and eat three or four dozen oysters."

"Are you kidding?" quipped Prof.

"Did you say 'gay' guys?" I asked.

"Yeah," said Martian. "Frank and Jerry; they're both gay."

I obviously had a puzzled look.

"Horsehead," interjected Bucky. "Please tell me that you know what 'gay' means."

"Well, I guess I do," I said, "but maybe I don't." I paused and said, "It used to mean 'happy,' didn't it. You know, like 'don we now our gay apparel' or 'the gay nineties.'"

Looking at each other, Bucky and Martian burst into laughter. Their reaction made me feel really dumb. I looked at Prof who also looked puzzled.

"Well," I said with a lot of irritation, "why don't you stop laughing and tell me what it means?"

"Horsehead, "giggled Bucky, "'gay' means 'queer'. You do know what 'queer' means, don't you?"

"Yes, I do," I replied. "Why didn't you just say that?"

Martian broke in, "Jimmy, 'gay' is the new word for 'queer', and Frank and Jerry are as queer as a three-dollar-bill."

"And they eat those oysters right off the shell?" asked Prof.

"Yep," said Bucky. "They come in around 7:00 every Friday night and start with a dozen oysters. They douse them in hot sauce, put the shell up to their mouths, and swallow them whole."

"How do you know that they are queers?" I asked.

With that, Bucky and Martian broke into laughter again. Prof and I did not say anything; we just looked at each other acknowledging that something weird was going on between Bucky and Martian.

"Should we tell them?" asked Martian looking intently at Bucky.

"I don't think so," said Bucky. "Prof would probably be all right, but Jimmy is too much of a Christ-er."

Again, Bucky and Martian started giggling. Prof and I just gave each other a puzzled look, wondering what was going on with these two.

When the giggling was over, Martian looked at Bucky and said, "If you're spending the night at my house, we need to go."

"Let's go then," replied Bucky.

They stood up and started walking down the porch steps. Buck turned and said, "I'll see you bastards."

***

A Place Called Viet Nam

Summer vacation of 1964 was somewhat abbreviated. The winter school closings had extended the school year through the second week of June. Summer was fading fast. The month of July had been a blur. On Monday, August 3, Dad and I opened the store at 6:30 a.m. Mondays were always slow and this one was no exception. After the regular early morning customers had left the store, I grabbed a comic book, turned the Philco to WKDA, and parked myself on the stool behind the counter.

Business was sporadic until a little after 9 a.m. After that, it was practically non-existent. I was spending my time reading about the adventures of Superman and listening to the Top Forty hits on the radio when an announcer interrupted *Rag Doll* by the Four Seasons: We interrupt this broadcast for a special news bulletin from NBC News." The news bulletin was brief and to the point. The previous day an American warship, the *U.S.S. Maddox*, was patrolling in international waters in the Gulf of Tonkin near North Viet Nam when the destroyer was attacked by two North Vietnamese torpedo boats. The announcement went on to say that the American destroyer had not suffered any damage, but the North Vietnamese vessels were badly damaged in the confrontation. Following the bulletin, WKDA resumed regular programming.

I really did not know what to make of the bulletin. No American was harmed in the attack and the *Maddox* had suffered no damage; however, the attack was on an American ship in international waters and appeared to be unprovoked. I wondered how the United States would respond.

Until the mid-1950's, the nations of North Viet Nam, South Viet Nam, Laos, and Cambodia were remnants of the old French empire. The area had been known as French Indochina. Following World War II, communist insurgents and non-communist nationalists had risen to overthrow French rule. After years of warfare, France concluded that holding onto Indochina was not worth the effort or cost. In 1955 France withdrew from the area. By international agreement in Geneva, Switzerland, the nations of Laos, Cambodia, and Viet Nam were created. Viet Nam was divided at the 17th Parallel into communist controlled North Viet Nam and democratically controlled South Viet Nam. Almost immediately, war broke out between North and South Viet Nam. The communist north was backed by the Soviet Union and Red China. Although the democratic government of South Viet Nam was extremely corrupt and persecuted its Buddhist minority, the United States backed South Viet Nam in the conflict with military advisors, equipment, and intelligence personnel. By the time of the attack on the *Maddox,* U.S. personnel in Viet Nam had grown to over 23,000. This was in keeping with the "containment" policy which began in the Truman Administration. It was believed that if one nation fell to communism, the philosophy would spread into neighboring areas and more nations would fall to communism. This "domino" theory led U.S. policy to use resources to contain the spread of communism. Although the "containment" policy grew out of the spread of Soviet communism in Eastern Europe,

Truman applied it to Asia in the Korean conflict. In the late 1950's, President Eisenhower applied it to Indochina. Presidents Kennedy and Johnson followed suit.

Two days following the attack on the *Maddox,* a second attack on American warships was reported. This prompted President Lyndon Johnson to inform the American people with a televised address on the evening of August 4.

"As President and Commander-in-Chief," he said, "it is my duty to the American people to report that renewed hostile actions against United States ships on the high seas in the Gulf of Tonkin have today required me to order military forces of the United States to take military actions in reply."

Mere hours following the speech, the United States launched air strikes against North Vietnamese forces. By the end of the week, both houses of the U.S. Congress had almost unanimously passed the Gulf of Tonkin Resolution allowing the U.S. to "take all necessary measures" to protect American forces in Viet Nam. The resolution had the same effect as a declaration of war giving the president a blank check to conduct military operations. The Viet Nam War was on.

Most Americans supported President Johnson's action. This was evidenced by his landslide victory in the presidential election the following November. Like my parents and I, people did not realize the cost in blood and treasure that the nation would sacrifice over the course of several years in this place called Viet Nam.

***

The Unspeakable and Sad Good-byes

"I don't know, Stone," said Mr. Gates. "What business do we have in a place nobody around here has ever heard of?"

"Communism is a cancer, Gates," said Officer Marcum. "If you don't stop it, it just keeps spreading. Just look at Eastern Europe, China, and Korea."

"Look," said Gates, "let me tell you where I'm coming from. My boy, Freddy, decided to make a career in the army. He just became sergeant, and I'm real proud of him. He may have to fight, and I'm scared. My son's life is too high of a price to pay to save some shit-hole country like Viet Nam from communism."

As Dad, Mr. Gates, and Officer Marcum stood near the front counter, I was listening with great interest to their mid-morning conversation. Dad and Mr. Marcum did not know how to reply to Mr. Gates' passionate comment. For the next several moments, the men were silent. National foreign policy is one thing, but when it lands at your front door, it's something else.

It had been a couple of weeks since the incident in the Gulf of Tonkin. Most people, like Mr. Marcum, supported the intervention in Viet Nam. Others, like Mr. Gates, were questioning the price that would be paid.

The silence was broken when the front door opened, and Tommy entered the store. He did not make his way to the drink box for his usual Dr. Pepper. A wrinkle on his forehead and the lack of his usual smile showed that something serious was on his mind.

"Officer Marcum," said Tommy, "can I talk to you for a minute?"

"Sure, Tommy," said Marcum.

"This is kinda private," said Tommy. "Can we go out on the porch?"

As Tommy and Marcum moved toward the door, Mr. Gates turned to Dad, "I better get on back home. I'll see you later."

As the three men exited the store, one of the Anderson children entered and handed me a short list of items.

"Hey, Dad," I said. "There's a pound of baloney on this list."

Dad journeyed back to the meat counter, and I collected the other items on the list. I checked out the order and held the receipt which would be paid on Saturday. When the Anderson child left the store, Marcum and Tommy were still engaged in conversation. I watched as the two shook hands, and Marcum entered his police cruiser to resume his patrol. Tommy stood on the porch and watched Marcum pull away and head down Fifth Avenue.

Tommy entered the store and retrieved a Dr. Pepper from the drink box. Placing a dime on the counter, Tommy said, "I just asked Mr. Marcum for a huge favor, and, Jim, I need to ask a favor of you."

"Sure, Tommy," I said. "Absolutely. Just ask."

"I've been drafted," said Tommy. "I got the letter the other day. On September 1, at 9:00 a.m. I have to be downtown at the First American Center. From there, they will ship me out for basic training."

"Man," I said.

"Well, I'm not worried about that," said Tommy. "What is bothering me is leave Momma."

"Okay," I said. "What can I do?"

"Jim, you know about my dad," said Tommy. "He's a mean drunk. Mr. Marcum said that he would check on Momma every day that he could, but I don't know how often that can be." After a brief pause, Tommy asked, "How often does Officer Marcum stop by here?"

"Four or five times a week," I said. "He and Dad have been friends for years."

"Well," said Tommy with some hesitation, "could you check on Momma after Daddy goes to work every day that you can?"

"I will," I said. "Miss Myrtle comes in at noon during the week. When she comes in, I'll go down there. When school starts next month, I'll check on her right after school."

"Jim," said Tommy, "if you see any bruises or scratches on Momma, can you get word to Mr. Marcum?"

"Yes," I replied. "I'll do that."

***

It was Monday, the last day of August. With school starting the next week, summer vacation had vanished. The early afternoon found Prof and I sitting under the sycamore tree at the pony field. We were relaxing, chewing on blades of grass, and lamenting the fact that we would be back in school the day after Labor Day.

"Have you seen Grasshopper lately?" asked Prof.

"It's been about a week since I saw him," I replied. "He and

Martian came into the store and got a cold drink. We talked for a while."

Since Bucky had taken the full-time job at the Bayou, he had become scarce. When I did see him, he was with Martian. The two had become inseparable.

"Speak of the devil," said Prof. "Look at what's coming across the field."

I looked up to see Bucky and Martian walking toward us.

"So, this is where you bastards are," shouted Bucky.

"This is where we are," I said. "Take a load off."

Bucky had no sooner sat down with us under the tree when he said, "I'm moving out next week."

"Are you kidding?" asked Prof.

"Nope," said Bucky. "Me and Martian found a place over in East Nashville. An old couple owns a big house with a two-room apartment in the attic that they rent out."

"Really," I said.

"Yeah," said Martian. "It comes with a couch, an easy chair, a coffee table, and a bed."

"We'll have to get a TV," added Bucky. "We'll be moving in next Tuesday."

"Wow," I said. "There's a lot of moving about to happen around here."

"What are you talking about, Horsehead?" asked Bucky.

"Tommy," I said. "He's been drafted. He's leaving for basic training in the morning."

"Are you kidding me?" asked Bucky rhetorically.

"Hasn't Bones told you?" I asked.

"Hell, Horsehead," said Bucky, "I haven't seen Bones in weeks."

"Well," I said, "Tommy has got to be at the First American Center at 9:00 in the morning."

"Damn," said Bucky.

"Hey, Buck. How much money are you paying for that apartment?" inquired Prof.

"Twenty dollars a week," Bucky replied.

"Ouch!" said Prof. "Can you afford that?"

"Hell, yeah," said Bucky. "There's two of us. That's just ten dollars apiece."

"Yeah," chimed Martian. "We can pay that with our part-time job."

"What part-time job?" I asked.

With that, Bucky and Martian broke into a very goofy giggle.

"What's so funny?" I asked with some irritation.

Martian turned to Bucky and said, "Maybe we should tell them."

"Do you bastards remember Frank and Jerry?" asked Bucky.

I shook my head, "Not really."

"Frank and Jerry are those two gay guys we told you about," said Martian.

"Oh," said Prof. "You mean those two queers that eat raw oysters."

"Yeah," chuckled Martian. "That's them. It's amazing. They are really gay, but they have families. They have wives and children."

"They also must have a lot of money," said Bucky. "Both of them live out in the Belmont area."

"And they give us a job making extra money every Friday night," added Martian.

"Yep," laughed Bucky. "We make ten dollars each."

Prof and I looked at each other. Both of us were reluctant to ask about the task they had to perform to earn that kind of money.

"So," said Martian, "we can use that extra money to pay our weakly rent."

With that, Bucky and Martian just looked at each other and snickered.

"Okay, I'll ask," said Prof. "What are you doing to make the ten dollars?"

"Come on, Buck," said Martian with a snicker. "Go on and tell them."

"Okay," said Bucky as he took a deep breath. "When me and Martian get off work on Friday nights, Jerry and Frank give us a ride home," said Bucky.

"But they don't take us straight home," giggled Martian.

"They take us to a motel down on Lafayette Street," laughed Bucky.

"A motel?" I asked. "Why?"

Prof gave me a look of disbelief and said," Are you kidding, Jimmy?"

"No," Bucky interjected quickly and sarcastically, "he's not kidding. Horsehead, let me spell it out for you."

Bucky went on to graphically detail the sexual act that

he and Martian allowed to be perpetrated upon them by Jerry and Frank. As Bucky described the raunchy details of the encounters, I found myself feeling nauseous. I found the narrative to be grossly repugnant. I found it difficult to accept that Bucky could describe the details with no feeling of shame. Looking at Prof, I sensed that he was having similar feelings.

As Bucky was completing his disgusting narrative, I did not wish to be condemning or self-righteous, but I also decided to stand up; I decided I would not go along to get along.

I leaned back against the sycamore tree and said, "Bucky, that's a disgusting way to make ten dollars."

Bucky looked at Martian and said, "Told you he couldn't handle it."

"Well," said Martian. "It doesn't matter if he can handle it or not. Let's go."

As Bucky and Martian stood and started walking away, Bucky turned and said, "See you bastards."

Prof leaned back against the tree and said, "See ya, Queer Bait."

***

About 7:40 a.m. the next day, Tommy entered the store carrying a duffle bag.

"Hey, Jimmy," said Tommy as he put his bag on the floor beside the ice cream freezer, "can I put my worldly possessions down here for a minute?"

"Sure, Tommy," I said.

Tommy proceeded to the drink box in the rear of the store

and extracted a Dr. Pepper. On the way back to the front, he stopped at the meat counter.

"Hey, Mr. Stone," said Tommy. "I guess this is good-bye for a while."

"Hate to see you go, Tommy," said Dad. "You will definitely be missed around here."

After a brief conversation, Tommy said, "Well, good-bye, Mr. Stone."

"Bye, Tommy," said Dad, "and take care of yourself."

Tommy walked up to the counter and put down a dime.

"Keep it, Tommy," I said. "This one is on the house."

"Jimmy, thanks for keeping tabs on Momma for me," said Tommy. "It means a lot to me."

"No problem," I said. "There's something I need to give you."

I tore a section of receipt paper from the adding machine and wrote the address of the store on it.

"When you get to boot camp," I said, "write me and give me your mailing address."

"Thanks, Jim," said Tommy. "I better get over to the bus stop. The bus will be here in a minute."

"Take the Dr. Pepper with you," I said. "I'll be looking for your letter."

I sadly watched as Tommy crossed Clay Street and stood at the bus stop. I watched as he boarded the bus for his trip downtown. As the bus pulled off, Dad moved up to the front window.

"That boy is a living miracle," said Dad.

***

"Bucky caught the bus hours ago," said Mom.

It was the day after Labor Day, the first day of school. Prof and I had practically run down Clay Street from North High School. We had hoped to see Bucky before he left to move into his apartment.

"Did he leave an address or a telephone number?" I asked.

"No," said Mom. "He came in around ten o'clock this morning and bought a pack of cigarettes. He walked over to the bus stop carrying a ratty-looking suitcase without saying anything to anybody."

It appeared to me that Mom was not sorry to see Bucky go. She believed that he was becoming a bad influence on me. Deep down, I knew that I should have been a better influence on him.

As Prof and I walked back to the drink box, Prof said, "Jimmy, you may never see Bucky again."

Prof was right. I never saw Bucky again.

***

Chapter 7

Spring 1966

In May 1965 I graduated from North Nashville High School. The night of my graduation was the only night that Dad had ever allowed the store to close early. Earlier that week he had driven to Schatten's Dry Goods Store and purchased a gray suit and a red tie to wear to my graduation. Mom wore a new dress. They looked great.

I spent the following summer working in the store and hanging out with Prof. In mid-July Aunt Elise drove Mom and I to Murfreesboro, Tennessee, which was the home of Middle Tennessee State University. The purpose of the trip was for me to pre-register for classes in the fall. With computers in their infancy, registration took several hours. By the end of the day, I was tired. I was also excited. My going to college was a goal that was going to be realized.

I moved into a freshman dormitory on the MTSU campus in September 1965. Although the campus was only forty miles from Nashville, my parents wanted me to have a full college experience. So did I.

I made several new friends and enjoyed my classes; however,

I did not like living in a dormitory. I found it to be a little chaotic—too many eighteen-year-olds in one place. That was one of the reasons that I went home every weekend. Another reason was I felt that I would be needed in the store on Saturdays. The real reason was that I got homesick during the week. I was only forty miles from home, but it may as well have been forty thousand.

Freshmen were not allowed to have cars on campus at MTSU. Each Sunday afternoon upon closing the store, Dad drove me to the Trailways bus station for my trip back to school. When I arrived at the bus station in Murfreesboro, I took a taxi to the dorm. I was one of many students who journeyed home every weekend. In fact, MTSU was known as a "suitcase college."

At the close of the fall semester, I found my grades to be mediocre. I earned an "A" in ROTC, a "B" in Western Civilization and Biology, and "C"s in English, Political Science, and Geography. When I registered for the spring semester in January, I was determined to rise from mediocrity. I had learned the hard way that college was not an extension of high school. I had to improve. I had not lost my goal of graduating from college and being accepted into Naval Officers Candidate School. I had to tighten up.

***

On Sunday morning, March 13, I drove Dad's '55 Chevy to church. Coming home every weekend, I continued to attend the little country-like church on Osage Street. Returning to the store, I was surprised to see Miss Myrtle working at the front counter. She never worked on weekends. Mom was working at the meat counter.

"Hey, Miss Myrtle," I said. "Where's Dad? Is he okay?"

"He's upstairs, Mr. Jim," she replied. "He's just a little under the weather."

Mom joined us at the front of the store and said, "Thanks for working today, Myrtle. We really appreciate it. You go on home now; Jimmy and I will be okay."

"Anytime, Miss Bess," said Miss Myrtle as she exited the store.

"Go ahead and lock the door, Jimmy," said Mom. "We're closing early today."

When Mom and I went upstairs, we found Dad sitting on the living room couch. He was bent slightly forward with his right hand on in stomach.

"Hey, Dad. Can I get you anything?" I asked.

"No, Son," he replied. "I'm just a little sick to my stomach. I'll be okay, just don't get between me and the bathroom."

Mom and I sat in the living room with Dad until it was time for me to begin my journey back to school. Dad was not feeling well enough to drive me to the bus station, and Mom had never learned to drive. Dad had tried to teach her on several occasions but concluded that it was hopeless. Mom called Checker Cab Company and instructed the driver to pull into the side parking area and sound his horn. When I heard the horn, I picked up my suitcase and took a few steps toward the door.

"Bye, Dad," I said. "I hope you get to feeling better."

My dad looked me in the eyes and said, "Good-bye, Son."

***

Arriving at the dorm, I found that my roommate had already returned from Chattanooga. After unpacking, I joined him at the two-person desk to do some studying that I had failed to do over the weekend. My studying did not last long. Although it was only a little after 8:00 p.m., I was extremely tired. I climbed onto the top bunk and immediately fell into a deep sleep.

Suddenly, both of my eyes opened, and I sat upright in the bunk. My heart was pounding as I turned and looked at the clock on the desk. The time was exactly 10:50 p.m.

"Are you alright?" asked my roommate who was still studying.

"Yeah, I guess," I said. After a pause, I said, "That was different."

"Well, go back to sleep," he chuckled.

I laid back and, again, fell into a deep sleep.

***

"Jimmy. Hey, Jimmy," said a voice from someone who was gently shaking my shoulder.

Opening my eyes, I saw that it was the voice of Uncle Henry.

"Hey, Jim," he said. "You need to wake up."

I raised up on one elbow and looked at the clock on the desk. It was almost 1 o'clock in the morning.

"Uncle Henry," I said. "What are you doing here?"

"I've got some bad news for you, Jim," said Uncle Henry. "Your dad passed away tonight."

I just looked at Uncle Henry for a few moments in disbelief. Not yet totally awakened, I said, "You're kidding."

"No, Jim," he replied. "Your dad died tonight." After a pause, he continued, "Bess is waiting for you at the funeral home."

***

Mom decided not to continue in the grocery business. Without Dad it would be too much of a burden, and she insisted that I finish college. Over the next couple of months, Mom was able to sell the store's inventory and all of Dad's cars except the '55 Chevy. During that time, she received considerable help and support from Uncle Henry and Aunt Elise. With the store closing, she moved into a house that she and Dad owned on Ninth Avenue. When the spring semester ended, Mom and I sold that house and purchased a small house in the Inglewood section of Nashville. Mom secured a job as a waitress at a café that was in walking distance of the house.

It was mid-July when Mom and I moved into the house in Inglewood. We were both still numb from the loss of Dad. The thread of our lives had changed. We were in a new house, in a new neighborhood, and—without Dad—in a new way of life. A new chapter was opening in our lives. With that new chapter opening, the Kalb Hollow chapter had come to a sad close.

Epilogue

Tommy Martin served in the Viet Nam War as a gunner on a helicopter gunship. After his discharge from the army, he returned to Viet Nam where he worked as a private contractor for over two years. With his earnings as a contractor, he founded a private security company in Franklin, Tennessee. He operated the company for over fifty years before turning the company over to his sons. Today, he and his wife live in an upscale area of Franklin. Raised in a three-room shotgun house with a dirt floor in Kalb Hollow, Tommy achieved the American dream.

Elizabeth "Bess" Stone worked as a waitress and assistant manager at the Inglewood Café until her retirement in 1982. She lived in quiet retirement enjoying her two grandchildren until her death in 1988.

Randall "Bones" Martin joined the Marine Corps in 1967. Bones was killed in action in Viet Nam in 1969.

Richard "Buzz" McNabb joined the Marine Corps along with Bones. Buzz survived the war in Viet Nam. Returning to Nashville after his discharge from the military, he drove eighteen-wheelers professionally until his retirement in 2005.

Silas Patterson attended Michigan State University on a

football scholarship. He graduated from MSU in 1970. Returning home, he became an executive with a large publishing firm in Nashville. Silas retired in 2015.

David "Prof" Denton went to work as a television repairman in Nashville following his graduation from high school in 1966. Prof and his wife moved to Gallatin, Tennessee in 1984. In the early 1990's. Prof transitioned into computer sales and repair. Prof passed away in 2019 leaving his wife, two sons, a daughter, and seven grandchildren.

Paul "Bucky" Thomas worked his way up to waiter at the Bayou. After the Bayou closed to make way for a luxury hotel on Commerce Street, Bucky continued to work in upscale restaurants in downtown Nashville. He suffered two failed marriages and remained childless. In the Spring of 1985, Bucky became mysteriously ill. He passed away suddenly in the summer of 1985.

Jim Stone never became a naval officer. As an only child and his mom a widow, he remained in Nashville. Beginning in 1969, he taught history at the high school and college level until his retirement in 2016. He and his wife of fifty-three years live in a modest suburb of Nashville. They love to spend time with their two children, three grandchildren, and a great grandchild.

***

Although I am in the winter of my life, I often remember those days in Kalb Hollow. The conflicts, disappointments, and tragedies do not usually come to mind; rather, I think of the baseball games at the Little League field, playing "strike-out" with Silas, the Sunday afternoon football games at Morgan Park, climbing the cliffs and roaming the bottoms with Bucky and Prof, listening to WKDA on Prof's porch, and sitting under the sycamore tree at the pony field. I also think of that very special place called North Nashville High School. Yes, I am in the winter of my life, but I am warmed by the memories that were created during the spring of my life in a place called Kalb Hollow.

Made in United States
Orlando, FL
16 August 2024